Here is an outstanding collection of imaginative and unusual science fiction from the pen of the world's masters of the *genre*.

THE GREAT ENGINE
THE GREAT JUDGE
SECRET UNATTAINABLE
THE HARMONIZER
HEIR UNAPPARENT
THE SECOND SOLUTION
FILM LIBRARY
ASYLUM

Eight masterpieces for the connoisseur.

'Van Vogt must be credited with plot ingenuity, skill in mystification, and a certain poignance . . .'

Chicago Tribune

D1434575

Also by A. E. van Vogt in Panther Books

A. E. van Vogt

Away and Beyond

Panther

Granada Publishing Limited
Published in 1963 by Panther Books Ltd
Frogmore, St Albans, Herts AL2 2NF
Reprinted 1968, 1970, 1973 (twice)

Made and printed in Great Britain by
C. Nicholls & Company Ltd
The Philips Park Press, Manchester
Set in Intertype Plantin

Contents

THE GREAT ENGINE

THE blue-gray engine lay half buried in a green hillside. It lay there in that summer of 1948, a soulless thing of metal and of forces more potent than life itself. Rain washed its senseless form. A July then an August sun blazed down upon it. In the night the stars looked down wanly, caring nothing for its destiny. The ship it drove had been nosing down into Earth's atmosphere when the meteorite plowed through the metal that held it in place. Instantly, in the irresistibleness of its terrible strength, the engine tore to shreds what remained of the framework and plunged through the gaping meteorite hole, down, down.

For all the weeks since then it had lain in the hillside seemingly lifeless but, actually, in its great fashion, alive. There was dirt in its force field, so tightly packed that it would have taken eagle eyes to see how swiftly it was spinning. Not even the boys who sat one day on a flange of the engine noticed the convulsions of the dirt. If one of them had poked a grimy hand into the inferno of energy that was the force field, muscles, bones, blood would have spurted like gas exploding.

But the boys went away; and the engine was still there on the day the searchers passed along the bottom of the hill. Discovery was as close as that. There were two of them, two alert, trained observers who anxiously scanned the hillside. But a cloud was veiling the brightness of the sun, and they passed on unseeing.

It was more than a week later, late in the afternoon, when a horse climbing the hill straddled the protruding bulge of the engine. The horse's rider proceeded to dismount in an astounding fashion. With his one hand he grasped the saddlehorn and *lifted* himself clear of the saddle. Casually, easily, he brought his left leg over, held himself poised in midair, and then dropped to the ground. The display of strength seemed all the more effortless because the action was automatic. His attention was concentrated the whole while on the thing in the ground.

His lean face twisted as he examined the machine. He glanced around, eyes suddenly narrowed. Then he smiled sardonically as he realized the thought in his mind. Finally, he shrugged. There was little chance of anybody seeing him out here. The town of Crescentville was more than a mile away; and there was no sign of life around the big white house which stood among the trees a third of a mile to the northwest.

He was alone with his horse and the machine. And, after a moment, his voice echoed with cool irony on the twilight air, "Well, Dandy, here's a job for us. This scrap should buy you quite a bit of feed. We'll haul it to the junk dealer after dark. That way she won't find out and we'll save some remnant of our pride."

He stopped. Involuntarily, he turned to stare at the garden-like estate whose width stretched for nearly a mile between himself and the town. A white fence, misty and halo-ish in the twilight, made a vast circuit around a green, verdant land of trees and pasture. The fence kept disappearing down gullies and into brush. It vanished finally in the north beyond the stately white house.

The man muttered impatiently, "What a fool I've been, hanging around Crescentville waiting for her." He cut the words with a mental effort and turned to stare down at the engine. "Have to get some idea of its weight," he thought. "Wonder what it is."

He climbed to the top of the hill and came down again carrying a piece of deadwood about four feet long and three inches in diameter. He began to pry the engine loose from the ground. It was awkward work with only a left arm. And so, when he noticed the dirt-plugged hole in the center, he jabbed the wood into it to get better leverage.

His shout of surprise and pain echoed hoarsely on the evening air.

For the wood jerked. Like a shot twisted by the rifled barrel of a gun, like a churning knife, it wrenched in his hand, tearing like a shredder, burning like fire. He was lifted up, up, and flung twenty feet down the hill. Groaning, clutching his tattered hand to his body, he stumbled to his feet.

The sound died on his lips, then, as his gaze fastened on the throbbing, whirling thing that had been a dead branch of tree. He stared. Then he climbed, trembling, onto the black horse. Nursing his bloodied hand, blinking from the agony, he raced the animal down the hill and toward the highway that led to the town.

A stone boat and harness for Dandy rented from a farmer, rope and tackle, a hand stiff with bandages, still numb with pain, a trek though darkness with a thrumming thing on the stone boat—for three hours Pendrake felt himself a creature in a nightmare.

But here was the engine now, on the floor of his stable, safe from discovery except for the sound that was pouring forth from the wood in its force field. It seemed odd now how his mind had worked. The determination to transport the engine secretly to his own cottage had been like choosing life instead of death, like swiftly picking up a hundred-dollar bill lying on a deserted street, so automatic as to be beyond the need of logic. It still seemed as natural as living.

The yellow glow from the lantern filled the interior of what had once been a large private garage and workshop. In one corner Dandy stood, black hide aglint, eyes glistening, as he turned his head to stare at the thing that shared his quarters. The not unpleasant smell of horse was thick now that the door was closed. The engine lay on its side near the door. And the main trouble was that the wood in it wasn't straight. It slogged away against the air like some caricature of a propeller, beating a sound out of the atmosphere by the sheer violence and velocity of its rotation.

Pendrake estimated its speed at about eight thousand revolutions a minute. He stood then, and strove to grasp the nature of a machine that could snatch a piece of wood and spin it so violently. His thought scattered before the mystery; and he gave it up. But a frown creased his face as he stared down at the speed-blurred wood. He couldn't just grab it. And, while undoubtedly there were a number of tools in the world that could grip a whirling bar and pull on it, they were not available here in this lantern-lighted stable.

He thought: "There must be a control, something to switch off the power."

But the bluish-gray, doughnut-shaped outer shell was glass smooth. Even the flanges that projected from four ends, and in which were the holes for bed bolts, seemed to grow out of the shell, as if they had been molded from the same block of metal, as if there had been a flowing, original design that spurned anything less than oneness. Baffled, Pendrake walked around the machine. It seemed to him that the problem was beyond the solution of a man who had as his working equipment one badly maimed and bandaged hand.

He noticed something. The machine lay solidly, heavily, on the floor. It neither jogged nor jumped. It made not the slightest effort to begin a sedate, reactionary creep in opposition to the insanely whirling thing that bristled from its middle. The engine was ignoring the law that action and reaction are equal and opposite.

With abrupt realization of the possibilities, Pendrake bent down and heaved at the metal shell. Instantly, knives of pain hacked at his hand. Tears shocked into his eyes. But when he finally let go, the engine was standing on one of its four sets of flanges. And the crooked wood was spinning, no longer vertically, but roughly horizontal to the floor.

The pulse of agony in Pendrake's hand slowed. He wiped tears from his eyes and proceeded to the next step in the plan that had occurred to him. Nails! He drove them into the bed bolt holes, and bent them over the metal. That was just to make sure the narrow-based engine wouldn't topple over in the event that he bumped too hard against the outer shell.

An apple box came next. Laid lengthwise on its side, it reached up to within half an inch of the exact center of the large hole, from the opposite side of which the wood projected. Two books held steady a piece of one-inch piping about a foot long. It was painful holding the small sledge hammer in that lame hand of his, but he struck true. The piece of piping recoiled from the hammer, banged the wood where it was held inside the hole of the engine, and knocked it out.

There was a crash that shook the garage. After a moment, Pendrake grew aware of a long, plintered slash in the ceiling, through which the four-foot piece of deadwood had bounced after striking the floor. Slowly, his reverberating mind gravitated into a rhythm with the silence that was settling. Pendrake drew a deep breath. There were still things to discover, a whole new machine world to explore. But one thing seemed clear:

He had conquered the engine.

At midnight he was still awake. He kept getting up, dropping the magazine he was reading, and going into the dark kitchen of the cottage to peer out at the darker garage. But the night was quiet. No marauders disturbed the peace of the town. Occasionally, a car motor sounded far away.

He began to realize the psychological danger when for the dozenth time he found himself pressing his face against the cool pane of the kitchen window. Pendrake cursed aloud and went back into the living room, muttering invective. What was he trying to do? He couldn't hope to keep that engine. It must be a new invention, a radical post-war development, lying on that hillside because of an accident that a silly ass who never read papers or listened to the radio wouldn't know anything about.

Somewhere in the house, he remembered, was a *New York Times* he'd bought not so long ago. He found the paper in his magazine rack with all the other old and unread papers and magazines he'd bought from time to time. The date at the top was June 7, 1947; and this was August 16th. Not too great a difference.

But this wasn't 1947. *This was* 1948!

With a cry, Pendrake leaped to his feet, then slowly sank back into his chair. It was an ironic picture that came then, a kaleidoscope of the existence of a man so untouched by the friction of time that fourteen months had glided by like so many days. Lazy, miserable hound, Pendrake thought in a blaze of fury, using his lost arm and an unforgiving woman as an excuse for lying down on life. That was over. All of it. He'd start again—

He grew aware of the paper in his hand. And all the anger went out of him as in a gathering excitement he began to glance at the headlines:

PRESIDENT CALLS ON NATION
FOR NEW INDUSTRIAL EFFORT
Two Hundred Billion Dollar National
Income Only Beginning, He Says

350,000 FAMILY PLANES SOLD
FIRST FIVE MONTHS OF 1947

IS THERE LIFE ON OTHER PLANETS?
Expect 200 Inch Telescope to
Provide New Evidence—To Be
Completed Next Year.

Pendrake's mind poised at that point, hard on the thought that came. "It was impossible! An engine that merely turned an axle in however wonderful a fashion wasn't a spaceship drive whatever else it might be."

The situation was really simple. He had crept away into this little cottage of his, almost right out of the world. Life had gone on dynamically. And somewhere, not so long ago, a tremendous invention had spawned out of that surging tide of will and ambition and creative genius. Tomorrow, he would try to get a mortgage on this cottage. That would provide him with a little cash, and break forever the thrall of the place. Dandy he'd send over to Eleanor in the same fashion that she had sent him three years ago, without a word. The green pastures of the estate would be like heaven for an animal that had starved too long now on an ex-airman's pension.

He must have slept at that point. Because he awoke at 3.00 a.m., sweating with fear. He was out in the night and clawing open the door of the garage-stable before he realized that he had had a bad dream. The engine was still there, the foot-long piece of piping in its force field. In the beam of his flashlight the piping glinted as it turned, shone with a brown glow that was hard to reconcile with the dirty, rusted, extruded metal thing he had ransacked out of his basement.

It struck Pendrake after a moment, and for the first time, that the pipe was turning far more slowly than had the piece of wood, not a quarter so fast, not more than fourteen or fifteen hundred revolutions per minute. The rate of rotation must be governed by the kind of material, based on atomic weight, or density, or something.

Uneasily, convinced that he mustn't be seen abroad at this hour, Pendrake shut the door and returned to the house. He felt no anger at himself, or at the brief frenzy that sent him racing into the night. But the implications were troubling.

It was going to be hard to give the engine up to its rightful owner.

The following day he went first to the office of the local newspaper. Forty issues of the weekly Crescentville *Clarion* yielded exactly nothing. Pendrake read the first two news pages of each edition, missing not a single heading. But there was no report of an air crash, no mention of a great new engine invention. He went out, finally, into the hot August morning, a haze of exhilaration tingling along his nerves. It couldn't be, it *couldn't* be. And yet, if this kept on, the engine was his.

The bank manager said, "A mortgage on the cottage. It isn't necessary. You have a large account here."

"Eh?" Pendrake said.

It was the expression on the man's smooth-jowled face, the faint, secret smile that warned him. The manager, whose name Pendrake remembered as Roderick Clay, said easily, "As you know, when you went to China with the Army Air Force, you signed all your possessions over to your wife, with the exception of the cottage where you now live. And that, as I understand it, was omitted accidentally."

Pendrake nodded, not trusting himself to speak. He knew now what was coming, and the manager's words merely verified his realization. The manager said, "At the end of the war, a few months after you and your wife separated, she secretly reassigned to you the entire property, including bonds, shares, cash, real estate, as well as the Pendrake estate, with the stipulation that

13

you not be advised of the transfer until you actually inquired, or in some other fashion indicated your need for money. She further stipulated that, in the interim, she be given the minimum living allowance with which to provide for the maintenance of herself and the Pendrake home.

"I may say"—the man was bland, smug, satisfied with the way he had carried off an interview that he must have planned in his idle moments with anticipatory thrills— "your affairs have prospered with those of the nation. Stocks, bonds, and cash on hand total about two hundred and ninety-four thousand dollars. Would you like me to have one of the clerks draw up a check for your signature? How much?"

It was hotter outside. Pendrake walked back to the cottage, thinking: He should have known Eleanor would pull something like that. These passionate, introvert women—Sitting there that day he had called, cold, remote, unable to break out of her shell of reserve. Sitting there knowing she had placed herself financially at his mercy. He'd have to think out the implications, plan his approach, his exact words and actions. Meanwhile, there was the engine.

It was still there. He glanced cursorily in at it, then padlocked the door again. On the way to the kitchen entrance he patted Dandy, who was staked out on the back lawn. Inside, he searched for, and found, the name of a Washington patent firm. He'd gone to China with the son of a member. Awkwardly, he wrote his letter. On his way to the post office to mail it, he stopped off at the only machine shop in town and ordered a wheel-like gripping device, a sort of clutch, the wheel part of which would whirl with anything it grasped

The answer to his letter arrived two days later, before the "clutch" was completed. The letter said:

Dear Mr. Pendrake:

As per your request, we placed the available members of our Research Department on your problem. All patent office records of engine inventions during the past three years were examined. In addition, I had a personal conversation with the director in charge of that particular

14

department of the patent office. Accordingly, I am in a position to state positively that no radical engine inventions other than jet variations have been patented in any field since the war.

For your perusal, we are enclosing herewith copies of ninety-seven recent engine patents, as selected by our staff from thousands.

Our bill is being sent to you by separate mail. Thank you for your advance check for two hundred dollars.

Sincerely yours,
N. V. Hoskins.

P.S.: I thought you were dead. I'll swear I saw your name in a casualty list after I was rescued, and I've been mourning you for three years. I'll write you a longer letter in a week or so. I'm holding up the patent world right now, not physically—only the great Jim Pendrake could do that. However, I'm playing the role of mental Atlas, and I sure got a lot of dirty looks for rushing your stuff through. Which explains the big bill. 'By for now.

Ned.

Pendrake was conscious of a choking sensation as he read and reread the note. To think how he'd cut himself off from all his friends. The phrase "—the great Jim Pendrake" made him glance involuntarily at the empty right sleeve of his sweater.

He smiled grimly. And several minutes passed before he remembered the engine. He thought then: "I'll order an automobile chassis and an engineless plane, and a bar made of many metals—have to make some tests first, of course."

He stopped, his eyes widening with the possibilities. Life was opening up again. But it was strangely hard to realize that the engine still had no owner but himself.

"What's that?" said a young man's voice behind Pendrake.

It was growing quite dark; and the truck he had hired seemed almost formless in the gathering night. Beside Pendrake the machine shop loomed, a gloomy, unpainted structure. The lights inside the building glimmered faintly through greasy windows.

The machine-shop employees, who had loaded the gripper on the truck for him, were gone through a door, their raucous good nights still ringing in his ears. Pendrake was alone with his questioner.

With a deliberate yet swift movement he pulled a tarpaulin over the gripper, and turned to stare at the man who had addressed him. The fellow stood in the shadows, a tall, powerful-looking young man. The light from the nearest street lamp glinted on high, curving cheekbones, but it was hard to make out the exact contours of the face.

It was the intentness of the other's manner that sent a chill through Pendrake. Here was no idler's curiosity, but an earnestness, a determination that was startling. With an effort, Pendrake caught himself. "What's it to you?" he said curtly.

He climbed into the cab. The engine purred. Awkwardly, Pendrake manipulated the right-hand gear shift and rolled off.

He could see the man in his rear-view mirror, still standing there in the shadows of the machine shop, a tall, strong figure. The stranger started to walk slowly in the same direction that Pendrake was driving. The next second Pendrake whipped the truck around a corner and headed down a side street. He thought, "I'll take a roundabout course to the cottage, then quickly return the truck to the man I rented it from, and then——"

Something damp trickled down his cheek. He let go of the steering wheel and felt his face. It was covered with sweat. He sat very still, thinking: "Am I crazy? I surely don't believe that someone is secretly searching for the engine."

His jumpy nerves slowly quieted. What was finally convincing was the coincidence of such a searcher standing near a machine shop of a small town at the very instant that Jim Pendrake was there. It was like an old melodrama where the villains were dogging the unsuspecting hero. Ridiculous! Nevertheless, the episode emphasized an important aspect of his possession of the engine: Somewhere that engine had been built. Somewhere was the owner.

He must never forget that.

It was darker when he was finally ready. Pendrake entered the garage-stable and turned on the light he had rigged up earlier in the day. The two-hundred-watt bulb shed a sunlike glare that somehow made the small room even stranger than it had been by lantern light.

The engine stood exactly where he had nailed it three nights before. It stood there like a swollen tire for a small, broad wheel; like a large, candied, blue-gray doughnut. Except for the four sets of flanges and the size, the resemblance to a doughnut was quite startling. The walls curved upward from the hole in the center; the hole itself was only a little smaller than it should have been to be in exact proportion. But there the resemblance to anything he had ever known ended. The hole was the damnedest thing that ever was.

It was about six inches in diameter. Its inner walls were smooth, translucent, nonmetallic in appearance; and in its geometrical center floated the piece of plumber's pipe. Literally, the pipe hung in space, held in position by a force that seemed to have no origin.

Pendrake drew a deep, slow breath, picked up his hammer and gently laid it over the outjutting end of the pipe. The hammer throbbed in his hand, but grimly he bore the pulsing needles of resuscitated pain, and pressed. The pipe whirred on, unyielding, unaffected. The hammer *brrred* with vibration. Pendrake grimaced from the agony and jerked the tool free.

He waited patiently until his hand ceased throbbing, then struck the protruding end of pipe a sharp blow. The pipe receded into the hole, and nine inches of it emerged from the other side of the engine. It was almost like rolling a ball. With deliberate aim, Pendrake hit the pipe from the far side. It bounced back so easily that eleven inches of it flowed out, only an inch remaining in the hole. It spun on like the shaft of a steam turbine, only there was not even a whisper of sound, not the faintest hiss.

Thoughtfully, his lips pursed, Pendrake sagged back and sat on his heels. The engine was not perfect. The ease with which the pipe and, originally, the piece of wood had been pushed in and out meant that gears or something would be needed. Something that would hold steady at high speeds under great strains. He climbed slowly to his feet, intent now. He dragged into position the device he had had constructed by the machine shop. It took

17

several minutes to adjust the gripping wheel to the right height. But he was patient.

Finally, he manipulated the control lever. Fascinated, he watched the two halves of the wheel close over the one-inch pipe, grip, and begin to spin. A glow suffused his whole body. It was the sweetest pleasure that had touched him in three long years. Gently, Pendrake pulled on the gripping machine, tried to draw it toward him along the floor. It didn't budge. He frowned at it. He had the feeling that the machine was too heavy for delicate pressures. Muscle was needed here, and without restraint. Bracing himself, he began to tug, hard.

Afterward, he remembered flinging himself back toward the door in his effort to get out of the way. He had a mental picture of the nails that held the engine to the floor pulling out as the engine toppled over toward him. The next instant the engine *lifted*, lifted lightly, in some incomprehensible fashion, right off the floor. It whirled there for a moment slowly, propeller-fashion, then fell heavily on top of the gripping machine.

With a crash the wooden planks on the floor splintered. The concrete underneath, the original floor of the garage, shattered with a grinding noise as the gripping machine was smashed against it fourteen hundred times a minute. Metal squealed in torment and broke into pieces in a shattering hail of death. The confusion of sound and dust and spraying concrete and metal was briefly a hideous environment for Pendrake's stunned mind.

Silence crept over the scene like the night following a day of battle, an intense, unnatural silence. There was blood on Dandy's quivering flank, where something had gashed him. Pendrake stood, soothing the trembling horse, assessing the extent of the destruction. He saw that the engine was lying on its face, apparently unaffected by its own violence. It lay, a glinting, blue-gray thing in the light from the miraculously untouched electric bulb.

It took half an hour to find all the pieces of what had been the gripping machine. He gathered the parts one by one and took them into the house. The first real experiment with the machine was over. Successfully, he decided.

He sat in darkness in the kitchen, watching. The minutes

ticked by, a calm succession. And there was still no movement outside. Pendrake sighed finally. It seemed clear that no one had paid any attention to the cataclysm in his garage. Or if they had they didn't give a damn. The engine was still safe.

The easing tension brought a curious awareness of how lonely he was. Suddenly, the very restfulness of the silence oppressed him. He had an abrupt, sharp conviction that his developing victory over the engine wasn't going to be any fun for one man cut off from the world by the melancholia in his character. He thought drably: "I ought to go and see her."

No—he shook himself—come to think of it, that wouldn't work. A genuine introvert like Eleanor acquired an emotional momentum in a given direction. Getting her out of that involved forces similar to the basic laws of hypnosis: The more direct the pressure to change her, the greater would be her innate resistance. Even if she herself willed to be free, the more determined she became about it, the more deeply she would become involved in the morass of emotions that was her psychic prison. Definitely, it wouldn't do any good to go and see her. But there was another possibility.

Pendrake put on his hat and went out into the night. At the corner drugstore, he headed straight for the phone booth. "Is Mrs. Pendrake in?" he asked when his call was answered.

"Yes, suh!" The woman's deep voice indicated that there was at least one new servant at the big white house. It was not a familiar voice. "Just a moment, suh."

A few seconds later, Eleanor's rich contralto was saying, "Mrs. Pendrake speaking."

"Eleanor, this is Jim."

"Yes?" Pendrake smiled wanly at the tiny change in her tone, the defensive edge that was suddenly in it.

"I'd like to come back, Eleanor," he said softly.

There was silence, then—

Click!

Out in the night again, Pendrake looked up at the starry heavens. The sky was dark, dark blue. The whole fabric of the universe of Occidental earth was well settled into night. Crescentville shared with the entire Eastern seaboard the penumbral shadows of the great mother planet. He thought: Maybe it had been a mistake, but now she knew. Her mind had probably gone dead slow on thoughts about him. Now it would come alive again.

He strolled up the back alley to his cottage. Reaching the yard, he suppressed an impulse to climb the tree from which the big white house was visible. He flung himself on the cool grass of the back lawn, stared at the garage, and thought shakily: An engine that would spin anything shoved into its force field or, if it resisted, smash it with the ease of power unlimited. An engine through which a shaft could be *pushed,* but from which it could not be *pulled.* Which meant that an airplane propeller need only be fastened to a bar of graded metals—graded according to atomic weight and density.

Someone was knocking at the front door of the cottage. Pendrake jumped physically and mentally. But presently he took the telegram from the boy who had disturbed him. The telegram read:

CABIN MODEL PUMA DELIVERED TO DORMANTOWN AIRPORT TOMORROW STOP SPECIAL ENGINE BRACES AND CONTROLS INSTALLED AS REQUESTED STOP MAGNESIUM ALLOY AND AEROGEL PLASTIC CONSTRUCTION STOP

ATLANTIC AIRCRAFT CORP.

Never, never, never had he been in a plane so fast. All the military machines he'd ever flown, the Lightnings, the Mustangs, Pumas, did not compare even remotely to the machine that quivered like vibrating bar steel before the power of the engine of dreams. The plane seemed to have no connection with earth. It was a creature of the sky, an arrow discharged by Jove. When he finally brought it down, Pendrake sat in the control seat, eyes closed, tugging his soul back from the upper heavens, where it had roamed, a free spirit.

He sat at last, sobered by the tremendous success. Because, what now? He could take other flights, of course, but sooner or later his machine, in its silent journeyings, would be remarked. And every day that passed, every hour that he clung to this secrecy, his moral position would grow worse. Somebody owned the engine. Owned it and wanted it. He must decide once and for all whether or not to advertise his possession of it. It was time to make up his mind.

He found himself frowning at the four men who were coming toward him along the line of sheds. Two of them were carrying between them a large tool case and one was pulling a small wagon which had other material on it. The group stopped fifty feet from Pendrake's plane. Then one of them came forward, fumbling in his pocket. He knocked on the cabin door.

"Something I'd like to ask you, mister!" he yelled.

Pendrake hesitated, cursing silently. He had been assured that no one else had rented a plane garage at this end of the field, and that the big sheds near by were empty, for use in future years only. Impatient, he activated the lever that opened the door. "What—" he began. He stopped, choked a little. He stared at the revolver that glittered at him from a hand that was rock steady, then glanced up at a face that—he saw with a start now—was covered by a flesh mask.

"Get out of there."

As Pendrake climbed to the ground, the man backed warily out of arm's reach and the other men ran forward, pulling their wagon, carrying their tools. They stowed the stuff into the plane and climbed in. The man with the gun paused in the doorway, drew a package out of the breast pocket of his coat and tossed it at Pendrake's feet.

"That'll pay you for the plane. And remember this, you will only make yourself look ridiculous if you pursue this matter further. This engine is in an experimental stage. We want to explore all its possibilities before we apply for a patent, and we don't inted to have simple secondary patents, improvements and what not hindering our development of the invention. That's all."

The plane began to move. In a minute it was lifting. It became a speck in the western sky and was merged into the blue haze of distance. The thought that came finally to Pendrake was: His decision had been made for him.

His sense of loss grew. And his blank feeling of helplessness.

For a while he watched the local planes taking off and landing on the northern runway; it was a mindless watch that left him after ten minutes still without a plan or purpose.

He could go home. He pictured himself sneaking into his cottage in Crescentville like a whipped dog, with the long, long evening still ahead of him. Or—the dark thought knit his brow —he could go to the police. The impulse jarred deeper and brought his first memory of the package that had been thrown at his feet. He stooped, picked it off the concrete, tore it open and counted the green bills inside. When he had finished, he mustered a wry smile. A hundred dollars more than he had paid for the Puma.

But it was a forced sale, and didn't count. With abrupt decision, Pendrake started the engine of his borrowed truck and headed for the Dormantown station of the state police. His doubts returned with a rush as the police sergeant, half an hour later, gravely noted down his charge.

"You found the engine, you say?" The policeman reached that point finally.

"Yes."

"Did you report your find to the Crescentville branch of the state police?"

Pendrake hesitated. It was impossible to explain the instinctive way he had covered up his possession of the engine without the engine as evidence of how unusual a find it was. He said at last, "I thought at first it was a piece of junk. When I discovered it wasn't, I quickly learned that no such loss had been reported. I decided on the policy of finders keepers."

'But the rightful owners now have it?"

"I would say so, yes," Pendrake admitted. "But their use of guns, their secrecy, the way they forced me to sell the plane convince me I ought to press the matter."

The policeman made a note, then, "Can you give me the manufacturer's number of the engine?"

Pendrake groaned. He went out finally into the gathering dusk feeling that he had fired a dud shot into impenetrable night.

He reached Washington by the morning plane from Dormantown and went at once to the office of Hoskins, Kendlon, Baker, and Hoskins, patent attorneys. A moment after his name had been sent in, a slim, dandified young man broke out of a door and came loping across the anteroom. Oblivious of the startled amazement of the reception clerk, he cried in an intense voice:

"The Air Force's Man of Steel. Jim, I—"

He stopped. His blue eyes widened. Some of the color went out of his cheeks and he stared with a stricken look at Pendrake's empty sleeve. Silently, he pulled Pendrake into his private office. He muttered, "The man who pulled knobs off doors when he was in a hurry and crushed anything in his hands when he got excited—" He shook himself, threw off the gloom with an effort. "How's Eleanor, Jim?"

Pendrake had known the beginning was going to be hard. As briefly as possible, he explained: "—You know what she was like. She held that job in the research department of the Hilliard Encyclopedia Company, an out-of-the-world existence that I pulled her away from, and—"

He finished after a moment and plunged instantly into a detailed account of the engine. By the time he reached the end of his story, Hoskins was pacing the office floor.

"A secret group with a new, marvelous engine invention. Jim, this sounds big to me. I'm well connected with the Air Force and know Commissioner Blakeley. But there's no time to waste. Have you plenty of money?"

Pendrake nodded doubtfully. "I guess so."

"I mean, we can't waste time on red tape. Can you lay out five thousand dollars for the electron image camera? You know, the one that was invented just at the end of the war? Maybe you'll get your money back, maybe you won't. The important thing is that you go to that hillside where you found the engine and photograph the soil electrons. We must have a picture of that engine to convince the type of cynic that's beginning to show himself in town again, the fellow who won't believe anything he doesn't see, and gives you a sustained runaround if you can't show him."

The man's excitement was contagious. Pendrake jumped up. "I'll leave at once. Where can I get one of those cameras?"

"There's a firm in town that sells them to the government and to various educational institutes for geologic and archaeologic purposes. Now, look, Jim, I hate to rush you off like this. I'd like you to come home and meet my wife; but time is of the essence in those photographs. That soil is exposed to the light, and the image will be fuzzy."

"I'll be seeing you," Pendrake said, and started for the door.

The prints came out beautifully clear, the image of the machine unmistakable. Pendrake was sitting in his living room admiring the glossy finish when the girl from the telephone office knocked.

"There's a long-distance call for you from New York," she said. "The party is waiting. Will you come to the exchange?"

"Hoskins," Pendrake thought, though he couldn't imagine what Ned would be doing in New York. The first sound of the strange voice on the phone chilled him. "Mr. Pendrake," it said quietly, "we have reason to believe that you are still attached to your wife. It would be regrettable if anything should happen to her as a result of your meddling in something that does not concern you. Take heed."

There was a click. The sharp little sound was still echoing in Pendrake's mind minutes later as he walked blankly along the street. Only one thing stood out clearly: The investigation was over.

The days dragged. For the first time it struck Pendrake that it was the engine that had galvanized him out of his long stupor. And that he had launched on the search as swiftly as he had because deep inside of him had been the realization that without the engine he would have nothing. It was worse than that. He tried to resume the old tenor of his existence. And he couldn't. The almost mindless rides on Dandy that once had lasted from dawn to dark ended abruptly before 10.00 a.m. on two successive days. And were not resumed. It wasn't that he no longer wanted to go riding. It was simply that life was more than an idler's dream. The three-years' sleep was over. On the fifth day, a telegram arrived from Hoskins:

WHAT'S THE MATTER? I'VE BEEN EXPECTING TO HEAR FROM YOU.

NED.

Uneasily, Pendrake tore the message to shreds. He intended to answer it, but he was still cudgeling his brain over the exact wording of his reply two days later when the letter arrived:

—cannot understand your silence. I have interested Air Commissioner Blakeley, and some technical staff officers have already called on me. In another week I'll look like a fool. You bought the camera; I checked up on that. You must have the pictures, so for Pete's sake let me hear from you—

Pendrake answered that:

I am dropping the case, I am sorry that I bothered you with it, but I have found out something which completely transforms my views on the affair, and I am not at liberty to reveal what it is.

Wouldn't reveal it would have been the truth, but it would be inexpedient to say so. These active Air Force officers—he had been one of them in his time—couldn't yet have got into their systems that fact that peace was radically different from war. The threat to Eleanor would merely make them impatient; her death or injury would constitute a casualty list so minor as to be beneath consideration. Naturally, they would take precautions. But to hell with them.

On the third day after he sent the letter, a taxi drew up before the gate of the cottage, and Hoskins and a bearded giant climbed out. Pendrake let them in, quietly acknowledged the introduction to the great Blakeley, and sat cold before the storm of questions. After ten minutes, Hoskins was as white as a sheet.

"I can't understand it," he raved. "You took the photos, didn't you?"

No answer.

"How did they come out?"

Silence.

"This thing you learned that transformed your views, did you obtain further information as to who is behind the engine?"

Pendrake thought in anguish that he should have lied outright in his letter, instead of making a stupidly compromising statement. What he had said had been bound to arouse intense curiosity and this agony of interrogation.

"Let me talk to him, Hoskins." Pendrake felt a distinct relief as Commissioner Blakeley spoke. It would be easier to deal with a stranger. He saw that Hoskins was shrugging as he seated himself on the chesterfield and nervously lighted a cigarette.

The big man began in a cool, deliberate tone: "I think what we have here is a psychological case. Pendrake, do you remember that fellow who in 1936 or thereabouts claimed to have an engine that got its power from the air? When the reporters swarmed over his car, they found a carefully concealed battery. And then," the cold, biting voice went on, "there was a woman who, two years ago, claimed to have seen a German submarine in Lake Ontario. Her story got wilder and wilder as the navy's investigation progressed, and finally she admitted she had told the story to friends to rouse interest in herself, and when the publicity started she didn't have the nerve to tell the truth. Now, in your case, you're being smarter."

The extent of the insult brought a twisted smile to Pendrake's face. He stood like that, staring at the floor, listening almost idly to the verbal humiliation he was being subjected to. He felt so remote from the hammering voice that his surprise was momentarily immense as two gigantic hands grabbed his lapels and the handsome, bearded face poked belligerently into his, and the scathing voice blared:

"That's the truth, isn't it?"

He hadn't thought of himself as being wrought up. He had no sense of rage as, with an impatient sweep of his hand, he broke the big man's double grip on him, whirled him around, caught him by the collar of his coat and carried him, kicking and shouting in amazement, into the hallway and through the screen door onto the verandah. There was a wild moment as Blakeley was heaved onto the lawn below. He came to his feet bellowing. But Pendrake was already turning away. In the doorway he met Hoskins. Hoskins had his coat and bowler hat. He said in a level voice:

"I'm going to remind you of something—" He intoned the words of the great pledge of men of honor. And he couldn't have known that he had won because he walked down the steps without looking back. The waiting taxi was gone before Pendrake grasped how completely those final words had defeated his own purpose.

That night he wrote the letter to Eleanor. He followed it the next day at the hour he had named: 3.30 p.m. When the plump Negress opened the door of the big white house, Pendrake had the fleeting impression that he was going to be told that Eleanor was out. But she wasn't. He was led through the familiar halls into the forty-foot living room. The Venetian blinds were drawn against the sun and so it took a moment for Pendrake to make out in the gloom the figure of the lithe young woman who had risen to meet him.

Her voice came, rich, familiar, questioning, out of the dimness: "Your letter was not very explanatory. However, I had intended to see you anyway; but never mind that. What danger am I in?"

He could see her more clearly now. And for a moment he could only stand there, drinking her in with his eyes—her slim body, every feature of her face, and the dark hair that crowned it. He grew aware that she was flushing under his intense scrutiny. Quickly, he began his explanation.

"My intention," he said, "was to drop the whole affair. But just as I thought I had ended the matter by tossing Blakeley out, I was reminded by Hoskins of my Air Force oath to my country."

"Oh!"

"For your own safety," he went on, more decisive now, "you must leave Crescentville for the time being, lose yourself in the vastness of New York until this matter has been probed to the bottom."

"I see!" Her dark gaze was non-committal. She looked oddly stiff, sitting in the chair she had chosen, as if she was not quite at ease. She said at last, "The voices of the two men who spoke to you, the gunman and the man on the phone—what were they like?"

27

Pendrake hesitated. "One was a young man's voice. The other, middle-aged."

"No, I don't mean that. I mean the texture, the command of language, the degree of education."

"Oh!" Pendrake stared at her. He said slowly, "I hadn't thought of that. Very well educated, I should say."

"English?"

"No, American."

"That's what I meant. Nothing foreign, though?"

"Not the slightest."

They were both, Pendrake realized, more at ease now. And he was delighted at the cool way she was facing her danger. After all, she wasn't trained to face down physical terrors; and being an introvert wouldn't help her any. Before he could think further, she said:

"This engine—what kind is it? Have you any idea?"

Did he have any idea! He who had racked his brain into the dark watches of a dozen nights! "It must," said Pendrake carefully, "have grown out of a tremendous background of research. Nothing so perfect could spring full grown into existence without a mighty base of other men's work to build on. Though even with that, somebody must have had an inspiration of pure genius." He finished quietly, "It's an atomic engine, I should say. It *can't* be anything else. There's no other comparable background."

She was staring at him, looking not quite sure of her next words. She said at last in a formal voice: "You don't mind my asking these questions?"

He knew what *that* meant. She had suddenly become aware that she was thawing. He thought: "Oh, damn these sensitives." He said quickly, earnestly, "You have already cleared up some important points. Just where they will lead is another matter. Can you suggest anything else?"

There was silence, then: "I realize," she said slowly, "that I am not properly qualified. I have no scientific knowledge, but I do have my research training. I don't know whether my next question is foolish or not, but—what is the decisive date for atomic energy?"

Pendrake frowned, said, "I think I see what you mean. What is the latest date that an atomic engine *couldn't* have been developed?"

"Something like that," she agreed. Her eyes were bright.

Pendrake was thoughtful. "I've been reading up on it lately. 1938 might fit, but 1940 is more likely."

"Ten years?"

Pendrake nodded. He knew what she was going to say, and that it was excellent, but he waited for her to say it. She did, after a moment. "Is there any way you can check up on the activities of every able person who has done atomic research in this country during that time?"

He inclined his head. "I'll go first," he said, "to my old physics professor. He's one of those perpetually young old men who keep abreast of everything."

Her voice, steady, cool, cut him off. "You're going to pursue this search in person?"

She glanced involuntarily at his right sleeve as she finished, then flushed scarlet. There was no doubt of the memory that was in her mind. Pendrake said swiftly, with a wan smile, "I'm afraid there's no one else. A soon as I've made a little progress I'll go to Blakeley and apologize for treating him as I did. Until then, right arm or not, I doubt if there's anyone more capable than I am." He frowned. "Of course, there is the fact that a one-armed man is easily spotted."

She had control of herself again. "I was going to suggest that you obtain an artificial arm and a flesh mask. Those people must have worn civilian masks if you recognized the disguise so quickly. You can secure the perfect soldier's type."

She stood up and finished in a level voice: "As for leaving Crescentville, I had already written my old firm, and they are hiring me in my former position. That was what I intended to see you about. I shall leave the house secretly tonight, and by tomorrow you should be free to pursue your investigations. Good luck."

They faced each other, Pendrake shocked to his core by the abrupt termination of the meeting, and by her words. They parted like two people who had been under enormous strain.

"And that," Pendrake thought as he stood out in the sun's glare, "is the truth."

It was after midnight, September 8th. Pendrake walked, head bent, into a strong east wind along a well-lighted street in the Riverdale section of New York City. He peered at the numbers of the houses as he pressed by: 418, 420, 432.

No. 432 was the third house from the corner; and he walked on past it to the lightpost. Back to the wind, he stood in the bright glow, once more studying his precious list—a final verification. His original intention had been to investigate every one of the seventy-three eastern Americans on that list, starting with the A's. On second thought, he had realized that scientists of firms like Westinghouse, the Rockefeller Foundation, private laboratories with small means, and physicists and professors who were carrying on individual research, were the least likely candidates, the former because of the impossibility of secrecy, the latter because that engine *must* have plenty of money behind it. Which left three private foundations. By far the wealthiest of these was the Lambton Institute, whose distinguished executive physicist, Dr. McClintock Grayson, lived in the third house from the corner.

He reached the front door of the darkened residence, and experienced his first disappointment. In a dim way he had hoped the door would be unlocked. It wasn't; and that meant all the doors he had opened in his life without ever noticing they were locked would now have to be precedents, proofs that a Yale lock could be broken silently. It seemed different doing it on purpose, but he tensed himself, and gripped the knob. The lock broke with the tiny click of metal that has been abruptly subjected to unbearable pressure.

In the inky hallway, Pendrake stood for a moment listening. But the only sound was the pounding of his heart. He went forward cautiously, using his flashlight as he peered into doors. Presently, he verified that the study must be on the second floor. He took the stairs four at a time.

The hallway of the second floor was large, with five closed doors and two open ones leading from it. The first open door led to a bedroom; the second into a large, cozy room lined with bookshelves. Pendrake sighed with relief as he tiptoed into it. There was a desk in one corner, a small filing cabinet and several floor lamps. After a swift survey, he closed the door behind him and turned on the trilight beside the chair next to the desk.

Once again he waited, listening with every nerve tensed. From somewhere near came a faint, regular breathing. But that was all. The *ménage* of Dr. Grayson was resting peacefully from its day's labors, which—Pendrake reflected as he seated himself at the desk—was where they ought to be. It would be unfair of fate to let him be interrupted now.

At two o'clock he had his man. The proof was a scrawled note abstracted from a mass of irrelevant papers that cluttered one drawer. It read:

The pure mechanics of the engine's operation depends on revolutions per minute. At very low r.p.m., *i.e.*, fifty to one hundred, the pressure will be almost entirely on a line vertical to the axial plane. If weights have been accurately estimated, a machine will at this stage lift buoyantly, but the forward movement will be almost zero—

Pendrake paused there, puzzled. It couldn't be anything but *the* engine that was being discussed. But what did it mean? He read on:

As the number of r.p.m. increases, the pressure will shift rapidly toward the horizontal, until, at about five hundred revolutions, the pull will be along the axial plane—and all counter or secondary pressure will have ceased. It is at this stage that the engine can be pushed along a shaft, but not pulled. The field is so intense that—

The reference to the shaft was ultimately convincing. He remembered only too well his own violent discovery that the shaft could not be pulled out of the engine.

The atomic wizard of the age was Dr. Grayson.

Quite suddenly, Pendrake felt weak. He lay back in the chair, strangely dizzy. He thought: "Got to get out of here. Now that I know, I can't take the chance of being caught."

The wild triumph came as the front door closed behind him. He walked down the street, his mind soaring with such a drunken exultancy that he swayed like an intoxicated person. He was eating breakfast at a lunch counter a mile away when the reaction came: So Dr. Grayson, famous *savant*, was the man behind the marvelous engine! So what now?

In the morning he phoned Hoskins long distance. "It's impossible," he thought, as he waited for the call to be put through, "that I carry on with this tremendous business all by myself."

If anything should happen to him, what he had discovered would dissolve into the great darkness, perhaps never to be reconstituted. After all, he was here because he had taken to heart a timeless oath of allegiance to his country, an oath that he had not, until reminded, considered relevant.

His reverie ended as the operator said: "Mr. Hoskins refuses to accept your call, sir."

His problem seemed as old as his existence. As he sat in the hotel library that afternoon, his mind kept coming back to the aloneness of his position, the reality that all decisions about the engine were his to make and his to act upon. What an incredible fool he was! He ought to put the whole miserable business out of his mind and go to a movie. Or return to Crescentville. The property there would need attention before winter. But he knew he wouldn't go. What would he do in that lonely town during the long days and the long nights of the coming years?

There was only the engine. All his interest in life, his rebirth of spirit dated from the moment that he had found the doughnut-shaped thing. Without the engine, or rather—he made the qualification consciously—without the search for the engine, he was a lost soul, wandering aimlessly through the eternity that was *being* on earth.

After a timeless period he grew aware suddenly of the weight of the book in his hands and remembered his purpose in coming to the library. The book was the 1948 edition of the *Hilliard*

Encyclopedia, and it revealed that Dr. McClintock Grayson had been born in 1897, that he had one daughter and two sons, and that he had made notable contributions to the fission theory of atomic science. Of Cyrus Lambton the *Encyclopedia* said:

—manufacturer, philanthropist, he founded the Lambton Institute in 1936. Since the war, Mr. Lambton has become actively interested in a Back to the Land Movement, the uniquely designed headquarters for this project being located at—

Pendrake went out finally into the warm September afternoon and bought a car. His days became a drab routine. Watch Grayson come out of his house in the morning, follow him until he disappeared into the Lambton Building, trail him home at night. It seemed endless, purposeless, hopeless. The world became a pattern of gray streets unreeling. He felt himself a wheel turning over and over on its axle, turning, turning, because it was easier to do that than to decide what else his life was good for.

On the seventeenth day the routine broke like a wave striking a wedge of rock. At one o'clock in the afternoon Grayson emerged briskly from the aerogel plastic structure that was the post-war abode of the Lambton Foundation.

The hour itself was startling. But immediately the difference of this day to the others showed more clearly. The scientist ignored his gray sedan parked beside the building, walked half a block to a taxi stand, and was driven to a twin-turreted building on Fiftieth Street; a plasto-glitter sign splashed across the two towers:

CYRUS LAMBTON LAND
SETTLEMENT PROJECT

As Pendrake watched, Grayson dismissed the taxi, and disappeared through a revolving door into one of the broad-based towers. Puzzled, but vaguely excited, Pendrake sauntered to a window that had a large glitter sign in it. The sign read:

wants earnest, sincere young couples who are willing to work hard to establish themselves on rich soil in a verdant and wonderful climate.

Former farmers, sons of farmers and their daughter-of-farmers' wives are especially welcome. No one who desires proximity to a city or who has relatives he must visit need apply. Here is a real opportunity under a private endowment plan.

Three more couples wanted today for the latest allotment, which will leave shortly under the monitorship of Dr. McClintock Grayson. Office open until 11 p.m.

HURRY!

It seemed meaningless and without connection to an engine lying on a hillside. But it brought a thought that wouldn't go away; a thought that was really a product of an urge that had been pressing at him for all the dreary days now past. For an hour he fought the impulse, then it grew too big for his brain, and projected down into his muscles, carried him unresisting to a phone booth. A minute later he was dialling the number of the Hilliard Encyclopedia Company.

There was a moment while she was being called to the phone. He thought a thousand thoughts, and twice he nearly hung up the receiver; and then:

"Jim, what's happened?"

The anxiety in her voice was the sweetest sound he had ever heard. Pendrake held himself steady as he explained what he wanted: "—you'll have to get yourself an old coat and put on a cheap cotton dress or something; and I'll buy some second-hand things. All I want is to find out what is behind that land-settlement scheme. We could go in before dark this evening. A simple inquiry shouldn't be dangerous."

His mind was blurred with the possibility of seeing her again. And so the uneasy idea of possible danger stayed deep inside him and did not rise to the surface until he saw her coming along the street. She would have walked right past, but he stepped out and said :

"Eleanor!"

She stopped short; and, looking at her, it struck him for the first time that the slip of a girl he had married six years before was grown up. She was still slim enough to satisfy any woman, but the richer contours of maturity were there, too. She said:

"I forgot about the mask, and the artificial arm. They make you look almost—"

Pendrake smiled grimly. "Almost human, eh?"

He knew instantly that he had said the wrong thing. She turned as pale as gray metal. For a panicky moment it seemed to Pendrake that she was going to faint. He caught her arm, cried, "I'm sorry, Eleanor. I'm a damned idiot. I ought to be shot."

"You had no right to say that," she breathed. "I know I was foolish that day three years ago when you returned from China. I ought not to have screamed when I saw your empty sleeve. But you should have written. You-should-have-written."

She made no move to withdraw her wrist from his fingers, and he could feel her trembling. He said in an intense voice, "Eleanor, it was all my fault. My walking out on you in front of all those people—it was the damnedest humiliation ever inflicted on a sensitive woman."

"You were overwrought from your terrible loss; and my scream—"

"I was a scoundrel. I deserve—"

He stopped because she was staring at him with a strange tenderness that made his mind reel. She said, "Let's forget it, Jim. And now, is that the building over there?"

"Eleanor, did you say—"

"We'll have to hurry if we intend to get in before it gets really dark."

"Eleanor, when you said 'let's forget it,' did you mean—"

But Eleanor stood staring across at the building, a complacent smile on her lips. "Aerogel turrets," she mused aloud, "a hundred and fifty feet high; one completely opaque, windowless, doorless —I wonder what that means—and the other—We'll be Mr. and

35

Mrs. Lester Cranston, Jim, of Winora, Idaho. And we were going to leave New York tonight but saw their sign. We'll love everything about their scheme."

She started across the street. And Pendrake, tagging along behind, was following her through the door before his senses snapped back into position. In one comprehensive leap of mind he saw that it was his own emotional desire to see her that had brought her here.

"Eleanor," he said tensely, "we're not going in."

He should have known it would be useless to speak. Inside, he followed her with reluctant steps to a girl who sat at a spacious plastic desk in the center of the room. He was seated before the glitter sign at the edge of the desk caught his eye:

MISS GRAYSON

Miss— What! Pendrake twisted in his chair, and then a vast uneasiness held him steady. Dr. Grayson's daughter! So the scientist's family was mixed up in this. It was even possible that two of the four men who had taken the plane from him had been sons. And perhaps Lambton also had sons. He couldn't remember what the *Encyclopedia* had said about the children of Lambton.

In the intensity of his thoughts he listened with half-attention to the conversation between Eleanor and Grayson's daughter. But when Eleanor stood up, he remembered that the talk had been of a psychological test in the back room. Pendrake watched Eleanor walk across to the door that led to the second tower, and he was glad when, after about three minutes, Miss Grayson said:

"Will you go in now, Mr. Cranston?"

The door opened into a narrow corridor, and there was another door at the end of it. As his fingers touched the knob of the second door, a net fell over him and drew taut.

Simultaneously, a slot opened to his right. Dr. Grayson, a syringe in his fingers, reached through, pushed the needle into Pendrake's right arm above the elbow, and then called over his shoulder to somebody out of sight:

"This is the last one, Peter. We can leave as soon as it gets dark."

The slot clicked shut.

Pendrake squirmed desperately. He fought there under that dim ceiling of light, striking against the net that held him. And every instant the terror grew, the terror that was in him, not for himself, but for Eleanor—Eleanor, who had gone through this door minutes before.

He would have cried out, but his rage was too great, his fear for her too near insanity. Eleanor, who had no artificial arm to take the shock of the dope from the syringe. He stopped the thought by an effort so violent that his whole being shook. He must pretend to have succumbed. Only thus could he avoid another syringe that might be more accurately aimed at a vital spot.

As he let himself slump, a voice said, "That fellow fought too hard. You'll have to increase the dose for these powerful-looking men."

The words were Pendrake's first knowledge that his struggle had been observed. He let himself slump farther, and after a moment realized that the net was moving, lifting. A door opened in the ceiling and brightness pressed against his eyelids.

"Lay him down here beside his wife."

His body touched a softness that seemed to yield endlessly like a bottomless cushion. The net writhed and wriggled from under him; and suddenly it was gone. The young man's voice said, "Look at this, he's severed four of the net strands. I thought this plastiwire was unbreakable."

The older man's voice came from a greater distance: "Strength is a curious quality. A dog can strain at a leash until it rots—or break it the first day if he lunges against it with enough snap. It—"

The scientist's voice faded, as if he had gone into another room and closed the door.

Gradually, as Pendrake lay there, he grew aware of breathing around him, the slow, measured breathing of many people. The sound, with all its implications of human beings still alive, eased the dreadful tightness in his throat. He slitted his eyes and saw that he was in a round metal room filled with scores of enormous hammocks that were suspended by cords attached to both the metal floor and the metal ceiling. Twice, Pendrake slid his leg over with the intention of dropping to the floor. But each time a vague snatch of sound made him sink back and slow his breath into rhythm with that of the others.

He was preparing for his third effort when his body was struck a sharp, all-over blow. Beneath him the hammock sagged at least two feet, and there was an awful emptiness inside him, like the nausea of sustained hunger. It was like that for a very long time, and actually there was no change in the fact. But his body grew accustomed to the relentless pressure. Finally, puzzled, he slid out of the voluminous folds of his hammock and dropped to the floor.

He fell hard. The violence of it strained his muscles, and there was a pressing weight on him that stunned because it was beyond all his experience. And because he recognized it. Acceleration! He must be in a ship. That damnable second tower had contained a ship powered by atomic engines. But what kind of a ship?

The thought faded as, with a blank will, he scrambled to his feet. There was a stairway leading to a closed door. But the door opened at his touch. One lightning glance revealed that no human beings were in the room. There was a window that showed a black sky punctuated with stars, and in the room itself, mounted on rigid metal bars, eight engines were spinning. For a moment, to his tensed mind, to his body concentrated on possible, impending danger, the scene seemed normal enough.

The number of engines didn't matter. If one existed, so could eight. And their unlimited power could surely raise a ship out of a hundred-and-fifty foot turret, though the speed of that rise in the night had been unnatural. Still, eight of those engines, spinning on their shafts, was quite an assembly.

The normalness shattered. Pendrake sent a glance wild with surmise at the engines. *The engines were spinning* on rigid shafts, and it should be the shafts that spun. His memory flung back to the night in his stable when the engine had lifted with strange buoyancy from the floor, spun slowly and—How could he have missed the significance? How *could* he?

With a hissing intake of his breath, he ran to the window. But the knowledge of what he would find was already in him. For a long moment he shivered with the physical daze of seeing interplanetary space, and then he drew his body and his mind into closer union and was himself. He reached the room where Dr. Grayson and the young men were lying in their hammocks. The latter he dealt one stunning blow—and tied them both with cords from their hammocks, tied them into their hammocks, wrapping the cords around and around.

There was silence in the control room. His mind felt far away, cold, joyless. His victory seemed somehow lacking. He couldn't quite place the missing factor, but perhaps it was the stunned expressions of the two prisoners. Uncertain, Pendrake studied the small instrument board. He thought finally: "That note I found in Dr. Grayson's study. All I've got to do is reduce the r.p.m. of the engines to less than five hundred. The pressure will gradually shift toward a line vertical to the axial plane and the spaceship will turn in a great circle and head back toward Earth."

He glanced at the men and then he walked slowly to an expanse of transparent aerogel, and stood staring out into the velvet, light-sprinkled night. The sun was a ghastly, flaring shape to his left. Pendrake said, without looking at the men:

"Where are you going? Mars, Venus, the Moon, or—" He stopped. He couldn't help it. Mars, Venus— He felt dizzy, then electrified. The wonders of the skies! The only divine cognomens that would survive all the ages of religion! "*Which one?*" Pendrake gasped. "Which planet?"

"Venus!" The answer sighed from the older man. "We have a coloney there. Quite a large one now. A ship with a hundred people leaves from one of our centers every three days—and there have been children."

Pendrake said sternly, "A hundred people kidnapped from Earth every three days—doped." He choked a little.

"Denilin sleep drug!" said Grayson. "Harmless, quick, no after effects. It saves simple people from their terror of something new, like space. When they get to Venus they don't mind. The planet is smaller, you know, than has been thought, not more than six thousand five hundred miles, more clouds high up, none below. But the brightness of the sun comes through without the heat; and all the glories of Earth cannot compare with the treasure land that is Venus, No, they don't mind when they see— You must be Pendrake—that stiff right arm—We wondered about you."

"Doped!" repeated Pendrake. But the miasma of his fears was fading. There was greater uncertainty in his voice as he said, "But why the secrecy? This great invention! Properly exploited it would be—"

"It would ruin everything!" It was the young man, his tone desperate. "Pendrake, we're not criminals. There are seventeen famous scientists and their families in this—the greatest names in atomic science. They decided in 1944 when the engine was invented, when the war was already won, that the planets should not inherit the bitterness of Earth. Don't you see, a scramble for territory would be hell? Our plan is to establish the nucleus of a new nation, modeled after the United States; and everybody who migrates becomes—a Venusian."

It was several hours later that the spaceship landed on a darkened lot. Pendrake and Eleanor climbed to the ground and stood silently watching the torpedo-shaped spaceship merge again with the clouded night sky.

The letter came to the big white house a week later:

Air Commissioner Blakeley has noted the names of the scientists on the list you submitted, but feels that further correspondence with you would be fruitless.

Pendrake grinned at his wife. "Now, everybody's satisfied. I *had* to report it, of course, but"—his expression grew thoughtful —"it is hard to believe the planets will have their chance because I tossed a loud-mouthed fool out on his ear one August afternoon."

THE GREAT JUDGE

"JUDGMENT," said the rad, "in the case of Douglas Aird, tried for treason on August 2nd, last—"

With a trembling movement of his fingers, Aird turned the volume control higher. The next words blared at him.

"—That Douglas Aird do surrender himself one week from this day, that is, on September 17, 2460 A.D., to his neighborhood patrol station, that he then be taken to the nearest converter, there to be put to death—"

Click!

He had no conscious memory of shutting off the rad. One instant the sound roared through his apartment, the next there was dead silence. Aird sank back in his chair and stared with sick eyes through the transparent walls out upon the shining roofs of The Judge's City. All these weeks he had known there was no chance. The scientific achievements that, he had tried to tell himself, would weigh the balance in his favor—even as he assessed their value to the race, he had realized that the Great Judge would not consider them from the same viewpoint as himself.

He had made the fatal error of suggesting in the presence of "friends" that a mere man like Douglas Aird could govern as well as the immortal Great Judge, and that in fact it might be a good idea if someone less remote from the needs of the mass of the people had a chance to promulgate decrees. A little less restriction, he had urged, and a little more individuality. With such abandon he had spoken on the day that he succeeded in transferring the nervous impulses of a chicken into the nervous system of a dog.

He had attempted to introduce the discovery as evidence that he was in an excited and abnormal state of mind. But the magistrate pronounced the reason irrelevant, immaterial, and facetious.

41

He refused to hear what the discovery was, ruling coldly: "The official science investigator of the Great Judge will call on you in due course, and you will then turn your invention over to him complete with adequate documentation."

Aird presumed gloomily that the investigator would call in a day or so. He toyed with the possibility of destroying his papers and instruments. Shudderingly, he rejected that form of defiance. The Great Judge's control of life was so complete that he permitted his enemies to remain at large until the day of their execution. It was a point made much of by the Great Judge's propaganda department. Civilization, it was said, had never before attained so high a level of freedom. But it wouldn't do to try the patience of the Great Judge by destroying an invention. Aird had a sharp conviction that less civilized methods might be used on him if he failed to carry through the farce.

Sitting there in his apartment, surrounded by every modern convenience, Aird sighed. He would spend his last week alive in any luxury he might choose. It was the final refinement of mental torture, to be free, to have the feeling that if only he could think of something he might succeed in escaping. Yet he knew escape was impossible. If he climbed into his hopjet, he'd have to swoop in at the nearest patrol station, and have his electronic registration "plates" stamped with a signal. Thereafter, his machine would continuously give off vibrations automatically advising patrol vessels of the time and space limitations of his permit.

Similar restrictions controlled his person. The electronic instrument "printed" on his upper right arm could be activated by any central, which would start a burning sensation of gradually increasing intensity.

There was absolutely no escape from the law of the Great Judge.

Aird climbed to his feet wearily. Might as well get his material ready for the science investigator. It was too bad he wouldn't have an opportunity to experiment with higher life forms but—

Aird stopped short in the doorway of his laboratory. His body throbbed with the tremendousness of the idea that had slammed into his mind. He began to quiver. He leaned weakly against the doorjamb, then slowly straightened.

"That's it!" He spoke the words aloud, his voice low and intense, simultaneously utterly incredulous and hopeful to the point of madness. It was the mounting hope that brought a return of terrible weakness. He collapsed on the rug just inside the laboratory, and lay there muttering to himself, the special insanities of an electronician.

". . . . have to get a larger grid, and more liquid, and—"

Special Science Investigator George Mollins returned to the Great Judge's Court, and immediately asked for a private interview with the Great Judge.

"Tell him," he told the High Bailiff of the Court, "that I have come across a very important scientific discovery. He will know what is meant if you simply say 'Category AA.'"

While he waited to be received, the Science Investigator arranged his instruments for readier transport, and then he stood idly looking around him at the dome-vaulted anteroom. Through a transparent wall he could see the gardens below. In the profusion of greenery, he caught the glint of a white skirt, which reminded him that the Great Judge was reputed to have at least seven reigning beauties in his harem at all times.

"This way, sir. The Great Judge will receive you."

The man who sat behind the desk looked about thirty-five years old. Only his eyes and his mouth seemed older. From bleak blue eyes and with thin-lipped silence, the immortal, ever-young Great Judge studied his visitor.

The latter wasted no time. The moment the door shut behind him, he pressed the button that released a fine spray of gas straight at the Great Judge. The man behind the desk simply sagged in his chair.

The visitor was calm but quick. He dragged the limp body around to his instrument case, and removed the clothes of the upper body. Swiftly, he swabbed the body with the liquid he had brought, and began to attach his nodes. Half a dozen on one side and a dozen on the other. The next step was to attach the wires to his own body, lie down, and press the activator.

The question that puzzled Douglas Aird on the day that he

succeeded in transferring the nervous impulses of a chicken into the nervous system of a dog was, how complete was the transference?

Personality, he argued with himself, was a complex structure. It grew out of many quadrillions of minute experiences and, as he had discovered, finally gave to each body its own special neural vibration.

Would it be possible by artificially forcing that exact vibration upon another body to establish a nerve energy flow between the two bodies? A flow so natural and easy that every cell would be impregnated with the thoughts and memories of the other body? A flow so complete, that, when properly channeled, the personality of one body would flow into the other?

The fact that a dog acted like a chicken was not complete proof. Normally, he would have experimented very carefully before trying it on a human being. But a man doomed to die didn't have to think of risks. When the Science Investigator called on him two days before the date of the execution, he gassed the man, and made the experiment then and there.

The transference was not absolutely complete. Blurred memories remained behind, enough to make the routine of going to the Great Judge's Court familiar and easy. He had worried about that. It was important that he follow the right etiquette in approaching a man who normally permitted no one near him but people he had learned to trust.

As it turned out, he did everything right. The moment he felt the blurring sensation which marked the beginning of the transfer of his personality from the body of the Science Investigator to the body of the Great Judge, Aird acted. He released a gas toward the Great Judge that would revive the man in about five minutes. Simultaneously, he sprayed his present body with instantaneous anaesthetic gas. Even as he sank into unconsciousness, he could feel the sharp, hard personality of the Great Judge slipping into the Investigator's body.

Five minutes later Douglas Aird, now in the body of the Great Judge, opened his eyes, and looked around him alertly. Carefully, he disconnected the wires, packed the instruments—

and then called a bailiff. As he had expected, no one questioned the actions of the Great Judge. It was the work of an hour to drive to the apartment of Douglas Aird, transfer the Great Judge's personality to the body of Douglas Aird—and at the same time return the personality of the Science Investigator into its proper body. As a precaution, he had the Science Investigator taken to a hospital.

"Keep him there for three days under observation," he commanded.

Back at the Great Judge's Court, he spent the next few days cautiously fitting himself into the pleasant routine of a life of absolute power. He had a thousand plans for altering a police state into a free state, but as a scientist he was sharply aware of the need for orderly transition.

It was at the end of a week that he inquired casually about a traitor named Douglas Aird. The story was interesting. The man had, it seemed, attempted to escape. He had flown some five hundred miles in an unregistered hopjet before being grounded by a local patrol. Immediately, he fled into the mountains. When he failed to report on the morning of the day set for his execution, the printed instrument on his right arm was activated. Shortly before dusk, a tired, distracted, staggering scarecrow of a man, screaming that he was the Great Judge, appeared in a mountain patrol station. The execution was then carried out with no further delay.

The report concluded: "Seldom in the experience of the attending patrol officers has a condemned man approached the converter with so much reluctance."

The Great Judge, sitting at his desk in the luxurious court, could well believe it.

SECRET UNATTAINABLE

THE file known as Secret Six was smuggled out of Berlin in mid-1945 when Russia was in sole occupation of the city. How it was brought to the United States is one of those dramatic true tales of World War II. The details cannot yet be published since they involve people now in the Russian zone of Germany.

All the extraordinary documents of this file, it should be emphasized, are definitely in the hands of our own authorities; and investigations are proceeding apace. Further revelations of a grand order may be expected as soon as one of the machines is built. All German models were destroyed by the Nazis early in 1945.

The documents date from 1937, and will be given chronologically, without reference to their individual importance. But first, it is of surpassing interest to draw attention to the following news item, which appeared in the New York *Sun*, March 25, 1941, on page 17. At that time it appeared to have no significance whatever. The item:

GERMAN CREEK BECOMES RIVER

London, March 24 (delayed): A Royal Air Force reconnaissance pilot today reported that a creek in northern Prussia, marked on the map as the Gribe Creek, has become a deep, swift river overnight. It is believed that an underground waterway burst its bounds. Several villages in the path of the new river showed under water. No report of the incident has yet been received from Berlin.

There never was any report from Berlin. It should again be pointed out that the foregoing news item was published in

1941; the documents which follow date from 1937, a period of four years. Four years of world-shaking history:

April 10, 1937

From   Secretary, Bureau of Physics
To   Reich and Prussian Minister of Science
Subject   10731—127—S—6

1. Inclosed is the report of the distinguished scientific board of inquiry which sat on the case of Herr Professor Johann Kenrube.

2. As you will see, the majority of the board oppose emphatically the granting of State funds for what they describe as a "fantastic scheme." They deny that a step-up tube would produce the results claimed, and refute utterly the number philosophy involved. Number, they say, is a function, not a reality, or else modern physics has no existence.

3. The minority report of Herr Professor Goureit, while thought-provoking, can readily be dismissed when it is remembered that Goureit, like Kenrube and Kenrube's infamous brother, was once a member of the SPD.

4. The board of inquiry, having in mind Hitler's desire that no field of scientific inquiry should be left unexplored, and as a generous gesture to Goureit, who has a very great reputation and a caustic pen, suggested that, if Kenrube could obtain private funds for his research, he should be permitted to do so.

5. Provided Geheime Staats Polizei do not object, I concur.

G.L.

Author's Note: *The signature G.L. has been difficult to place. There appear to have been several secretaries of the Bureau of Physics Research, following one another in swift order. The best accounts identify him as Gottfried Lesser, an obscure B Sc. who early joined the Nazi party, and for a period was its one and only science expert. Geheime Staats Polizei is of course Gestapo.*

MEMO   April 17, 1937
From   Chief, Science Branch, Gestapo

If Kenrube can find the money, let him go ahead. Himmler concurs, provided supervision be strict.

K. Reissel

COPY ONLY   June 2, 1937
From   Co-ordinator Dept., Deutsche Bank
To   Gestapo

The marginally noted personages have recently transferred sums totaling Reichsmarks four million five hundred thousand to the account of Herr Professor Johann Kenrube. For your information, please.

J Pleup.

June 11, 1937
From   Gestapo
To   Reich and Prussian Minister of Science
Subject   Your 10731—127—S—6

Per your request for further details on the private life of J. Kenrube since the death of his brother in June, 1934, in the purge.

We quote from a witness, Peter Braun: "I was in a position to observe Herr Professor Kenrube very closely when the news was brought to him at Frankfort-on-Main that August, his brother, had been executed in the sacred blood purge.

"Professor Kenrube is a thin, good-looking man with a very wan face normally. This face turned dark with color, then drained completely of blood. He clenched his hands and said: 'They've murdered him!' Then he rushed off to his room.

"Hours later, I saw him walking, hatless, hair disarrayed, along the bank of the river. People stopped to look at him, but he did not see them. He was very much upset that first day. When I saw him again the next morning, he seemed to have recovered.

He said to me: 'Peter, we must all suffer for our past mistakes. The tragic irony of my brother's death is that he told me only a week ago in Berlin that he had been mistaken in opposing the National-sozialistiche Arbeitspartei. He was convinced they they were doing great things. I am too much of a scientist ever to have concerned myself with politics.' "

You will note, Excellency, that this is very much the set speech of one who is anxious to cover up the indiscreet, emotional outburst of the previous day. However, the fact that he was able to pull himself together at all seems to indicate that affection of any kind is but shallowly rooted in his character. Professor Kenrube returned to his laboratories in July, 1934, and has apparently been hard at work ever since.

There has been some discussion here concerning Kenrube, by the psychologists attached to this office; and the opinion is expressed, without dissent, that in three years the professor will almost have forgotten that he had a brother.

K. Reissel.

MEMO AT BOTTOM OF LETTER:

I am more convinced than ever that psychologists should be seen and not heard. It is our duty to watch every relative of every person whose life is, for any reason, claimed by the State. If there are scientific developments of worthwhile nature in this Kenrube affair, let me know at once. His attainments are second to none. A master plan of precaution is in order.

Himmler.

October 24, 1937

From   Secretary, Bureau of Physics
To   Reich and Prussian Minister of Science
Subject   Professor Johann Kenrube

The following report has been received from our Special Agent Seventeen:

"Kenrube has hired the old steel and concrete fortress, Gribe Schloss, overlooking the Gribe Creek, which flows into the Eastern Sea. This ancient fortress was formerly located on a small hill in a valley. The hill has subsided, however, and is now virtually level with the valley floor. We have been busy for more than a month making the old place livable, and installing machinery."

For your information, Agent Seventeen is a graduate in physics of Bonn University. He was for a time professor of physics at Muenchen. In view of the shortage of technicians, Kenrube has appointed Seventeen his chief assistant.

G.L.

May 21,1938

From   Science Branch, Gestapo
To   Reich and Prussian Minister of Science
Subject 10731—127—S—6

Himmler wants to know the latest developments in the Kenrube affair. Why the long silence? Exactly what is Professor Kenrube trying to do, and what progress has he made? Surely, your secret agent has made reports.

K. Reissel.

June 3, 1938

From   Secretary, Bureau of Physics
To   Chief, Science Branch, Gestapo
Subject Professor Johann Kenrube

Your letter of the 21st ultimo has been passed on to me. The inclosed précis of the reports of our Agent Seventeen will bring you up to date.

Be assured that we are keeping a careful watch on the developments in this case. So far, nothing meriting special attention has arisen.

G.L.

Our agent reports that Professor Kenrube's first act was to place him, Seventeen, in charge of the construction of the machine, thus insuring that he will have the most intimate knowledge of the actual physical details.

When completed, the machine is expected to occupy the entire common room of the old fortress, largely because of the use of step-up vacuum tubes. In this connection, Seventeen describes how four electric dynamos were removed from Kenrube's old laboratories, their entire output channeled through the step-up tubes, with the result that a ninety-four per cent improvement in efficiency was noted.

Seventeen goes on to state that orders for parts have been placed with various metal firms but, because of the defense program, deliveries are extremely slow. Professor Kenrube has resigned himself to the possibility that his invention will not be completed until 1944 or '45.

Seventeen, being a scientist in his own right, has become interested in the machine. In view of the fact that, if successful, it will insure measureless supplies of raw materials for our Reich, he urges that some effort be made to obtain priorities.

He adds that he has become quite friendly with Kenrube. He does not think that the Herr Professor suspects how closely he is connected with the Bureau of Science.

June 4, 1938

From   Gestapo
To   Reich and Prussian Minister of Science
Subject 10731—127—S—6

Raw materials! Why was I not informed before that Kenrube was expecting to produce raw materials? Why did you think I was taking an interest in this case, if not because Kenrube is a genius of the first rank; and therefore anything he does must be examined with the most minute care? But—raw materials! Are you all mad over there, or living in a world of pleasant dreams?

You will at once obtain from Herr Professor Kenrube the full plans, the full mathematics of his work, with photographs of the machine as far as it has progressed. Have your scientists prepare a report for me as to the exact nature of the raw materials that Kenrube expects to obtain. Is this some transmutation affair, or what is the method?

Inform Kenrube that he must supply this information or he will obtain no further materials. If he satisfies our requirements, on the other hand, there will be a quickening of supplies. Kenrube is no fool. He will understand the situation.

As for your agent, Seventeen, I am at once sending an agent to act as his bodyguard. Friendly with Kenrube indeed!

Himmler.

June 28, 1938

From   Gestapo
To   Secretary, Bureau of Physics
Subject   Secret Six

Have you received the report from Kenrube? Himmler is most anxious to see this the moment it arrives.

K. Reissel.

July 4, 1938

From   Gestapo
To   Secretary, Bureau of Physics
Subject   Secret Six

What about the Kenrube report? Is it possible that your office does not clearly grasp how important we regard this matter? We have recently discovered that Professor Kenrube's grandfather once visited a very curious and involved revenge on a man whom he hated years after the event that motivated the hatred. Every conceivable precaution must be taken to see to it that the

Kenrube machine can be duplicated, and the machine itself protected.

Please send the scientific report the moment it is available.

K. Reissel.

July 4, 1938

From   Secretary, Bureau of Physics
To   Chief, Science Branch, Gestapo
Subject Professor Johann Kenrube

The report, for which you have been asking, has come to hand, and a complete transcription is being sent to your office under separate cover. As you will see, it is very elaborately prepared; and I have taken the trouble to have a précis made of our scientific board's analysis of the report for your readier comprehension.

G.L.

PRÉCIS
OF
SCIENTIFIC ANALYSIS OF KENRUBE'S REPORT
ON HIS INVENTION

General Statement of Kenrube's Theory: That there are two kinds of space in the universe, normal and hyper-space.

Only in normal space is the distance between star systems and galaxies great. It is essential to the nature of things, to the unity of material bodies, that intimate cohesion exist between every particle of matter, between, for instance, the earth and the universe as a whole.

Kenrube maintains that gravity does not explain the perfect and wonderful balance, the singleness of organism that is a galactic system. And that the theory of relativity merely evades the issue in stating that planets go around the sun because it is easier for them to do that than to fly off into space.

Kenrube's thesis, therefore, is that all the matter in the universe conjoins according to a rigid mathematical pattern, and that this conjunction presupposes the existence of hyper-space.

Object of Invention: To bridge the gap through hyper-space between the Earth and any planet, or any part of any planet. In effect, this means that it would not be necessary to drill for oil in a remote planet. The machine would merely locate the oil stratum, and tap it at any depth; the oil would flow from the orifice of the machine which, in the case of the machine now under construction, is ten feet in diameter.

A ten-foot flow of oil at a pressure of four thousand feet a minute would produce approximately six hundred thousand tons of oil every hour.

Similarly, mining could be carried on simply by locating the ore-bearing veins, and skimming from them the purest ores.

It should be pointed out that, of the distinguished scientists who have examined the report, only Herr Professor Goureit claims to be able to follow the mathematics proving the existence of hyper-space.

COPY ONLY   July 14, 1938

TRANSCRIPTION OF INTERVIEW BY HERR HIMMLER OF PROFESSOR H. KLEINBERG, CHAIRMAN OF THE SCIENTIFIC COMMITTEE OF SCIENCE BRANCH, GESTAPO, INVESTIGATING REPORT OF HERR PROFESSOR JOHANN KENRUBE.

Q. You have studied the drawings and examined the mathematics?
A. Yes.
Q. What is your conclusion?
A. We are unanimously agreed that some fraud is being perpetrated.
Q. Does your verdict relate to the drawings of the invention, or to the mathematics explaining the theory?
A. To both. The drawings are incomplete. A machine made

from those blueprints would hum with apparent power and purpose, but it would be a fraudulent uproar; the power simply goes oftener through a vacuumized circuit before returning to its source.

Q. I have sent your report to Kenrube. His comment is that almost the whole of modern electrical physics is founded on some variation of electricity being forced through a vacuum. What about that?

A. It is a half truth.

Q. What about the mathematics?

A. There is the real evidence. Since Descartes—

Q. Please abstain from using these foreign names.

A. Pardon me. Since Llibniz, number has been a function, a variable idea. Kenrube treats of number as an existing *thing*. Mathematics, he says, has living and being. You have to be a scientist to realize how incredible, impossible, ridiculous, such an idea is.

WRITTEN COMMENT ON THE ABOVE

I am not a scientist. I have no set ideas on the subject of mathematics or invention. I am, however, prepared to accept the theory that Kenrube is withholding information, and for this reason order that:

1. All further materials for the main machine be withheld.
2. Unlimited assistance be given Kenrube to build a model of his machine in the great government laboratories at Dresden. When, and not until, this model is in operation, permission will be given for the larger machine to be completed.
3. Meanwhile, Gestapo scientists will examine the machine at Gribe Schloss, and Gestapo construction experts will, if necessary, reinforce the building, which must have been damaged by the settling of the hill on which it stands.
4. Gestapo agents will hereafter guard Gribe Schloss.

Himmler.

From   Secretary, Bureau of Physics
To   Chief, Science Branch, Gestapo
Subject   Herr Professor Kenrube

Inclosed is the quarterly précis of the reports of our Agent Seventeen.

For your information, please.

August Buehnen

Author's Note: *Buehnen, a party man who was educated in one of the Nazi two-year Science Schools, replaced G.L. as secretary of the Bureau of Physics about September, 1938.*

It is not known exactly what became of Lesser, who was a strong party man. There was a Brigadier General G. Lesser, a technical expert attached to the Fuehrer's headquarters at Smolensk. This man, and there is some evidence that he is the same, was killed in the first battle of Moscow.

QUARTERLY PRÉCIS OF REPORTS
OF
AGENT SEVENTEEN

1. Herr Professor Kenrube is working hard on the model. He has at no time expressed bitterness over the enforced cessation of work on the main machine, and apparently accepts readily the explanation that the government cannot afford to allot him material until the model proves the value of his work.

2. The model will have an orifice of six inches. This compares with the ten-foot orifice of the main machine. Kenrube's intention is to employ it for the procuration of liquids, and believes that the model will of itself go far to reducing the oil shortage in the Reich.

3. The machine will be in operation sometime in the summer of 1939. We are all eager and excited.

February 7, 1939

From   Secretary, Bureau of Physics
To   Gestapo
Subject   Secret Six

The following precautions have been taken with the full knowledge and consent of Herr Professor Kenrube:

1. A diary in triplicate is kept of each day's progress. Two copies are sent daily to our office here. As you know, the other copy is submitted by us to your office.

2. Photographs are made of each part of the machine before it is installed, and detailed plans of each part are kept, all in triplicate, the copies distributed as described above.

3. From time to time independent scientists are called in. They are invariably impressed by Kenrube's name, and suspicious of his mathematics and drawings.

For your information, please.

August Buehnen.

March 1, 1939

From   Reich and Prussian Minister of Science
To   Herr Heinrich Himmler, Gestapo
Subject   The great genius, Herr Professor Kenrube

It is my privilege to inform Your Excellency that the world-shaking invention of Herr Professor Johann Kenrube went into operation yesterday, and has already shown fantastic results.

The machine is not a pretty one, and some effort must be made to streamline future reproductions of this model, with an aim toward greater mobility. In its present condition, it is strung out over the floor in a most ungainly fashion. Rough metal can be very ugly.

Its most attractive feature is the control board, which consists of a number of knobs and dials, the operator of which, by an arrangement of mirrors, can peer into the orifice, which is located on the right side of the control board, and faces away from it. (I do not like these awkward names, orifice and hyper-space. We must find a great name for this wonderful machine and its vital parts.)

When Buehnen and I arrived, Professor Kenrube was busy opening and shutting little casements in various parts of that sea of dull metal. He took out and examined various items.

At eleven forty-five, Kenrube stationed himself at the control board, and made a brief speech comparing the locator dials of the board to the dial on a radio which tunes in stations. His dials, however, tuned in planets; and, quite simply, that is what he proceeded to do.

It appears that the same planets are always on exactly the same gradation of the main dial; and the principle extends down through the controls which operate to locate sections of planets. Thus it is always possible to return to any point of any planet. You will see how important this is.

The machine had already undergone its first tests, so Kenrube now proceeded to turn to various planets previously selected; and a fascinating show it was.

Gazing through the six-inch orifice is like looking through a glassless window. What a great moment it will be when the main machine is in operation, and we can *go* through the ten-foot orifice.

The first planet was a desolate, frozen affair, dimly lighted by a remote red sun. It must have been airless because there was a whistling sound, as the air rushed out of our room into that frigid space. Some of that deadly cold came trickling through, and we quickly switched below the surface of the planet.

Fantastic planet! It must be an incredibly heavy world, for it is a treasure house of the heavier metals. Everywhere we turned, the soil formation showed a shifting pattern of gold, silver, zinc, iron, tin—thousands of millions of tons.

At Professor Kenrube's suggestion, I put on a pair of heavy gloves, and removed a four-inch rock of almost pure gold. It simply lay there in a gray shale, but it was so cold that the moisture of the room condensed on it, forming a thick hoarfrost. How many ages that planet must have frozen for the cold to penetrate so far below the surface!

The second planet was a vast expanse of steaming swamps and

tropical forests, much as Earth must have been forty million years ago. However, we found not a single trace of animal, insect, reptile, or other non-floral life.

The third, fourth, and fifth planets were devoid of any kind of life, either plant or animal. The sixth planet might have been Earth, except that its green forests, its rolling plains showed no sign of animal or intelligent life. But it is on this planet that oil had been located by Kenrube and Seventeen in their private tests. When I left, a pipe line, previously rigged up, had been attached to the orifice, and was vibrating with oil at the colossal flow speed of nearly one thousand miles per hour.

This immense flow has now been continuous for more than twenty-four hours; and I understand it has already been necessary to convert the great water reservoir in the south suburbs to storage space for oil.

It may be *nouveau riche* to be storing oil at great inconvenience, when the source can be tapped at will. But I personally will not be satisfied until we have a number of these machines in action. It is better to be childish and have the oil than logical and have regrets.

I cannot conceive what could go wrong now. Because of our precautions, we have numerous and complete plans of the machines. It is necessary, of course, to ensure that our enemies do not learn our secret, and on this point I would certainly appreciate your most earnest attention.

The enormous potentialities of this marvelous instrument expand with every minute spent in thinking about it. I scarcely slept a wink last night.

March 1, 1939

From   Chief, Criminal Investigation Branch, Gestapo
To   Reich and Prussian Minister of Science
Subject Secret Six

Will you please inform this office without delay of the name of every scientist or other person who has any knowledge, however meager, of the Kenrube machine?

Reinhard Heydrich

Author's Note: *This is the Heydrich, handsome, ruthless Heydrich, who in 1941 bloodily repressed the incipient Czech revolt, who after the notorious Himmler became Minister of the Interior, succeeded his former master as head of the Gestapo, and who was subsequently assassinated.*

March 2, 1939

From   Secretary, Bureau of Physics
To   R. Heydrich
Subject Secret Six

The list of names for which you asked is herewith attached.

August Buehnen

COMMENT AT BOTTOM OF LETTER

In view of the importance of this matter, some changes should be made in the precautionary plan drawn up a few months ago with respect to these personages. Two, not one, of our agents, must be assigned to keep secret watch on each of these individuals. The rest of the plan can be continued as arranged with one other exception: In the event that any of these men suspect that they are being watched, I must be informed at once. I am prepared to explain to such person, within limits, the truth of the matter, so that he may not be personally worried. The important thing is we do not want these people suddenly to make a run for the border.

Himmler.

SPECIAL DELIVERY
PERSONAL

From   Reich and Prussian Minister of Science
To   Herr Heinrich Himmler
Subject Professor Johann Kenrube

I this morning informed the Fuehrer of the Kenrube machine. He became very excited. The news ended his indecision about the Czechs. The army will move to occupy.

For your advance information, please.

March 13, 1939

From   Gestapo
To   Reich and Prussian Minister of Science
Subject The Dresden Explosion

The incredibly violent explosion of the Kenrube model must be completely explained. A board of discovery should be set up at Dresden with full authority. I must be informed day by day of the findings of this court.

This is a very grim business. Your agent, Seventeen, is among those missing. Kenrube is alive, which is very suspicious. There is no question of arresting him; the only thing that matters is to frustrate future catastrophes of this kind. His machine has proved itself so remarkable that he must be conciliated at all costs until we can be sure that everything is going right.

Let me know *everything*.

Himmler.

PRELIMINARY REPORT OF AUGUST BUEHNEN

When I arrived at the scene of the explosion, I noticed immediately that a solid circle, a remarkably precise circle, of the wall of the fifth floor of the laboratories—where the Kenrube machine is located—had been sliced out as by some inconceivable force.

Examining the edges of this circle, I verified that it could not have been heat which performed so violent an operation. Neither the brick nor the exposed steel was in any way singed or damaged by fire.

The following facts have been given to me of what transpired:

It had been necessary to cut the flow of oil because of the

complete absence of further storage space. Seventeen, who was in charge—Professor Kenrube during this whole time was at Gribe Schloss working on the main machine—was laboriously exploring other planets in search of rare metals.

The following is an extract from my interview with Jacob Schmidt, a trusted laboratory assistant in the government service:

Q. You say, Herr—(Seventeen) took a piece of ore to the window to examine it in the light of the sun?

A. He took it to the window, and stood there looking at it.

Q. This placed him directly in front of the orifice of the machine?

A. Yes.

Q. Who else was in front of the orifice?

A. Dobelmanns, Minster, Freyburg, Tousand-freind.

Q. These were all fellow assistants of yours?

A. Yes.

Q. What happened then?

A. There was a very loud click from the machine, followed by a roaring noise.

Q. Was anyone near the control board?

A. No, sir.

Q. It was an automatic action of the machine?

A. Yes. The moment it happened we all turned to face the machine.

Q. All of you? Herr—(Seventeen), too?

A. Yes, he looked around with a start, just as Minster cried out that a blue light was coming from the orifice.

Q. A blue light. What did this blue light replace?

A. A soil formation of a planet, which we had numbered 447—711—Gradation A—131—8, which is simply its location on the dials. It was from this soil that Herr—(Seventeen) had taken the ore sample.

Q. And then, just like that, there was the blue light?

A. Yes. And for a few instants that was all there was, the blue light, the strange roaring sound, and us standing there half paralyzed.

Q. Then it flared forth?
A. It was terrible. It was such an intense blue it hurt my eyes, even though I could only see it in the mirror over the orifice. I have not the faintest impression of heat. But the wall was gone, and all the metal around the orifice.
Q. And the men?
A. Yes, and the men, all five of them.

March 18, 1939

From   Secretary, Bureau of Physics
To   Chief, Science Branch, Gestapo
Subject   Dresden Explosion

I am inclosing a précis of the report of the Court of Inquiry, which has just come to hand. The report will be sent to you as soon as a transcription has been typed.

For your information, please.

August Buehnen

PRÉCIS OF REPORT OF COURT OF INQUIRY

1. It has been established:
   (A) That the destruction was preceded by a clicking sound.
   (B) That this click came from the machine.
   (C) That the machine is fitted with automatic finders.
2. The blue flame was the sole final cause of the destruction.
3. No theory exists, or was offered, to explain the blue light. It should be pointed out that Kenrube was not called to testify.
4. The death of Herr—(Seventeen) and of his assistants was entirely due to the momentary impulse that had placed them in the path of the blue fire.
5. The court finds that the machine could have been tampered with, that the click that preceded the explosion could have been the result of some automatic device previously set to tamper with the machine. No other evidence of sabotage exists, and no one in the room at the time was to blame for the accident.

March 19, 1939

From   Major H.L. Guberheit
To   Minister for Air
Subject   Destruction of plane, type JU-88

I have been asked to describe the destruction of a plane under unusual circumstances, as witnessed by several hundred officers and men under my command.

The JU-88, piloted by Cadet Pilot Herman Kiesler, was approaching the runway for a landing, and was at the height of about five hundred feet when there was a flash of intense blue—and the plane vanished.

I cannot express too strongly the violence, the intensity, the blue vastness of the explosion. It was titanic. The sky was alive with light reflections. And though a bright sun was shining, the entire landscape grew brilliant with that blue tint.

There was no sound of explosion. No trace of this machine was subsequently found, no wreckage. The time of the accident was approximately ten thirty a.m., March 13th.

There has been great uneasiness among the students during the past week.

For your information, please.

H. L. Guberheit
Major, C. Air Station 473

COMMENT AT BOTTOM OF LETTER

Excellency—I wish most urgently to point out that the time of this unnatural accident coincides with the explosion of "blue" light from the orifice of the Kenrube machine.

I have verified that the orifice was tilted ever so slightly upward, and that the angle would place the beam at a height of five hundred feet near the airport in question.

The staggering feature is that the airport referred to is *seventy-five miles* from Dresden. The greatest guns ever developed can scarcely fire that distance, and yet the incredible power of the blue energy showed no diminishment. Literally, it disintegrated metal and flesh—everything.

I do not dare to think what would have happened if that devastating flame had been pointed not away from but at the ground.

Let me have your instructions at once, because here is beyond doubt the weapon of the ages.

August Buehnen

March 19, 1939

From   Chief, Science Branch, Gestapo
To   Reich and Prussian Minister of Science
Subject   Secret Six

In perusing the report of the inquiry board, we were amazed to note that Professor Kenrube was not questioned in this matter.

Be assured that there is no intention here of playing up to this man. We absolutely require an explanation from him. Send Herr Buehnen to see Kenrube and instruct him to employ the utmost firmness if necessary.

K. Reissel

March 21, 1939

From   Secretary, Bureau of Physics
To   Chief, Science Branch, Gestapo
Subject   Dresden Explosion

As per your request, I talked with Kenrube at Gribe Schloss.

It was the second time I had seen him, the first time being when I accompanied his Excellency, the Minister of Science, to Dresden to view the model; and I think I should point out here that Herr Professor Kenrube's physical appearance is very different from what I had been led to expect from the description recorded in File Secret Six. I had pictured him a lean, fanatic-eyed type. He *is* tall, but he must have gained weight in recent years, for his body is well filled out, and his face and eyes are serene, with graying hair to crown the effect of a fine, scholarly, middle-aged man.

It is unthinkable to me that this is some madman plotting against the Reich.

The first part of his explanation of the blue light was a most curious reference to the reality of mathematics, and, for a moment, I almost thought he was attempting to credit the accident to this *actuality* of his incomprehensible number system.

Then he went on to the more concrete statement that a great star must have intruded into the plane of the planet under examination. The roaring sound that was heard he attributed to the fact that the component elements of the air in the laboratory were being sucked into the sun, and destroyed.

The sun, of course, would be in a state of balance all its own, and therefore would not come into the room until the balance had been interfered with by the air of the room.

(I must say my own explanation would be the reverse of this; that is, the destruction of the air would possibly create a momentary balance, a barrier, during which time nothing of the sun came into the room except light reflections. However, the foregoing is what Kenrube said, and I presume it is based on his own mathematics. I can only offer it for what it is worth.)

Abruptly, the balance broke down. For a fraction of an instant, then, before the model hyper-space machine was destroyed, the intolerable energies of a blue-white sun poured forth.

It would have made no difference if the airplane that was caught in the beam of blue light had been farther away from Dresden than seventy-five miles—that measureless force would have reached seven thousand five hundred miles just as easily, or seventy-five thousand.

The complete absence of visible heat is no evidence that it was not a sun. At forty million degrees Fahrenheit, heat, as we know it, does not exist.

The great man went on to say that he had previously given some thought to the danger from suns, and that in fact he was in the late mathematical stage of developing an attachment that would automatically reject bodies larger than ten thousand miles in diameter.

In his opinion, efforts to control the titanic energies of suns

66

should be left to a later period, and should be carried out on uninhabited planets by scientists who have gone through the orifice and who have been then cut off from contact with earth.

August Buehnen

COMMENT ATTACHED

Kenrube's explanation sounds logical, and it does seem incredible that he would meddle with such forces, though it is significant that the orifice was tilted "slightly upward." We can dispense with his advice as to when and how we should experiment with sun energies. The extent of the danger seems to be a momentary discharge of inconceivable forces, and then destruction of the machine. If at the moment of discharge the orifice was slightly tilted toward London or New York, and if a sufficient crisis existed, the loss of one more machine would be an infinitesimal cost.

As for Kenrube's fine, scholarly appearance, I think Buehnen has allowed himself to be carried away by the greatness of the invention. The democrats of Germany are not necessarily madmen, but here, as abroad, they are our remorseless enemies.

We must endeavor to soften Kenrube by psychological means.

I cannot forget that *there is not now a working model of the Kenrube machine in existence*. Until there is, all the fine, scholarly-looking men in the world will not convince me that what happened was entirely an accident.

The deadly thing about all this is that we have taken an irrevocable step with respect to the Czechs; and war in the west is now inevitable.

Himmler

May 1, 1939

From   Chief, Science Branch, Gestapo
To   Reich and Prussian Minister of Science
Subject   Secret Six

The Fuehrer has agreed to exonerate completely August

Kenrube, the brother of Herr Professor Kenrube. As you will recall, August Kenrube was killed in the sacred purge of June, 1934. It will now be made clear that his death was an untimely accident, and that he was a true German patriot.

This is in line with our psychological attack on Professor Kenrube's suspected anti-Nazism.

K. Reissel.

June 17, 1939

From   Secretary, Bureau of Physics
To   Chief, Science Branch, Gestapo
Subject Professor Johann Kenrube

In line with our policy to make Kenrube realize his oneness with the community of German peoples, I had him address the convention of mathematicians. The speech, of which I inclose a copy, was a model one; three thousand words of glowing generalities, giving not a hint as to his true opinions on anything. However, he received the ovation of his life; and I think he was pleased in spite of himself.

Afterward, I saw to it—without, of course, appearing directly—that he was introduced to Fräulein Ilse Weber.

As you know, the Fräulein is university educated, a mature, modern young woman; and I am sure that she is merely taking on one of the many facets of her character in posing to Kenrube as a young woman who has decided quite calmly to have a child, and desires the father to be biologically of the highest type.

I cannot see how any human male, normal or abnormal, could resist the appeal of Fräulein Weber.

August Buehnen.

July 11, 1939

From   Chief, Science Branch, Gestapo
To   Secretary, Bureau of physics
Subject Secret Six

Can you give me some idea when the Kenrube machine will

be ready to operate? What about the duplicate machines which we agreed verbally would be built without Kenrube's knowledge? Great decisions are being made. Conversations are being conducted that will shock the world, and, in a general way, the leaders are relying on the Kenrube machine.

In this connection please submit as your own some variation of the following memorandum. It is from the Fuehrer himself, and therefore I need not stress its urgency.

K. Reissel.

MEMORANDUM OF ADOLF HITLER

Is it possible to tune the Kenrube machine to our own earth?

July 28, 1939

From   Secretary, Bureau of Physics
To   Chief, Science Branch, Gestapo
Subject   Secret Six

I enclose the following note from Kenrube, which is self-explanatory. We have retained a copy.

August Buehnen

NOTE FROM KENRUBE

Dear Herr Buehnen:

The answer to your memorandum is yes.

In view of the international anxieties of the times, I offer the following suggestions as to weapons that can be devised from the hyper-space machine:

1. Any warship can be rendered noncombatant at critical moments by draining of its oil tanks.

2. Similarly, enemy oil-storage supplies can be drained at vital points. Other supplies can be blown up or, if combustible, set afire.

3. Troops, tanks, trucks, and all movable war materials can

be transported to any point on the globe, behind enemy lines, into cities, by the simple act of focussing the orifice at the desired destination—and driving it and them through. I need scarcely point out that my machine renders railway and steamship transport obsolete. The world shall be transformed.

4. It might even be possible to develop a highly malleable, delicately adjusted machine, which can drain the tanks of airplanes in full flight.

5. Other possibilities, too numerous to mention, suggest themselves with the foregoing as a basis.

Kenrube.

COMMENT ATTACHED

This machine is like a dream. With it, the world is ours, for what conceivable combination of enemies could fight an army that appeared from nowhere on their flank, in the centers of their cities, in London, New York, in the Middlewest plains of America, in the Ural Mountains, in the Caucasus? Who can resist us?

K. Reissel.

ADDITIONAL COMMENT

My dear Reissel:

Your enthusiasm overlooks the fact that the machine is still only in the building stage. What worries me is that our hopes are being raised to a feverish height—what greater revenge could there be than to lift us to the ultimate peak of confidence, and than smash it in a single blow?

Every day that passes we are involving ourselves more deeply, decisions are being made from which there is already no turning back. When, oh, when will this machine be finished?

H.

July 29, 1939

From   Secretary, Bureau of Psysics
To   Chief, Science Branch, Gestapo
Subject   Secret Six

The hyper-space machine at Gribe Schloss will be completed in February, 1941. No less than five duplicate machine are under construction, unknown to Kenrube. What is done is that, when he orders an installation for the *Gribe Schloss* machine, the factory turns out five additional units from the same plans.

In addition, a dozen model machines are being secretly constructed from the old plans, but, as they must be built entirely from drawings and photographs, they will take not less, but more, time to build than the larger machines.

August Buehnen

August 2, 1939

From   Secretary, Bureau of Physics
To   Herr Heinrich Himmler
Subject Professor Johann Kenrube

I have just now received a telegram from Fräulein Ilse Weber that she and the Herr Professor were married this morning, and that Kenrube will be a family man by the middle of next summer.

August Buehnen

COMMENT WRITTEN BELOW

This is great news indeed. One of the most dangerous aspects of the Kenrube affair was that he was a bachelor without ties. Now, we have him. He has committed himself to the future.

Himmler.

FURTHER COMMENT

I have advised the Fuehrer, and our great armies will move into Poland at the end of this month.

H.

August 8, 1939

From   Gestapo
To   Reich and Prussian Minister of Science
Subject Secret Six

I have had second thought on the matter of Fräulein Ilse Weber, now Frau Kenrube. In view of the fact that a woman, no matter how intelligent or objective, becomes emotionally involved with the man who is the father of her children. I would advise that Frau Kenrube be appointed to some great executive post in a war industry. This will keep her own patriotism at a high level, and thus she will continue to have exemplary influence on her husband. Such influence cannot be overestimated.

                                        Himmler.

January 3, 1940

From   Secretary, Bureau of Physics
To   Chief, Science Branch, Gestapo

In glancing through the correspondence, I notice that I have neglected to inform you that our Agent Twelve has replaced Seventeen as Kenrube's chief assistant.

Twelve is a graduate of Munich, and was for a time attached to the General Staff in Berlin as a technical expert.

In my opinion, he is a better man for our purpose than was Seventeen, in that Seventeen, it seemed to me, had toward the end a tendency to associate himself with Kenrube in what might be called a scientific comradeship, and intellectual fellowship. He was in a mental condition where he quite unconsciously defended Kenrube against our suspicion.

Such a situation will not arise with Twelve. He is a practical man to the marrow. He and Kenrube have nothing in common.

Kenrube accepted Twelve with an attitude of what-does-it-matter-who-they-send. It was so noticeable that it is now clear that he is aware that these men are agents of ours.

Unless Kenrube has some plan of revenge which is beyond all

precautions, the knowledge that he is being watched should exercise a restraint on any impulses to evil that he may have.

August Buehnen.

Author's Note: *Most of the letters written in the year 1940 were of a routine nature, consisting largely of detailed reports as to the progress of the machine. The following document, however, was an exception:*

December 17, 1940

From   Reich and Prussian Minister of Science
To   Herr Heinrich Himmler
Subject Secret Six

The following work has now been completed on the fortress *Gribe Schloss,* where the Kenrube machine is nearing completion:

1. Steel doors have been fitted throughout.

2. A special, all-steel chamber had been constructed, from which, by an arrangement of mirrors, the orifice of the machine can be watched without danger to the watchers.

3. This watching post is only twenty steps from a paved road which runs straight up out of the valley.

4. A concrete pipe line for the transportation of oil is nearing completion.

August Buehnen.

MEMO AT BOTTOM OF LETTER

To Reinhard Heydrich:

Please make arrangements for me to inspect personally the reconstructed *Gribe Schloss.* It is Hitler's intention to attend the official opening.

The plan now is to invade England via the Kenrube machine possibly in March, not later than April. In view of the confusion that will follow the appearance of vast armies in every part of the country, this phase of the battle of Europe should be completed by the end of April.

In May, Russia will be invaded. This should not require more than two months. The invasion of the United States is set for July or August.

Himmler.

January 31, 1941

From   Secretary, Bureau of Physics
To   Chief, Science Branch, Gestapo
Subject   Secret Six

It will be impossible to complete the five extra Kenrube machines at the same time as the machine at *Gribe Schloss*. Kenrube has changed some of the designs, and our engineers do not know how to fit the sections together until they have studied Kenrube's method of connection.

I have personally asked Kenrube the reason for the changes. His answer was that he was remedying weaknesses that he had noticed in the model. I am afraid that we shall have to be satisfied with this explanation, and complete the duplicate machines after the official opening, which is not now scheduled until March 20th. The delay is due to Kenrube's experimentation with design.

If you have any suggestions, please let me hear them. I frankly do not like this delay, but what to do about it is another matter.

August Buehnen.

February 3, 1941

From   Chief, Science Branch, Gestapo
To   Secretary, Bureau of Physics
Subject   Secret Six

Himmler says to do nothing. He notes that you are still taking the precaution of daily photographs, and that your agent, Twelve, who replaced Seventeen, is keeping a diary in triplicate.

There has been a meeting of leaders, and this whole matter discussed very thoroughly, with special emphasis on critical analysis of the precautions taken, and of the situation that would exist if Kenrube should prove to be planning some queer revenge.

You will be happy to know that not a single additional precaution was thought of, and that our handling of the affair was commended.

K. Reissel.

February 18, 1941

From   Gestapo
To   Reich and Prussian Minister of Science
Subject   Secret Six

In view of our anxieties, the following information, which I have just received, will be welcome:

Frau Kenrube, formerly our Ilse Weber, has reserved a private room in the maternity ward of the Prussian State Hospital for May 7th. This will be her second child, another hostage to fortune by Kenrube.

K. Reissel.

COPY ONLY
MEMO   March 11, 1941

I have today examined *Gribe Schloss* and environs and found everything according to plan.

Himmler

March 14, 1941

From   Secretary, Bureau of Physics
To   Herr Himmler, Gestapo
Subject   Secret Six

You will be relieved to know the reason for the changes in design made by Kenrube.

The first reason is rather unimportant; Kenrube refers to the mathematical structure involved, and states that, for his own elucidation, he designed a functional instrument whose sole purpose was to defeat the mathematical reality of the machine. This is very obscure, but he had referred to it before, so I call it to your attention.

The second reason is that there are now two orifices, not one. The additional orifice is for focusing. The following illustration will clarify what I mean:

Suppose we had a hundred thousand trucks in Berlin, which we wished to transfer to London. Under the old method, these trucks would have to be driven all the way to the *Gribe Schloss* before they could be transmitted.

With the new two-orifice machine, one orifice would be focused in Berlin, the other in London. The trucks would drive through from Berlin to London.

Herr Professor Kenrube seems to anticipate our needs before we realize them ourselves.

August Buehnen.

March 16, 1941

From   Gestapo
To   Secretary, Bureau of Physics
Subject   Secret Six

The last sentence of your letter of March 14th to the effect that Kenrube seems to anticipate our needs made me very uncomfortable, because the thought that follows naturally is: Is he also anticipating our plans?

I have accordingly decided at this eleventh hour that we are dealing with a man who may be our intellectual superior in every way. Have your agent advise us the moment the machine has undergone its initial tests. Decisive steps will be taken immediately.

Himmler.

DECODED TELEGRAM

KENRUBE MACHINE WAS TESTED TODAY AND WORKED PERFECTLY.

AGENT TWELVE:

COPY ONLY
MEMO   March 19, 1941

To Herr Himmler:

This is to advise that Professor Johann Kenrube was placed under close arrest, and has been removed to Gestapo Headquarters, Berlin.

R. Heydrich.

March 19, 1941

DECODED TELEGRAM

REPLYING TO YOUR TELEPHONE INSTRUCTIONS, WISH TO STATE ALL AUTOMATIC DEVICES HAVE BEEN REMOVED FROM KENRUBE MACHINE. NONE SEEMED TO HAVE BEEN TAMPERED WITH. MADE PERSONAL TEST OF MACHINE. IT WORKED PERFECTLY.

TWELVE

COMMENT WRITTEN BELOW

I shall recommend that Kenrube be retired under guard to his private laboratories, and not allowed near a hyper-space machine until after the conquest of the United States.

And with this, I find myself at a loss for further precautions. In my opinion, all thinkable possibilities have been covered. The only dangerous man has been removed from the zone where he can be actively dangerous; a careful examination has been made to ascertain that he has left no automatic devices that will cause havoc. And, even if he has, five other large machines and a dozen small ones are nearing completion, and it is impossible that he can have tampered with them.

If anything goes wrong now, thoroughness is a meaningless word.

Himmler.

March 21, 1941

From   Gestapo
To   Secretary, Bureau of Physics
Subject   Secret Six

Recriminations are useless. What I would like to know is: What in God's name happened?

Himmler.

March 22, 1941

From   Secretary, Bureau of Physics
To   Herr Heinrich Himmler
Subject   Secret Six

The reply to your question is being prepared. The great trouble is the confusion among the witnesses, but it should not be long before some kind of coherent reply is ready.

Work is being rushed to complete the duplicate machines on the basis of photographs and plans that were made from day to day. I cannot see how anything can be wrong in the long run.

As for Number One, shall we send planes over with bombs?

August Buehnen.

COPY ONLY
MEMO   March 23, 1941

From   Detention Branch, Gestapo

The four agents, Gestner, Luslich, Heinreide, and Muemmer,

who were guarding Herr Professor Johann Kenrube, report that he was under close arrest at our Berlin headquarters until six p.m., March 21st. At six p.m., he abruptly vanished.

S. Duerner

COMMENT WRITTEN BELOW

Kenrube was at *Gribe Schloss* before two p.m., March 21st. This completely nullifies the six p.m. story. Place these scoundrels under arrest, and bring them before me at eight o'clock tonight.

Himmler.

COPY ONLY
EXAMINATION BY HERR HIMMLER OF F. GESTNER

Q. Your name?
A. Gestner. Fritz Gestner. Long service.
Q. Silence. If we want to know your service, we'll check it in the record.
A. Yes, sir.
Q. That's a final warning. You answer my questions, or I'll have your tongue.
A. Yes, sir.
Q. You're one of the stupid fools set to guard Kenrube?
A. I was one of the four guards, sir.
Q. Answer yes or no.
A. Yes, sir.
Q. What was your method of guarding Kenrube?
A. By twos. Two of us at a time were in the great white cell with him.
Q. Why weren't the four of you there?
A. We thought—
Q. You thought! Four men were ordered to guard Kenrube and—By God, there'll be dead men around here before this

79

night is over. I want to get this clear: There was never a moment when two of you were not in the cell with Kenrube?

A. Always two of us.

Q. Which two were with Kenrube at the moment he disappeared?

A. I was. I and Johann Luslich.

Q. Oh, you know Luslich by his first name. An old friend of yours, I suppose?

A. No, sir.

Q. You knew Luslich previously, though?

A. I met him for the first time when we were assigned to guard Herr Kenrube.

Q. Silence! Answer yes or no. I've warned you about that.

A. Yes, sir.

Q. Ah, you admit knowing him?

A. No, sir. I meant—

Q. Look here, Gestner, you're in a very bad spot. Your story is a falsehood on the face of it. Tell me the truth. Who are your accomplices?

A. None, sir.

Q. You mean you were working this alone?

A. No, sir.

Q. You damned liar! Gestner, we'll get the truth out of you if we have to tear you apart.

A. I am telling the truth, Excellency.

Q. Silence, you scum. What time did you say Kenrube disappeared?

A. About six o'clock.

Q. Oh, he did, eh? Well, never mind that. What was Kenrube doing just before he vanished?

A. He was talking to Luslich and me.

Q. What right had you to talk to the prisoner?

A. Sir, he mentioned an accident he expected to happen at some official opening somewhere.

Q. He what?

A. Yes, sir; and I was desperately trying to find out where, so that I could send a warning.

Q. Now, the truth is coming. So you do know about this business, you lying rat! Well, let's have the story you've rigged up.

A. The dictaphone will bear out every word.

Q. Oh, the dictaphone was on.

A. Every word is recorded.

Q. Oh, why wasn't I told about this in the first place?

A. You wouldn't lis—

Q. Silence, you fool! By God, the coöperation I get around this place. Never mind. Just what was Kenrube doing at the moment he disappeared?

A. He was sitting—talking.

Q. Sitting? You'll swear to that?

A. To the Fuehrer himself.

Q. He didn't move from his chair? He didn't walk over to an orifice?

A. I don't know what you mean, Excellency.

Q. So you pretend, anyway. But that's all for the time being. You will remain under arrest. Don't think we're through with you. That goes also for the others.

AUTHOR'S NOTE:

The baffled fury expressed by the normally calm Himmler in this interview is one indication of the dazed bewilderment that raged through high Nazi circles. One can imagine the accusation and counter-accusation and then the slow, deadly realization of the situation.

March 24, 1941

From   Gestapo
To   Reich and Prussian Minister of Science
Subject Secret Six

Inclosed is the transcription of a dictaphone record which was made by Professor Kenrube. A careful study of these deliberate

words, combined with what he said at *Gribe Schloss,* may reveal
his true purpose, and may also explain the incredible thing
that happened.

I am anxiously awaiting your full report.

Himmler.

TRANSCRIPTION OF DICTAPHONE RECORD P-679-423-1; CON-
VERSATION OF PROFESSOR JOHANN KENRUBE IN WHITE CELL
26, ON 3/21/41.

(Note: K. refers to Kenrube, G. to any of the guards.)

K. A glass of water, young man.

G. I believe there is no objection to that. Here.

K. It must be after five.

G. There is no necessity for you to know the time.

K. No, but the fact that it is late is very interesting. You see, I
have invented a machine. A very queer machine it is
going to seem when it starts to react according to the laws
of real as distinct from functional mathematics. You have
the dictaphone on, I hope?

G. What kind of a smart remark is that?

K. Young man, that dictaphone had better be on. I intend
talking about my invention, and your masters will skin you
alive if it's not recorded. Is the dictaphone on?

G. Oh, I suppose so.

K. Good. I may be able to finish what I have to say. I may not.

G. Don't worry. You'll be here to finish it. Take your time.

K. I had the idea before my brother was killed in the purge,
but I thought of the problem then as one of education.
Afterward, I saw it as revenge. I hated the Nazis and all
they stood for.

G. Oh, you did, eh? Go on.

K. My plan after my brother's murder was to build for the
Nazis the greatest weapon the world will ever know, and
then have them discover that only I, who understood and
who accordingly *fitted* in with the immutable laws involved
—only I could ever operate the machine. And I would

have to be present physically. That way I would prove my indispensability and so transform the entire world to my way of thinking.

G. We've got ways of making indispensables work.

K. Oh, that part is past. I've discovered what is going to happen —to me as well as to my invention.

G. Plenty is going to happen to you. You've already talked yourself into a concentration camp.

K. After I discovered that, my main purpose was simplified. I wanted to do the preliminary work on the machine and, naturally, I had to do that under the prevailing system of government—by cunning and misrepresentation. I had no fear that any of the precautions they were so laboriously taking would give them the use of the machine, not this year, not this generation, not ever. The machine simply cannot be used by people who think as they do. For instance, the model that—

G. Model! What are you talking about?

K. Silence, please. I am anxious to clarify for the dictaphone what will seem obscure enough under any circumstances. The reason the model worked perfectly was because I fitted in mentally and physically. Even after I left, it continued to carry out the task I had set it, but as soon as Herr— (Seventeen) made a change, it began to yield to other pressures. The accident—

G. Accident!

K. Will you shut up? Can't you see that I am trying to give information for the benefit of future generations? I have no desire that my secret be lost. The whole thing is in under- standing. The mechanical part is only half the means. The mental approach is indispensable. Even Herr—(Seventeen), who was beginning to be *sympathique* could not keep the machine sane for more than an hour. His death, of course, was inevitable, whether it looked like an accident or not.

G. Whose death?

K. What it boils down to is this. My invention does not fit into our civilization. It's *the next*, the coming age of man. Just as modern science could not develop in ancient Egypt because the whole mental, emotional, and physical attitude was wrong, so my machine cannot be used until the thought structure of man changes. Your masters will have some further facts soon to bear me out.

G. Look! You said something before about something happening. What?

K. I've just been telling you: I don't know. The law of averages says it won't be another sun, but there are a thousand deadly things that can happen. When Nature's gears snag, no imaginable horror can match the result.

G. But something is going to happen?

K. I really expected it before this. The official opening was set for half-past one. Of course, it doesn't really matter. If it doesn't happen today, it will take place tomorrow.

G. Official opening! You mean an accident is going to happen at some official opening?

K. Yes, and my body will be *attracted*. I—

G. What— Good God! He's gone!

(Confusion. Voices no longer audible.)

March 25, 1941

From   Reich and Prussian Minister of Science
To   Herr Himmler
Subject   Destruction of *Gribe Schloss*

The report is still not ready. As you were not present, I have asked the journalist, Polermann, who was with Hitler, to write a description of the scene. His account is inclosed, with the first page omitted.

You will note that in a number of paragraphs he reveals incomplete knowledge of the basic situation, but except for this, his story is, I believe, the most accurate we have.

The first page of his article was inadvertently destroyed. It was simply a preliminary.

For your information.

84

—The first planet came in an unexpected fashion. I realized that as I saw Herr—(Twelve) make some hasty adjustments on one of his dials.

Still dissatisfied, he connected a telephone plug into a socket somewhere in his weird-looking asbestos suit, thus establishing telephone communication with the Minister of Science, who was in the steel inclosure with us. I heard His Excellency's reply:

"Night! Well, I suppose it has to be night some time on other planets. You're not sure it's the same planet? I imagine the darkness is confusing."

It was. In the mirror, the night visible through the orifice showed a bleak, gray, luminous landscape, incredibly eerie and remote, an unnatural world of curious shadows, and not a sign of movement anywhere.

And that, after an instant, struck us all with an appalling effect, the dark consciousness of that great planet, swinging somewhere around a distant sun, an uninhabited waste, a lonely reminder that life is rarer than death in the vast universe. Herr —(Twelve) made an adjustment on a dial; and, instantly, the great orifice showed that we were seeing the interior of the planet. A spotlight switched on, and picked out a solid line of red earth that slowly, as the dial turned, became clay; then a rock stratum came into view, and was held in focus.

An asbestos-clothed assistant of Herr—(Twelve) dislodged a piece of rock with a pick. He lifted it, and started to bring it toward the steel inclosure, apparently for the Fuehrer's inspection.

And abruptly vanished.

We blinked our eyes. But he was gone, and the rock with him. Herr—(Twelve) switched on his telephone hurriedly. There was a consultation, in which the Fuehrer participated. The decision finally was that it had been a mistake to examine a doubtful planet, and that the accident had happened because the rock had been removed. Accordingly, no further effort would be made to remove anything.

Regret was expressed by the Fuehrer that the brave assistant should have suffered such a mysterious fate.

We resumed our observant positions, more alert now, conscious of what a monstrous instrument was here before our eyes. A man whisked completely out of our space simply because he had touched a rock from a planet in hyper-space.

The second planet was also dark. At first it, too, looked a barren world, enveloped in night; and then—wonder. Against the dark, towering background of a great hill, a city grew. It spread along the shore of a moonlit sea, ablaze with ten million lights. It clung there for a moment, a crystalline city, alive with brilliant streets. Then it faded. Swiftly it happened. The lights seemed literally to slide off into the luminous sea. For a moment, the black outline of the city remained, then that, too, vanished into the shadows. Astoundingly, the hill that had formed an imposing background for splendor, distorted like a picture out of focus, and was gone with the city.

A flat, night-wrapped beach spread where a moment before there had been a world of lights, a city of another planet, the answer to ten million questions about life on other worlds—gone like a secret wind into the darkness.

It was plain to see that the test, the opening, was not according to schedule. Once more, Herr—(Twelve) spoke through the telephone to His Excellency, the Minister of Science.

His Excellency turned to the Fuehrer, and said, "He states that he appears to have no control over the order of appearance. Not once has he been able to tune in a planet which he had previously selected to show you."

There was another consultation. It was decided that this second planet, though it had reacted in an abnormal manner, had not actually proved dangerous. Therefore, one more attempt would be made. No sooner was this decision arrived at, than there was a very distinctly audible click from the machine. And, though we did not realize it immediately, the catastrophe was upon us.

I cannot describe the queer loudness of that clicking from the machine. It was not a metallic noise. I have since been informed that only an enormous snapping of energy in motion could have made that unusual, unsettling sound.

My own sense of uneasiness was quickened by the sight of Herr—(Twelve) frantically twisting dials. But nothing happened for a few seconds. The planet on which we had seen the city continued to hold steady in the orifice. The darkened beach spread there in the half-light shed by a moon we couldn't see. And then—

A figure appearred in the orifice. I cannot recall all my emotions at the sight of that manlike being. There was a wild thought that here was some supercreature who, dissatisfied with the accidents he had so far caused us, was now come to complete our destruction. That thought ended as the figure came out onto the floor and one of the assistants swung a spotlight on him. The light revealed him as a tall, well-built handsome man, dressed in ordinary clothes.

Beside me, I heard someone exclaim: "Why, it's Professor Kenrube!"

For most of those present, everything must have, in that instant, been clear. I, however, did not learn until later that Kenrube was one of the scientists assigned to assist Herr—(Twelve) in building the machine, and that he turned out to be a traitor. He was suspected in the destruction of an earlier model, but as there was no evidence and the suspicion not very strong, he was permitted to continue his work.

Suspicion had arisen again a few days previously, and he had been confined to his quarters, from whence, apparently, he had now come forth to make sure that his skillful tampering with the machine had worked out. This, then, was the man who stood before us. My impression was that he should not have been allowed to utter his blasphemies, but I understand the leaders were anxious to learn the extent of his infamy, and thought he might reveal it in his speech. Although I do not profess to understand the gibberish, I have a very clear memory of what was said, and set it down here for what it is worth.

Kenrube began: "I have no idea how much time I have, and as I was unable to explain clearly to the dictaphone all that I had to say, I must try to finish here." He went on, "I am not

87

thinking now in terms of revenge, though God knows my brother was very dear to me. But I want the world to know the way of this invention."

The poor fool seemed to be laboring under the impression that the machine was his. I did not, and do not, understand his reference to a dictaphone. Kenrube went on:

"My first inkling came through psychology, the result of meditating on the manner in which the soil of different parts of the earth influences the race that lives there. This race-product was always more than simply the end-shape of a seacoast, or a plains, or a mountain environment. Somehow, beneath adaptations, peculiar and unsuspected relationships existed between the properties of matter and the phenomena of life. And so my search was born. The idea of revenge came later.

I might say that in all history there has never been a revenge as complete as mine. Here is your machine. It is all there; yours to use for any purpose—provided you first change your mode of thinking to conform to the reality of the relationship between matter and life.

"I have no doubt you can build a thousand duplicates, but beware—every machine will be a Frankenstein monster. Some of them will distort time, as seems to have happened in the time of my arrival here. Others will feed you raw material that will vanish even as you reach forth to seize it. Still others will pour obscene things into our green earth; and others will blaze with terrible energies, but you will never know what is coming, you will never satisfy a single desire.

"You may wonder why everything will go wrong. Herr— (Twelve) has, I am sure, been able to make brief, successful tests. That will be the result of my earlier presence, and will not recur now that so many alien presences have affected its— sanity!

"It is not that the machine has will. It reacts to laws, which you must learn, and in the learning it will reshape your minds, your outlook on life. It will change the world. Long before that, of course, the Nazis will be destroyed. They have taken irrevocable steps that will insure their destruction.

"Revenge! Yes, I have it in the only way that a decent human being could desire it. I ask any reasonable being how else these murderers could be wiped from the face of the earth, except by other nations, who would never act until *they* had acted first?

"I have only the vaguest idea what the machine will do with me—it matters not. But I should like to ask you, my great Fuehrer, one question: Where now will you obtain your raw material?"

He must have timed it exactly. For, as he finished, his figure dimmed. Dimmed! How else describe the blur that his body became? And he was gone, merged with the matter with which, he claimed, his life force was attuned.

The madman had one more devastating surprise for us. The dark planet, from which the city had disappeared, was abruptly gone from the orifice. In its place appeared another dark world. As our vision grew accustomed to this new night, we saw that this was a world of restless water; to the remote, dim horizon was a blue-black, heaving sea. The machine switched below the surface. It must have been at least ten hellish miles below it, judging from the pressure, I have since been informed.

There was a roar that seemed to shake the earth.

Only those who were with the Fuehrer in the steel room succeeded in escaping. Twenty feet away a great army truck stood with engines churning—it was not the first time that I was thankful that some car engines are always left running wherever the Fuehrer is present.

The water swelled and surged around our wheels as we raced up the newly paved road, straight up out of the valley. It was touch and go. We looked back in sheer horror. Never in the world has there been such a titanic torrent, such a whirlpool.

The water rose four hundred feet in minutes, threatened to overflow the valley sides, and then struck a balance. The great new river is still there, raging toward the Eastern Sea.

Author's Note: *This is not quite the end of the file. A few more letters exist, but it is unwise to print more, as it might be possible for the GPU to trace the individual who actually removed the file Secret Six from its cabinet.*

It is scarcely necessary to point out that we subsequently saw the answer that Hitler made to Professor Kenrube's question: "Where now will you obtain your raw materials?"

On June 22nd, three months almost to the day after the destruction of Gribe Schloss, the Nazis began their desperate invasion of Russia. By the end of 1941, their diplomacy bankrupt, they were at war with the United States.

THE HARMONIZER

AFTER it had sent two shoots out of the ground, the ibis plant began to display the true irritability of intelligent living matter. It became aware that it was growing.

The awareness was a dim process, largely influenced by the chemical reaction of air and light upon the countless membranes that formed its life structure. Tiny beads of acid were precipitated on these delicate colloidal films. The rhythm of pain-pleasure that followed surged down the root.

It was a very early stage in the development of an ibis plant. Like a new-born puppy, it reacted to stimuli. But it had no purpose as yet, and no thought. And it did not even remember that it had been alive previously.

Slash! Snip! The man's hoe caught the two silvery shoots and severed them about two inches below the ground.

"I thought I'd got all the weeds out of this border," said the man.

His name was Wagnowski, and he was a soldier scheduled to leave for the front the next day. He didn't actually use the foregoing words, but the gist of his imprecation is in them.

The ibis plant was not immediately aware of what had happened. The series of messages that had begun when the first shoot pushed up through the soil were still trickling down the root, leaving the impact of their meaning on each of a multitude of colloidal membranes. This impact took the form of a tiny chemical reaction, which in its small way caused a sensation.

Instant by instant, as those messages were transmitted by the slow electricity that obtained in the membranous films, the ibis plant came more alive. And tiny though each chemical consciousness was in itself, *no subsequent event could cancel it in the slightest degree*.

The plant was alive, and knew it. The hoeing out of its shoots and the upper part of its root merely caused a second wave of reactions to sweep downward. The chemical effect of this second wave was apparently the same as the earlier reaction: Beads of acid composed of not more than half a dozen molecules each formed on the colloid particles. The reaction seemed the same, but it wasn't. Before, the plant had been excited, almost eager. Now, it grew angry.

After the manner of plants, the results of this reaction were not at once apparent. The ibis made no immediate attempt to push up more shoots. But on the third day a very curious thing started to happen. The root near the surface came alive with horizontal sub-roots. These pushed along in the soil darkness, balancing by the simple process of being aware, like all plants, of gravitation.

On the eighth day one of the new roots contacted the root of a shrub, and began to wind in and around it. Somehow, then, a relation was established, and on the fifteenth day a second set of shoots forced the soil at the base of the shrub and emerged into the light, The radical, the astounding thing about this second set of shoots was that they were not of a silvery hue. They were a dark green. In color, shape, and texture the leaves, as they developed, seemed more and more exact duplicates of the leaves of the shrub.

Rapidly the new shoots shot up. As the weeks sped by, the "fear" that had induced chameleonism faded, and the leaves reverted to their silver color. Slowly, the plant became conscious of human and animal thoughts. But not until two hundred days later did the ibis begin to show its basic sensitivity. The reaction which followed was as potent and far reaching as had been the results of that same sensitivity in its previous existence.

That was eighty million years before.

The ship, with the ibis plants aboard, was passing through the solar system when the catastrophe occurred.

It came down onto an earth of marsh, fog, and fantastic reptilian monsters. It came down hard and out of control. Its speed as it struck the thick atmosphere was approximately colossal. And there was absolutely nothing that the superbeings aboard could do about it.

What had happened was a precipitation of the matter held in suspension in the drive chambers. As a result of condensation, the crystalloids in the sub-microscopic twilight zone above the molecule state lost surface area. Surface tensions weakened to a tenth, a hundredth, a thousandth of what was necessary. And at that moment, by the wildest accident, the ship passed near Earth and tangled with the dead mass of the gigantic planet's magnetic field.

Poor ship! poor beings! Crashed now, dead now nearly eighty thousand years.

All that day and night, remnants of the ship burned and fused, and flared again in a white, destroying incandescence. When that first fire-shattered darkness ended, not much remained of what had been a mile-long liner. Here and there over the cretaceous land and water and primeval forest, unburnt sections lay, jagged lumps of metal rearing up toward the perpetually muggy heavens, their lower parts sunk forever into a thick, fetid soil that would eat and eat at their strength until at last, the metal defeated, its elements would dissolve into earth and become earth.

Long before that happened, the ibis that were still alive had reacted to the dampness, and sent creepers out over the broken metal of what had been their culture room, out towards the gaping holes that opened into the soil. There had been three hundred plants, but in that last terrible period before the crash some effort had been made to destroy them.

Altogether, eighty-three ibis survived the deliberate attempt at their destruction; and among them there was a deadly race to take root. Those that came last knew instinctively that they had better move on. Of these latter, weakened by an injury in the crash, was *the* ibis. It reached the life-giving earth last of all. There followed a painful and timeless period when its creepers and its roots forced their way among the massed tangle of its struggling fellows towards the remote edge of the gathering forest of silver shrubs.

But it got there. It lived. And, having survived, having taken possession of a suitable area in which to develop without interference, it lost its feverishness, and expanded into a gracious, silver-hued tree.

A hundred, a hundred and fifty, two hundred feet tall it grew. And then, mature and satisfied, it settled down to eternal existence in a grotesque yet immensely fertile land. It had no thought. It lived and enjoyed and experienced existence. For a thousand years no acid beads formed on its colloidal membranes except the acids of reaction to light, heat, water, air, and other extrania of simply being alive.

The idyllic life was interrupted one gray soggy morning by a dull but tremendous thunder and a shaking of the ground. It was no minor earthquake. Continents shook in the throes of rebirth. Oceans rushed in where there had been land; and land surged wetly out of the warm seas. There had been a wide expanse of deep marsh water separating the forest of ibis trees from the mainland. When the shuddering of the tortured planet ended in the partial stability of that uneasy age, the marsh was joined to the distant higher ground by a long, bare, hill-like ridge.

At first it was merely mud, but it dried and hardened. Grass sprouted and shrubs made a tangle of parts of it. Trees came up from drift seed. The young growth raced for the sky, and simultaneously waged a bitter battle for space, but all that was unimportant beside the fact that the ridge existed. The gap that isolated the ibis had been bridged. The new state of things was not long in manifesting. One timeless day a creature stamped boldly along the height, a creature with a rigidly upheld armored tail, teeth like knives, and eyes that glowed like fire with the fury of unending bestial hunger.

Thus came *Tyrannosaurus Rex* to the peaceful habitat of the ibis, and awakened from a latent condition a plant that had been cultivated and developed by its creators for one purpose only.

Animals were no new thing to the ibis trees. The surrounding marshes swarmed with great placid vegetarians. Gigantic snakes crawled among the ferns at the water's edge, and writhed through the muddy waters. And there was an endless scurrying of young, almost mindless beasts in and out among the silver trees.

It was a world of hungry life, but the hunger was for vegetation, or for living things that were scarcely more than plants, for the long, lush marsh grass, the leaf-laden shrubs, the soggy roots of water plants and the plants themselves, for primitive fish, for wriggling things that had no awareness of pain or even of their fate. In the quiet torpor of their existence, the plant-eating reptiles and amphibians were little more than Gargantuan plants that could move about.

The most enormous of all these well-behaved creatures, the long-necked, long-tailed brontosaurus, was eating of the generous leaves of a tall fern on the morning that the flesh-eating dinosaur walked onto the scene with all the tact of a battering ram.

The struggle that followed was not altogether one-sided. The brontosaurus had, above everything else, weight and a desire to escape, something that proved especially difficult because *Tyrannosaurus Rex* had his amazing teeth sunk into the thick lower part of the big fellow's neck, and also, he had dug his claws into the thick meat of the great side to which he was clinging. Movement for the brontosaurus was limited by the necessity of carrying along the multi-ton dinosaur.

Like a drunken giant, the great beast staggered blindly toward the marsh water. If it saw the ibis tree, it was a visualization that meant nothing. The crash knocked the brontosaurus off its feet, a virtual death sentence for a creature that, even under the most favorable circumstances, required ten minutes to stand up. In a few minutes, the dinosaur administered the *coup de grâce*, and, with a slobbering bloody ferocity, started gorging.

It was still at this grisly meal half an hour later when the ibis began reacting in a concrete fashion.

The initial reactions had begun almost the moment the dinosaur arrived in the vicinity. Every sensitive colloid of the tree caught the blasts of palpable lusts radiated by the killer. The thought waves of the beast were emitted as a result of surface tensions on the membranes of its embryo brain; and as these were electric in nature, their effect on the delicately balanced films of the ibis's membranes was to set off a feverish manufacture of acids. Quadrillions of the beads formed; and, though once again they seemed no different from similar acids created as a result of other irritants, the difference began to manifest itself half an hour after the brontosaurus grunted its final agony.

The ibis tree and its companions exuded a fragrance in the form of billions on billions of tiny dust motes. Some of these motes drifted down to the dinosaur, and were gulped into its lungs from where, in due course, they were absorbed into its bloodstream.

The response was not instantly apparent. After several hours, the dinosaur's gigantic stomach was satiated. It stalked off to wallow and sleep in a mudhole, quickly made extra-odorous by its own enormous droppings and passings, a process that continued as easily in sleep as during consciousness.

Waking, it had no difficulty scenting the unrefrigerated meat of its recent kill. It raced over eagerly to resume feeding, slept, and ate again, and then again. It took several days for its untiring digestion to absorb the brontosaurus, and then it was once more ravenously hungry.

But it didn't go hunting. Instead, it wandered around aimlessly and restlessly, looking for carrion. All around, amphibians and snakes moved and had their being, ideal prey. The dinosaur showed no interest. Except for an inadequate diet of the carrion of small reptiles, it spent the next week starving to death in the midst of plenty.

On the fifteenth day a trio of small, common dinosaurs came across its wasted body, and ate it without noticing that it was still alive.

On the wings of a thousand breezes, the fragrant spores drifted. There was no end to them. Eighty-three ibis trees had started manufacturing that for which they had been created. Once started, there was no stopping.

The spores did not take root. That wasn't what they were for. They drifted. They hung in the eddies above quiet glades, sinking reluctantly towards the dank earth, but always swift to accept the embrace of a new wind, so light, so airy themselves that journeys half-way around the earth proved not beyond their capabilities. In their wake they left a trail of corpses among the killer reptiles. Once tantalized by the sweet-scented motes, the most massive murderers in the history of the planet lost their brutality, their will to kill, and died like poisoned flies.

It took time, of course, but of that at least there was a plenitude. Each dead carnivore provided carrion meat for the hungry hordes that roamed the land; and so after a fashion, over the decades, tens of thousands of individuals lived on because of the very abundance of dead meat-eaters. In addition there was a normal death rate among the none-meat-eaters that had always provided a measure of easy food; since there were fewer meat-eaters every year, the supply of meat per capita increased, at first gradually, and then with a suddenness and totality that was devastating.

The death of so many killers had created an imbalance between the carnivores and their prey. The vegetarians in their already huge numbers began to breed almost without danger. The young grew up in a world that would have been idyllic except for one thing: There was not enough food. Every bit of reachable green, every root, vegetable, and shoot was snatched by eager jaws before it could begin to mature.

For a time the remnants of the killers feasted. And then, once more, a temporary balance was struck. But again and again the prolific vegetarians dropped their young into a world made peaceful by the exudation of plants that couldn't stand brutality, yet felt nothing when death came by starvation.

The centuries poured their mist of forgetfulness over each bloody dip of that fateful seesaw. And all the while, as the millenniums slipped by, the ibises maintained their peaceful existence. For long and long it *was* peaceful, without incident of any kind. For a hundred thousand years the stately silver trees stood on their almost-island, and were content. During that vast expanse of time, the still unstable earth had rocked many times to the shattering and re-forming fury of colossal earthquakes, but it was not until the trees were well into their second hundred thousandth year that they were again affected.

A continent was rift and torn. The gap was about a thousand miles long, and in some places as much as twenty-five miles deep. It cut the edge of the island, and plummeted *the* ibis tree into an abyss three miles deep. Water raged into the hole, and dirt came roaring down in almost liquid torrents. Shocked and buried, the ibis tree succumbed to its new environment. It sank rapidly to the state of a root struggling to remain alive against hostile forces.

It was three thousand years later that the second last act of the ibis trees was played out on the surface of the planet.

A ship clothed in myriad colors slipped down through the murk and the gloom of the steaming jungle planet that was cretaceous earth. As it approached the silver-hued grove, it braked its enormous speed and came to a full stop directly over the island in the marsh.

It was a much smaller machine that the grand liner that had crashed to a fiery destruction so many, many years before. But it was big enough to disgorge, after a short interval, six graceful patrol boats.

Swiftly, the boats sped to the ground.

The creatures who emerged from them were two-legged and two-armed, but there the resemblance to human form ended. They walked on rubbery land with the ease and confidence of absolute masters. Water was no barrier; they strode *over* it as if they were made of so much buoyant fluff. Reptiles they ignored; and, for some reason, whenever a meeting threatened, it was the beasts that turned aside, hissing with fear.

The beings seemed to have a profound natural understanding of purposes, for there was no speech among them. Without a sound or waste motion, a platform was floated into position above a small hill. The platform emitted no visible or audible force, but beneath it the soil spumed and ripped. A section of the drive chamber of the old, great ship catapulted into the air, and was held captive by invisible beams.

No dead thing this. It sparkled and shone with radiant energy. Exposed to the air, it hissed and roared like the deadly machine it was. Torrents of fire poured from it until something—*something green*—was fired at it from a long gun-like tube. The greenness must have been *a*-energy, and potent out of all proportion to its size. Instantly, the roaring, the hissing, the flaring of the energy in the drive chamber were snuffed out. As surely as if it were a living thing mortally struck, the metal lost its life.

The super-beings turned their concentrated attention on the

grove of ibis trees. First they counted them. Then they cut incisions into several roots, and extracted a length of white pith from each. These were taken to the parent ship, and subjected to chemical examination. It was in this way that the discovery was made that there had been eighty-three trees. An intensive search for the missing tree began.

But the mighty rent in the planet's great belly had been filled in by drift and mud and water. Not a trace of it remained.

"It must be concluded," the commander noted finally in his logbook, "that the lost ibis was destroyed by one of the calamities so common on unfinished planets. Unfortunately, great damage has already been done to the natural evolution of the jungle life. Because of this accelerated development, intelligence, when it finally does emerge, will be dangerously savage in its outlook. The time lapse involved precludes all advance recommendations for rectification."

Eighty million years passed.

Wagnowski hurried along the quiet suburban road and through the gate. He was a thick, beefy soldier with cold blue eyes, coming home on leave; and at first, as he kissed his wife, he didn't notice that there had been bomb damage to his house.

He finally saw the silver tree. He stared. He was about to exclaim, when he noticed that one whole wing of the house was an empty shell, a single wall standing vacuously in a precarious balance.

"The !-!-?-! American fascists!" he bellowed murderously. "!-! ? !-!"

It was less than an hour later that the sensitive ibis tree began to give off a delicious perfume. First Russia, then the rest of the world breathed the spreading "peace."

World War III ended.

HEIR UNAPPARENT

IT was an uneasy, all-pervading sensation, a threat of pain to come combined with the beginning of the pain itself. The old man saw that Doctor Parker was looking at him startled.

"Good heavens, sire," the physician said. "You've been given Blackmail poison. This is incredible."

Arthur Clagg sat very still in the bed, his eyes narrowed, his thought a slow pattern of reception to impression. His gaze took in the chunky, red-faced Parker, the enormous bedroom, the shaded windows. At last, grimly, he shook his shaggy old head, and said: "When will the crisis come in a man of my age?"

"About four days. The development is progressive, and the pain increases hour after hour by infinitesimal increments to a pitch of—"

The doctor broke off in a thin-lipped fury. "By God, this is the damnedest crime in the history of the world. Poisoning a man ninety-four years of age. Why, it's—"

He must have noticed the scornful quality of Arthur Clagg's gaze. He stopped. He looked abashed. He said: "I beg your pardon, sire."

Arthur Clagg said coldly: "I once defined you, Doctor, as a person with an adult mind and the emotional capacity of a child. It still seems to fit."

He paused. He sat in the bed, cold-faced, thoughtful. He said finally in a precise, almost stately voice: "You will refrain from informing anyone of what has happened, not even my great-granddaughter and her husband. No one! And"—a bleak smile touched his gray lips—"do not be too outraged by the crime. A man who dares to hold the reins of government is subject to all the risks of the trade, regardless of his age. In fact—"

He paused again. His smile twisted ironically as he went on: "In fact, as is already apparent, the struggle for succession to the power of an old dictator is bound to be ferocious. . . . A year ago a battery of doctors, including yourself, said I had at least fifteen more years of life ahead of me. That was very welcome news because I had, and have still, to decide who shall be my successor."

He smiled again, but there was a harshness in his voice as he went on: "I now find that I have four days in which to make my decision. That is, I *think* I have four days. Is there anything in the news that will cut me down to even less time than that?"

The doctor was silent for a moment, as if he were organizing his mind, then: "Your armies are still retreating, sire. Machine guns and rifles out of museums are almost useless against the forbidden atomic weapons of the rebel, General Garson. At their present rate of advance, the rebels should be here in six days. During the night they captured—"

Arthur Clagg scarcely heard. His mind was concentrating on the words "six days." That was it, of course. The power group in the palace wanted to force his hand before the arrival of the rebels. . . . He grew aware again of Doctor Parker's voice.

". . . Mr. Medgerow thinks that only the fewness of their numbers prevents them from making a break-through. They—"

"Medgerow!" echoed Arthur Clagg blankly. "Who's Medgerow? Oh, I remember. That's the inventor whose writings you once tried to bring to my attention. But, as you know, science no longer interests me."

Doctor Parker clicked his tongue apologetically. "I beg your pardon, sire. I used his name quite inadvertently."

The old man made a vague it-doesn't-matter movement. He said: "Send in my valet, as you go out."

The doctor turned at the doorway. A grim look crept over his thick face. "Sire," he said, "I hope I will not seem presumptuous when I say that your friends and well-wishers will wait anxiously for you to turn *the* weapon on all your enemies."

He went out.

Arthur Clagg sat there, icily satiric. Fifty years, he thought, for fifty years the world had been educated against war, against the use of weapons. For fifty years he had poured the wealth of

101

the earth into contructive channels, into social security, public works that *were* public and not merely political catchpolls.

The continents had been transformed; every conceivable idea for improvement within the bounds of scientific possibility had been subjected to the marvelous pressures of money and labor.

Green and fruitful in summer, gorgeously scientized in winter, peaceful and prosperous the year round, earth turned its made-over face towards its sun, a smiling, happy face. There was not an honest man alive who ought not to glory in the miracle that had been wrought during the brief span of half a century.

He had taken over a world devastated by atomic energy misused, and had changed it almost overnight into a dream of a billion wonders. And now—

Arthur Clagg suddenly felt his age. It seemed incredible that the first crisis could evoke the oldest evil impulse in human nature. Kill! Destroy all your enemies. Be merciless. Bring out the irresistible weapon.

The surge of bitter thought quieted, as a discreet knock came at the door. Arthur Clagg sat heavy with his problem as his valet entered.

At last his mind calmed with the beginning of, not decision, but purpose.

The day passed. There was nothing to do but carry on his routine—and wait for his poisoners to come to him. They knew they had only four days in which to act. They wouldn't waste any time.

The intermediary would be Nadya or Merd.

It was like a thousand other days of his old age. All around him was movement, footsteps hurrying to and from his apartment, secretaries, department heads, police agents, an almost endless line of the people who kept him in touch with what was going on. A world of low voices telling him the many facts about a gigantic government whose every action was taken in his name.

The details only had to be left out. Except for that, everything absorbed him. . . . Trouble in Chinese Manchuria. . . . Renewed guerrilla activity in the virgin forest land of what had once been

Europe. . . . The cities controlled by the rebel, General Garson, were loosely held, and were not dangerous in themselves. "Very well. Go on sending them food. . . ." Of all the government scientists, only a man called Medgerow had a wide acquaintance among important personages in the citadel.

"Hmmm," the old man mused aloud. "Medgerow! The name has already come up once today. What's he like?"

The chief of the state police shrugged. "Cultured conversationalist, abnormal though fascinating personality. But we've got nothing on him except that a lot of people go to see him. If I may ask, sire, why this interest in scientists?"

Arthur Clagg said slowly, "To my mind, no group either inside or outside the citadel would dare to act against me in this machine age, without a scientific adviser."

The police officer said matter-of-factly: "Shall I pick him up, and put on the pressure?"

"Don't be silly." Curtly. "If he's a good scientist, the simple little games you play with mechanical hypnotism and lie detectors won't catch him. But your action would have meantime served to warn the bigger game. You have given me the information I desire: so far as you know, there is no secret revolutionary force operating inside the citadel?"

"That is correct, sire."

When the police chief had gone, Arthur Clagg sat sunk in thought. There no longer seemed any doubt. His first suspicion was correct. The poisoners were his own people.

It was the implication that was disturbing. Was it possible that, no matter how honorably a dictator might rule, his very existence kept *in* existence the violences of human power lusts, made bloodshed inevitable and, in its intensional structure, held the seeds of a far-wider, greater chaos than the democracy which, for ten years, he had been considering restoring?

It seemed so; only—you couldn't bring back democracy with all *its* implications in three days.

The day dragged. At four o'clock Nadya, made up and glittering like a movie star, came in with a rustling of silk and a clack-clack of high heels. She brushed his cheek with her perfumed lips, then lighted a cigarette and flung herself on a settee.

He thought: Nadya, poisoner. Earlier, the idea had been easy enough to accept, part of the life of intrigue that sinuated around him.

But *his* great-granddaughter! The last blood tie he had with the human race. All the rest, the noble Cecily, the quiet intellectual Peter, the first and loveliest Nadya, and the others, had slipped away into their graves, leaving him alone with this— this sanguinary betrayer and murderess.

The dark mood passed as swiftly as it had come, as Nadya said, "Grandfather, you're impossible!"

Arthur Clagg studied her with abrupt but detached good humor. Nadya was twenty-eight. She had a pretty face, but her eyes were hard and bright, calculating rather than thoughtful.

She had once had great influence over him, and the old man realized with a cool objectivity why that had been so: her youth! The vibrant, purely animal spirits of a young girl had blinded him to the fact that she was just one more stranger not too cleverly out for what she could get.

That was over.

He waited. She went on earnestly. "Grandfather, what is in your mind? Are you going to permit the rebel Garson and that upstart parliament which is sponsoring him—are you going to let yourself be shoved aside? Are you giving up without a fight, letting us all go down to ridicule and ruin because of your refusal to face the fact that human nature hasn't changed?"

Arthur Clagg asked softly, "What would you do in my place, Nadya?"

It was not an answer to her tirade; it was designed purely and simply to draw her out. Up to a year before, whenever he had given in to her wishes, that was the question that had always preceded the act of his yielding.

He saw from the way she was stiffening, that she recognized the phrase. A brilliant smile lighted her berouged face. Her eyes widened, grew eager.

"Grandfather, it's no exaggeration to say that you're probably the greatest man who has ever lived. In spite of your age and the fact that you have delegated so many of your powers, your prestige is so great that, in spite of gathering confusion resulting from the rebel march on the citadel, your world is holding together. But before you, and terribly near now, is the most important decision of your life: you must decide to use your potent weapon. For fifty years you've kept it hidden, but now you must bring it forth, and use it. With it you can decide what the future shall be. Medgerow says there is no record in history of a decision of such importance being defaulted because of the refusal of—"

"Medgerow!" ejaculated Arthur Clagg. He stopped himself. "Never mind. Go on."

Nadya was looking at him. "He's a horrible little man with a personality and an extraordinary self-confidence that make him interesting in spite of his appearance. An inventor attached to the government science bureau, I believe."

She hesitated. She seemed to realize that the full force of her argument had to be rebuilt now that it had been interrupted.

"Grandfather, in spite of all your repugnance, the fact is that good men have already died. If you don't kill the rebels, they'll go on exterminating your loyal army, and will eventually reach the citadel. I am going to suspend judgment as to what they will do to us when they get here. But it's a point you ought to consider. You can't just leave it to chance."

She stopped; she drew a deep breath; then: "You have asked me for my opinion. As plainly as I can, I want to say that I think you should disarm the rebels, and then turn your weapon over to Merd. Only through him and me can your life work be saved from violent transformations. The laws of political accession are such that other groups would have to tear down at least part of the edifice you have so carefully built up. The world might even dissolve once more into separate contending states. The death toll *could* reach fantastic proportions.

"Can't you see"—she was so earnest that her voice trembled—"it is to our interest, and ours alone in all this wide world, to keep things as they are. Well"—she finished with an effort at casualness—"what do you say?"

It took a moment for the old man to realize that, for the time at least, she had finished.

After a moment, it struck him that he was not altogether displeased with her verbal picture. For all its cold-bloodedness, it was a gentle solution to a deadly situation. For, as she had said, the choice was no longer between killing and not killing. Government soldiers had already died before the blast of atomic cannon, and, according to reports, mobile artillery had wrought havoc in the rebel ranks.

Death was definitely involved.

Nevertheless only a monstrosity of a man would hand a world and its helpless people over to a gang of poisoners.

He saw that Nadya was watching him anxiously. Arthur Clagg laughed, a silent, bitter laugh. He parted his lips, but before he could speak, the young woman said, "Grandfather, I know you've hated me ever since I married Merd. You may not be aware of that dislike, but it's there; and the reason for it is emotional reaction. I haven't dared mention it to you before, but this is an ultimate crisis. Within six days atomic cannon will be burning at this citadel; and in the fire of such a reality, not even the feelings of an old man can be spared."

"Hated you!" said Arthur Clagg.

It was not a reaction. It was a pure expression, a sound having no origin in thought. He did note in a remote part of his mind that she had said six days, not four. She apparently did not anticipate a crisis at the moment of his death. The implication, that she knew nothing of the poisoning, was startling.

She could of course have such firm mental control over herself that the seemingly unconscious reaction was actually deliberate. ... There was no time to think about that. Nadya was speaking.

"You've hated me in a perversion of love. I was all you had, and then I got married, and, naturally, thereafter Merd and the children came first. Grandfather, don't you see—that is why you hate me."

The gathered effects of the poison made thinking hard. The old man remained stiff, and, at first, hostile. He began to brace himself mentally. With a sudden, reaching effort, he threw off the queasy weight of his sickishness. Briefly, his mind drummed with energy. Thought came in the old, flashing way.

He relaxed finally, astounded. Why, you old fool, he thought. She's right. That *is* why you disliked her. Jealousy!

He studied her from under shaggy eyebrows, curious, conscious that earlier impressions were now subject to revision. In many ways Nadya's was a distinctive face, not so good-looking but definitely aristocratic. Funny how people got that way. He himself had always had a professorish sort of countenance; and yet here was his great-granddaughter looking like a patrician.

Why was it that no one had ever adduced the natural laws that would explain why the grandchildren of people who ruled all had the same expressions on their faces?

Arthur Clagg shook himself and drew his mind back to Nadya. She had on, he decided after a moment, severely, too much make-up, almost as much as some of the hussies who fluttered around the citadel. You could scarcely blame a woman, though, for being in style.

The old man began to feel staggered. What was happening to his case against her?

Here she sat, a lean, aristocratic woman, anxious to retain her high position—who wouldn't in her place?—clever rather than intellectual, a little callous, perhaps. But all people who commanded had to harden their hearts to individual suffering.

He who had lived in an age where a tornado of atomic energy killed a billion human beings *had* to have as successor a person who, in the final issue, was capable of exterminating anyone daring once more to precipitate such a holocaust. And now that there was doubt as to whether Nadya was a party to the poisoning, she was again eligible.

But if she and Merd weren't guilty, who was?

The old man sat shaken, uncertain. He might never find out, of course, in spite of the fact that the need to know was rapidly becoming an obsession. But he couldn't condemn anyone without proof. He said slowly, "Leave me now, Nadya. You have presented your case well, but I have not decided. Tomorrow, I intend to . . . Never mind."

He waited till, with puzzled side-glances, she had left. Then he picked up his private radio phone. It took a moment to establish the connection.

"Well?" said Arthur Clagg.

The police chief's voice came. "The arrangements are made. The meeting will take place in No-Man's Land. He agrees to the presence of three bodyguards." The officer broke. "Sire, this is a most dangerous business. If anything should go wrong—"

The old man said curtly, "You are having the mobile unit outfitted according to my instructions?"

"Yes, but—" Earnestly, "Sire, I ask again, what is your purpose in talking to General Garson?"

The old man only smiled tightly, and hung up. He had not one but two purposes in meeting Garson. It wouldn't do to tell anyone that he intended to size up the rebel chieftain as a possible successor to himself. There was no use broadcasting his second reason either.

"Remember," said Arthur Clagg to his chief officer, "take no action till I tug at my ear."

The unpleasant part of the whole business was walking fifty feet from his mobile to where the tables and chairs had been set up in the open meadow. Every step he took twisted his insides. Gasping, he sank into one of the chairs.

He was almost at the table when a lanky individual in an ill-fitting blue uniform descended the steps of the second mobile and strode across the grass. The man's movements had something of the awkward confidence of a man who was very sure of himself but lacked good manners.

Recognition was unmistakable. The lean, bony face with its lantern jaw had already stared at Arthur Clagg several times from photographs. Even without the countenance, the nasal-twanged voice, which had sounded many times on the radio, would have made the identification inevitable. Rebel General Garson was photo- and voco-genic.

He said, "Old Man, I hope you haven't got some slick scheme up your sleeve."

It was loudly said; too loudly to be polite. But Arthur Clagg was intent and curious. Nor did he think immediately of replying. He was conscious of a genuine absorption in this man who dared oppose the irresistible weapon.

Garson had brown eyes and uncombed sandy hair. He sank into his chair, and stared unsmilingly at his aged opponent. Once more it was Garson who spoke, snappingly this time. "Get to the point, man."

Arthur Clagg hardly heard. Nor did the details of physical appearance interest him now. It was the man, his boldness in organizing a small army in a vast land, his defiance of death for an ideal—a defiance that almost in itself merited success for his enterprise.

The old man straightened his anguished body and said with dignity, "General Garson—as you will notice, I am recognizing your military title—to me you represent a trend of thought in the country. And as a result I might, if you can give me some dialectical arguments, allow parliament to be re-established under your mentorship. I am not opposed to democracy, because, except for the disaster in which it involved itself half a century ago, it was a vigorous, marvellously growing organism. I have no doubt it can be so again. The danger is the free use of atomic energy—"

"Don't worry about that—" Garson waved a gaunt hand. "My congress and I will keep it to ourselves."

"Eh!" Arthur Clagg stared across the table, not sure that he had heard correctly. He had the sudden, blank feeling that meaningless words had been projected at him.

Before he could speak, or think further, the lanky man leaned forward. The small brown eyes peered at him.

"See here, Mr. Dictator Clagg, I don't know just what you had in mind, asking me to come over. I thought maybe you wanted to surrender, now that I've called your bluff. Here's my offer: I understand you've got some kind of estate down south. Okeh. I'll let you and your granddaughter and family live there under guard. If anybody starts something, naturally they get killed. My congress will set me up as president, and I'll just slip into your position as quickly as I can. In a few months everything'll be going along as smooth as ever. That clear?"

The shock was greater. There seemed nothing to think. At

109

last Arthur Clagg expostulated, "But see here, you haven't got a congress yet. A congress is a governing body elected by a secret ballot by the vote of all the people. Two hundred men can't just organize and call themselves congress. They—"

His voice trailed, as the implications penetrated of what he was saying. It seemed incredible but—was this man so ignorant of history that he didn't know what representative government was?

The old man tried to picture that. The psychology of it finally grew plausible. Like so many human beings, Garson was only dimly aware that there had been life before his own ego emerged from the mists of childhood. To him, that pre-Garson period must be an unsubstantial hodgepodge. Somehow the words "congress" and "president" had come down to him. And he had made his own definitions.

With an effort Arthur Clagg drew his attention back to Garson. And the thought came finally: After all, it was the courage of this creature that was fascinating. A man who had the boldness to defy *the* weapon must be amenable to reason and to a partial re-education.

"Boy!" Garson's voice twanged. "You sure have been smart, Clagg. All these years pretending you had a super weapon, and fixing up books and motion pictures and things to make people think it all happened the way you said. You never fooled me though; and so now you've had your day. I'll sure carry on with that weapon game, though. It—"

His voice went on, but Arthur Clagg did not listen. He waited until the sound stopped, and then with a casual gesture tugged at his ear.

He saw Garson stiffen, as the mechanical hypnotic waves struck at him. The old man wasted no time.

"Garson," he intoned, "Garson, you will be glad to tell me, tell me, tell me who gave you the blueprints for atomic cannon. Garson, was it someone in the government? Garson, it is so easy to tell me."

"But I do not know." The man's voice was far away somehow, and vaguely surprised. "They were given me by a man I do not know. He said he was an agent, an agent—"

"An agent for whom?" Arthur Clagg pressed.

"I do not know."

"But didn't you care? Didn't it worry you?"

"No, I figured as soon as I had the cannon, the other fellow would have to start worrying."

After three minutes, Arthur Clagg tugged at his ear— and Garson came back to normal life. He looked a little startled, but the old man was not worried about the suspicions of a so completely ignorant man. He said, "Since I gave you my word, Mister, you may depart at once in perfect safety. I would advise you, however, to keep on traveling, because tomorrow no one in the vicinity of an atomic cannon will be alive. In any event I shall advise"—pause—"my great-grandson-in-law, my heir and successor, to hunt you down and have you brought to justice."

He was thinking as he finished: there was no time for further choice.

The house was one of a row of pleasant mansions that stood amid greenery in the shadow of the towering peak of a building that was the citadel.

The outer door must have opened by remote electrical control because, When Doctor Parker had gone through, he found himself in a narrow metal hallway. A tiny bulb in the ceiling shed a white glow upon a second door, which was all metal. The doctor stood motionless, then he called, shrilly, "Medgerow, what's all this?"

There was a mechanical chuckle from one of the walls. "Don't get excited, Doctor. As you know, the whole situation is now entering the critical stage, and I am taking no chances."

"B-but I've been here a hundred times before, and I've never seen any of this—this fortification."

"Good!" Medgerow's voice came again through the wall-speaker. He sounded pleased. "It would take an atomic cannon or"—pause—"Arthur Clagg's Contradictory Force to blast me out of this. But come in."

The second door opened into a panelled hallway and clanged behind Parker. A small man was waiting there for him. He chuckled as he saw Parker, then said curtly, "Well, your report, man! You administered the poison successfully?"

The doctor did not reply as he followed the other into the living room. These first moments in the presence of Medgerow always made him uneasy.... Adjustment from normalcy to abnormalcy was a semi-involved process.

It wasn't so much, Parker realized bleakly for the hundredth time, that Medgerow's ugliness by itself was so jarring. A thousand males picked up at random from the streets outside would have yielded a dozen whose physical characteristics were less prepossessing. Medgerow differed in that he exuded a curious, terrible aura of misshapen strength. His personality had the concreteness of the hump of a hunchback. It seemed to make him not quite human. Parker had discovered that, by letting only the corner of his eyes be aware of the man, he could tolerate his presence. That was what he did now.

"Yes, I administered the poison last night. And all day he has been feeling the first effects."

The image in the corner of the doctor's vision stood stock still. "He will die in four days?"

"About midnight on the fourth day."

There was silence. The figure remained still. But at last Medgerow said with a compelling quietness, "I shall not make the mistake of the new princes of history. I have no desire to be dragged, as was Cromwell, out of my grave and hanged as a public spectacle. Nor shall I be so slow in starting my executions as were the early French revolutionists. And as for those talkative idiots, Felix Pyat and Delescluze in 1871 Paris—it makes me sick just to think about them. Mussolini was caught in the same net. He allowed his potential destroyers and betrayers to remain alive. Hitler, of course, had half his work done for him when the Allies rid Germany of the Hohenzollern regime. He made one mistake: the United States."

The quiet voice grew abruptly savage. "But enough of this. I shall be ruthless. The possessor of Arthur Clagg's Contradictory Force weapon rules the world, provided he makes certain that no possible assassin remains alive on the face of the earth."

"But are you sure?" Parker interrupted anxiously. "Are you absolutely sure that you can nullify his weapon long enough to seize control of it? How can you be positive that he will even use it, and so give you a chance to seize it?"

Medgerow clicked his tongue impatiently. "Of course, I'm not sure. I am basing my estimations on the character of a man whose actions, speeches, and writings I have studied for years. At this very moment, I'll warrant, the old man has practically decided to use the weapon in one way or another. In my opinion, he will use it to act against the rebels, and will then turn the weapon over to his son-in-law. This is all to the good. I want him to stamp out the rebel force before I move against him.

"All this, however, will not happen tomorrow. If I read Arthur Clagg aright, he will first seek a meeting with General Garson, the rebel leader. He will find a man who embodies the worst features of the demagogue. And, besides, Garson has dared to use atomic power. That, as I have told you, will balance in the old man's mind his suspicion that his great-granddaughter helped to poison him. Oh, yes, he'll use the weapon. And that"—the little monstrosity of a man chuckled—"is where I come in. Little did Arthur Clagg realize fifty years ago that he established a precedent, and became the first, not the last, of the scientist leaders. Now that men's minds accept such a possibility, scientists will begin to think in that direction, unconsciously molding their lives and their works with the hope of power in their minds. Such are the laws of dialectical materialism. But now—"

He broke off, and there was suddenly a more savage intensity; he grew quiet. "Thanks for coming, Doctor. As you know, we couldn't take the chance of a phone call being intercepted, particularly as the secret police have been making guarded inquiries about me."

As they shook hands, Medgerow, his blue eyes glistening, said, "You've done well, Parker. I'm sorry you were too squeamish to use the real poison, but that can be remedied when I get into power. As it is, your assistance in helping me force the old man to bring out his weapon will gain you the reward you desire. Arthur Clagg's great-granddaughter, Nadya, will be *given* you

113

in marriage as soon as her husband has been decently disposed of."

"Thank you," said Parker quietly.

Contemptuous-eyed, the little man watched him go. He thought coldly: silly ass! Couldn't he see that the public necessities of the situation required that the only natural heir of the *former* dictator marry the new ruler? Pawns didn't take queens in this game.

For old Arthur Clagg speed was essential. He sent the invitations to Merd and Nadya for that afternoon. They arrived shortly after lunch. In spite of himself, the old man found himself staring at his great-grandson-in-law, seeking in the man's lean face reassurance that the colossal trust he was about to receive would not be misused. He saw gray eyes, dark hair, a rather fine, sensitive face with stern lips—exactly the same physical characteristics, the same person, he had so violently disliked from the very first announcement of Nadya's betrothal. The body, not the mind, was visible.

It was not enough. The thought was a pain briefly greater than the agony of the poison. Outward appearances didn't count. And yet, the decision was made. A man with two days to live couldn't think of anything but the easy solution. Arthur Clagg said curtly, "Lock all the doors. We're going to uncover the weapon. It will require most of the afternoon."

Merd said explosively. "You mean, it's *here*?"

The old man ignored that. He went on drably. "The weapon is mounted inside a plastic airplane powered by four gas turbine jets and strato rockets. This machine is hidden in the east wing of the citadel which, as you perhaps know, was built by workers from every part of the world. The employment of men from far places who did not speak the same language made it possible to construct a hiding place without anyone guessing its true purpose."

He broke off, fumbled in his coat pocket, and produced a key.

"This will unlock a tool cupboard next to my bathroom. Bring the tools in here. You will need them all to uncover and then activate the mechanical keys that will open the hidden chamber."

114

It took time, the two young people silent and intent on their unaccustomed work, carting machine saws, atomic drills, mobile planes into various indicated parts of the living room. When all the tools were gathered, the old man motioned them to the settee near him, and began. "There has been a great deal of wild talk about the nature of my weapon. The speculation was quite unnecessary because many years ago I very foolishly gave out some of the theory in a series of articles published in the government science gazette. It was foolish, not because anyone will be able to duplicate the weapon but because—"

He broke off, frowning. "Never mind. I'll explain that later."

He went on, quietly, "The theory behind the Contradiction Force penetrates to the inner core of the meanings of life and of movement. Life, as you know, has been defined as orderly movement. There is movement also in inorganic matter, but this is a primitive version and is explained by the larger concept. What makes movement possible? Why does not matter, organic or inorganic, simply collapse into its basic components, and, thus inert, fulfill its apparently senseless destiny?

"You might answer that things are as they are because electrons whirl in orbits according to fixed laws, forming atoms which, in their turn, have a physically logical relationship to the larger structure of molecules, and so on. But that would be merely evading the issue.

"Movement occurs in an object because *in* it, in its very basic oneness, there is an antithesis, a contradiction. It is only because a thing contains a contradiction within itself that it moves and acquires impulse and activity.

"The theory by itself suggested the nature of the research: I found first what were the laws governing the contradiction in various types of matter, and I then started to develop a force to interfere with it. The mechanical problem of practicalizing the theory involved in its simplest functions the procuration of a force that would cause the contradiction in any given matter to operate, not in the orderly fashions that nature has laboriously evolved, but uncontrollably. Those who have not seen it in action cannot imagine how terrible the result is. It is not, has no relation to, atomic energy. As a destructive force, the hellish active area in

115

the interior of a nova sun possibly equals it in violence, but such a sun cannot even theoretically surpass it.

"Fortunately, heat is not a by-product, as would be the case if the force were related to atomic or electrical energy. It was only long after the weapon was an actuality that I discovered that I had hit on a billion-to-one chance, that my discovery was an accident that cannot be repeated in a million years. Tomorrow you will see it in action."

He paused and frowned, partly with pain, partly because he was worried.

"The weapon has only one aspect that is dangerous to us. It can be nullified by a simple, electrically induced magnetic flow in the object on which it is focused. That is why I was foolish in giving out the theory. Someday, somewhere, a smart scientist will discover the nullifying principle—and the weapon will cease to be a factor in world politics. I must confess I have worried about that in the dark watches of many nights. But now"—he straightened slowly—"let us get to work. . . ."

Minute by minute, as the hours passed, his choice seemed more and more final.

The third day dawned cloudless. It was one of those brightly perfect spring mornings. The world below the plane was a panorama of emerging green. Even now, with the anguish tearing at his body, it was hard for Arthur Clagg to realize that, in this setting of eternally youthful soil, his mortality was finding its final expression.

They came to the rebel lines, and began to circle. The telescopes showed metal glinting among the trees below—and Arthur Clagg, with Nadya leaning over his shoulder, examined the maps the army had supplied.

"Climb higher," he ordered finally. And again, minutes later, "Higher."

"But we're up about thirty-five miles," Merd protested. "We've already used up three-quarters of our rocket fuel."

"Higher!" said the old man inexorably. "The problem at all times with this weapon is to remain clear of the explosion. When I first estimated mathematically its power, I hardly believed my figures. Fortunately, I had the sense to rig up a device that would cut off the force after one millionth of a second. If I do that now, and set this dial to '*metal*,' only the outermost rim of atoms on the one cannon below that I'm aiming at will be affected."

He finished, "When you have five minutes' fuel left, tell me."

Merd's voice came over the earphones. "Less than five minutes left now. I'll have to turn over to the jets."

"Steady!" said Arthur Clagg.

He had left the telescopic sights, and was swinging the gun around, locking it into place. Once more he looked through the sights. He pressed the trigger.

The ground below turned bluer than the sky. For a long moment, it looked like a placid lake in a glacier. Then the lake was gone. And where there had been trees and green beauty was a gray-black hole thirty miles in diameter.

Desert!

"Grandfather," Nadya cried. "The gun is swinging back. It'll hit you."

The old man did not move from the sights. The gun swung in a one-hundred-and-eighty-degree arc, and clicked back into position just beside his head. He said, without looking up, "It's all right I made it that way."

A moment longer he looked, then he straightened. Awareness came that the plane was shuddering with speed, the jets whistling shrilly.

He sat down. He leaned back, weary, feeling strangely old. Slowly he straightened, fighting the pain and the fatigue. Merd's voice came over the phones.

"Grandfather, there's news coming through from the citadel. Some idiot has started a revolution. Listen!"

A strange voice sounded: ". . . . A rebellion in the air force . . . uprising in the citadel garrison, with fighting now going on in the gardens. A man named Medgerow has declared himself to be the new dictator—"

There was more, but Arthur Clagg's mind followed it no further. Medgerow. Funny, how the name had come up so often

117

the last few days, almost like predestination. Nadya had mentioned him, and Parker.

The old man sagged a little. Parker . . . poison. For a moment, the connection seemed impossible. What could be the man's motive? Except for a tendency to lose control of his emotions, Parker was a timid, cautious fellow with a reasonably good mind.

Arthur Clagg sighed. There was no use thinking about it. Medgerow had precipitated a palace revolution before the arrival of Garson. Like Garson, the new usurper was apparently not taking the slightest notice of an old man and his mythical Contradictory Force.

Perhaps he should have announced in advance his intention to use it.

No use worrying about that now. The die was cast, and there were things to do. He straightened.

"Nadya."

"Yes, Grandfather."

"Jump."

He had almost forgotten that people never disobeyed him when he took that tone, that manner; it was so long since he had used it.

One measured look she gave him. Then she was running forward to Merd. She came back, tears in her eyes. Her lips touched his. She said, "I shall join the children at the Lodge, and wait till I hear from you."

He watched her fall into the blue haze. It was five minutes later that Merd's voice came over the radio.

"There're some planes following us, Grandfather. What—"

Three times Arthur Clagg pressed the trigger of the Contradictory Force weapon, but the planes came on, untouched, unharmed. At last he whispered his defeat over the phone. "Better obey their signal, Merd, and go down. There's nothing we can do."

They were actually landing before he realized he was still holding the weapon. He stared down grimly at the now useless double cone, and then let it slip clear of his fingers. He watched it swing back in its one-hundred-eighty-degree arc, and click metallically into its rest position.

It lay in its cradle, still omnipotent under the right conditions. But by the time it was used again, Merd and he would be dead, and the law and order world he had created would be scrambled by the passions of men. And it would take a hundred years to put all the pieces together again.

The devil of it, the irony, was that Medgerow had no reason to use it immediately. . . . He felt the plane settling on its jets. Gently it touched the ground. Merd left the controls and came back to him.

"They're signalling us to get off," he said quietly.

Arthur Clagg nodded. In silence they climbed to the ground. They were about a hundred feet away when the other planes began to disgorge men, most of whom carried tubes of rocket fuel to the big plane. One of the men, however, a tall chap in air force uniform, came over.

He said insolently, "The Medgerow orders that you be searched."

The Medgerow. Merd submitted stonily, but the old man watched the procedure with a bleak admiration for its thoroughness.

When the man had finished, Arthur Clagg said, "Satisfy my curiosity. Why did you rebel?"

The officer shrugged. "The—deadness—you created was killing my will to live. The Medgerow is going to release atomic energy. We're going to the planets, perhaps even the stars, in my lifetime."

When the officer had gone, Arthur Clagg turned to Merd.

"My desire for order grew out of the hideous misuse of atomic energy. But I always knew that man was the Contradictory Force of the organic universe, and that sooner or later, for better or worse, he must again be allowed to play with that ultimate fire. Apparently, the time has come."

A small man was climbing out of the nearest plane. He carried an atomic blaster in one hand. He came forward briskly. And even though he had never seen Medgerow before, it seemed to Arthur Clagg that he would have recognized him anywhere, without any more description that he had already received by chance.

Merd was speaking distastefully, "I've discovered that by letting only the corner of my eyes be aware of him, I can stand his presence."

It was an odd and altogether fascinating statement. The words drew the old man's attention briefly away from Medgerow. He felt momentarily absorbed by the insight they gave into Merd's character.

He found himself liking his son-in-law better.

There was no time to think about either Merd or his words. Medgerow stood before them.

He looked abnormal. It wasn't so much, Arthur Clagg decided bleakly, that Medgerow's ugliness was jarring in itself. A thousand males picked at random would have yielded a dozen whose physical characteristics were less prepossessing.

Perhaps it was the triumphant smile on his face, with its frank and unashamed arrogance. It was hard to tell. The man exuded a curious, terrible aura of misshapen strength. His personality protruded with the concretness of the hump of a hunchback.

Gazing at him, old Arthur Clagg felt a chill, a sick consciousness of the extent of his failure. It seemed incredible that he had let himself be panicked into using his weapon, and had not once suspected that that was exactly what his hidden enemy was working for.

He thought: *The* Medgerow, heir of earth. . . . The very idea was shattering.

Medgerow broke the silence, coolly. "In a moment I shall get into your plane and start climbing. As soon as I have reached a safe height, I shall fire at this"—he drew a strip of metal from his pocket, and tossed it onto the ground—"with your weapon. I like ironies like that."

For a moment, the old man could not believe that he had heard aright. The intention, so deliberately stated, was so far-reaching in its implications, so unexpected, that it seemed impossible. He opened his mouth, then closed it again. The hope that came shook his very bones; it had no parallel in the long history of his career.

It was Merd who finally reacted vocally, Merd who said

120

violently, "But there's a city of fifty thousand over there about eight miles. You can't fire the weapon so near it."

Arthur Clagg fumbled at Merd's arm. He wanted to tell the young fool to stop arguing. Couldn't he see that Medgerow was playing into their hands?

Merd cried, "Put a bullet through our brains, you damned murderer. You can't destroy a whole city. You *can't*!"

Once more, in a haze of anxiety now, Arthur Clagg parted his lips to utter words that would silence Merd. Just in time, he saw the look on Medgerow's face. And closed them again.

No words were needed. The best ally he had in this fateful moment was *the* Medgerow himself.

The little man stood, head flung back proudly. His eyes blazed with sardonic joy. "Force and terror—those are the weapons that win, when there are no undefeated armies extant to support opposition groups. I shall use the weapon on you because I have to test its operation anyway. I shall do this here and now because nothing will better convince the world of my unalterable determinations than the destruction of a city. So true is this that, if the city had not been to hand, it would have been necessary for me to transport all of us to its vicinity."

He finished cynically, "It will be a simple matter, once I am established, to propagandize people into believing that it was you, not I, who destroyed it."

Merd said tensely, "You can't do this. It's not human."

Firmly, this time, the old man caught his arm. "Merd," he said resonantly, "can't you see it's useless? We're dealing with a man who has a plan, a settled policy of conquest."

The remark seemed to please Medgerow. He said with satisfaction, "That's right. Argument is useless. I never missed a bet in my strategy. You did everything exactly as I intended you to. Your decision had to be made too swiftly. You had no time to think."

"My foolishness," said Arthur Clagg quietly, "was in thinking all these days and years that there was a decision to be made. I've just realized that, actually, I made my choice long ago. I chose, not self, but the good of all mankind, whereas you have chosen self."

121

"Eh!" Medgerow stared at him intently, as if searching for a hidden meaning. He laughed. Then he said, arrogantly, "Enough of this chatter. You ruined yourself twenty years ago, Arthur Clagg, when you ignored the letters sent you by a struggling science student, myself. I realize now you probably didn't even receive them. But that excuse doesn't apply to later years when powerful friends tried to draw my work to your attention and you wouldn't even look at it."

He was suddenly livid with rage. He spat. "Twenty years of obscurity. . . . During the next twenty minutes I'll let you think of what might have been if you had treated me from the beginning according to my merits."

He whirled away. The plane door clanged behind him. The gas turbines whined. The jets hissed. Lightly, swiftly, the plane rose into the sky. It became a dot.

After a minute, the other planes took off; the two men were alone.

There was a long silence. At last, cold and contemptuous, Merd said, "This creature cannot see that you are not, and never were, his type of dictator. The history of democracies teaches that in emergencies people will temporarily surrender their liberties. No greater emergency ever existed than the release of atomic energy. The period of control has been a long one, because the world had to be reorganized; and, like a new mold, allowed to set. In my considered opinion, the people are ready again to take over; and no one, not Medgerow, not me, not all the force anyone can possibly exert will stop them."

"Why, Merd," said Arthur Clagg, "I didn't know you felt like that. In fact, you have provided me with a whole series of pleasant shocks. Under pressure, you have showed a very great number of golden attributes. Accordingly, I herewith commission you to begin re-establishing democracy as soon as we return to the citadel."

The young man gazed at him thoughtfully. At last, shakily, he asked, "W-what did you say? Back to the citadel. . . ."

Arthur Clagg felt a sudden sympathy for his great-grandson-in-law, a sharp understanding of the agonized turmoil being experienced by a man who had geared himself to death, and now was confronted by the possibility of life.

It seemed curiously important that Merd suffer no more than he had to. The old man said grimly, "I was terrified that someday the Contradictory Force would be set off accidentally. I therefore constructed the weapon so that its muzzle resembled its stock. I placed it so that it would swing around automatically after I had fired it, and point up towards the sky or towards any stranger who might be impelled to fire it. *That is the position it is in this very moment, as Medgerow stands aiming it.*"

Old Arthur Clagg finished in a ringing tone, "Not with Medgerow, but in your hands, Merd, lies the destiny of mankind."

He did not know then that the poison inside him was only a substitute, and that he would be the wise old mentor of the new and lusty civilization of the stars.

THE SECOND SOLUTION

THE little, thin chap with the too-sharp voice was saying, "My point is, we didn't need Edison, Paladine, Clissler, or any particular scientist. It is the mass mind that moves inevitably in certain directions. The inventions, the ideas of individuals grow out of that mass. They would occur regardless of the birth or early death of any individual genius, so-called. There's always a second solution."

Somebody disagreed. "Inventions change the course of history. A new weapon wins a war because it was introduced when it was. A year later would have been too late."

The big man cleared his throat, drawing our attention to him. I had noticed him idle over from the club bar a few minutes earlier, and listen with that bored contempt which deep-space men have for groundlings. He had the tan of space in his hawk-like countenance. He looked as if this were between voyages for him, and he didn't know what to do with himself. "I hate to enter an impractical discussion," he said, "but it just happens I can illustrate your argument. You all remember the experience some years ago of Professor Jamieson with a full-grown ezwal in the ocean jungle of Eristan II—how they captured a Rull lifeship intact, and eventually escaped with its secret of perfect antigravity, and prevented a revolution and a massacre on Carson's Planet?"

We all recalled it. The big man went on, "Actually, Professor Jamieson had captured two ezwals on that visit of his to Carson's Planet. One was a male, which he took with him on his own ship, and with which he was later wrecked on Eristan II. The other was a female, which he had dispatched to Earth on an earlier ship. En route, this female gave birth to a male about as big as a lion. The young one grew about a foot on the trip, but that wouldn't have mattered in itself. What precipitated the

124

whole thing was the antigravity converters, the old, imperfect pre-Rull type. In their fashion, they began to discharge torrents of free energy; and that's where the story begins."

"Does it prove my point or his?" asked the little chap with the sharp voice.

The big man grimaced at him. And silence settled over our little group.

He began his story.

The grim face of Commander McLennan twisted toward the two officers. "Absolutely out of control!" he said. "The ship will strike Earth in fifteen minutes somewhere in the great Toganna Forest Reserve in northern Canada." He broke off. "Carling, get the men into the lifeboats, then make contact with the superintendent of the Reserve. Tell him we've got two ezwals of Carson's Planet aboard, who'll probably live through the crash. Tell him to prepare for any eventualities; and that I'll be down to take charge of the wreck in half an hour. Brenson!"

"*Yessir!*" The white-faced younger officer sprang to attention as Carling whirled out of the room.

"Go down and kill those two ezwals, mother and son. We can't take a chance on those two beasts getting loose on Earth. They'll murder a thousand people before they can be killed—if they ever get free! You know what they're like. Anybody who's been to Carson's Planet—" He shook his head angrily. "Damn Jamieson for having ezwals brought to Earth. I was against it from the—" He caught himself. "And Brennan, be at the lifeboats in seven—no, make it six minutes for safety. Even if they're not dead! Now, *run!*"

The young man blanched whiter still. "Yessir!" he breathed again, and was gone, tugging at his gun.

For McLennan there were vital things to do, valuable papers to retrieve. And then the time was up. He plunged through the door of a lifeboat, and asked, "Brenson here yet?"

"No, sir!"

They waited. One minute slipped by. Two. Then it was Carling who whispered, "We've got to leave, sir. He can use that empty lifeboat, if he comes. We've *got* to leave."

125

McLennan looked blank. "He's the son of old Rock Brenson. What'll I tell my old pal?"

Carling made no reply. And McLennan's lips twisted to the shaping of a curse, but no sound came, and, actually, no violent words were in his mind. As he slid the lifeboat smoothly into safety of space, he heard the fierce whisper of one of the men:

"It was a mistake to send Brenson down. He's got the killer mind. That's what's holding him. He's got to kill—"

From above the young ezwal sounded the terrible snarl of his mother; and then her thoughts, as hard and sharp as crystal: "Under me for your life! The two-legged one comes to kill!"

Like a streak, he leaped from his end of the cage, five hundred pounds of dark-blue monstrosity. Razor-clawed hands rattled metallically on the steel floor. and then he was into the blackness under her vast form, pressing into the cave of soft, yielding flesh that she made for him. He took unbreakable holds with his six hands, so that, no matter what the violence of her movements or the fury of her attacks, he would be there safe and sound, snugly deep in the folds between her great belly muscles.

Her thought came again: "Remember all the things I've told you. The hope of our race is that men continue to think us beasts. If they suspect our intelligence, we are lost. And someone does suspect it. If that knowledge lives, our people die!"

Faster came her thought: "Remember, your weaknesses in this crisis are those of youth. You love life too much. Fight the resulting fear, for fear it is. Accept death if the opportunity comes to serve your race by so doing."

Her brain slowed. She grew calm. He watched with her then, clinging to her mind with his mind as tightly as his body clung to her body. He saw the thick steel bars of the cage, and, half-hidden by their four-inch width, the figure of a man. He saw the *thoughts* of the man!

"Damn you!" those thoughts came. "If it wasn't for you being on this ship I'd be out of danger now. I—"

The man's hand moved. There was a metallic glint as he pushed the weapon between the bars. It spurted white fire.

For a moment, the mental contact with his mother blackened. It was his own ears that heard the gasping roar; his own flat

126

nostrils that smelled the odor of burning flesh. And there was no mistaking the tangible, physical reality of her wild charge straight at the merciless flame gun projecting between the bars.

The fire clicked off. The blackness vanished from his mother's mind. The young ezwal saw that the weapon and the man had retreated from the reaching threat of those mighty claws.

"Damn you!" the man flared. "Well, take it from here, then!"

There must have been blinding pain, but none of it came through into his brain. His mother's thoughts remained at a mind shaking pitch of malignance; and not for an instant did she remain still. She ducked this way and that way. She ran with twisting, darting, rolling, sliding movements as she fought for life in the narrow confines of the cage.

Like a squirrel she raced twenty feet up the bars of the cage; and then, at the ceiling, she swung along with the agility of a monkey from bar to thick bar. But always, in spite of her desperation, a part of her mind remained untouched and unhurried. The tearing fire followed her, missing her, then hitting her squarely, hitting her so often that finally she could no longer hold back the knowledge that her end was near. And with that thought came another, his first awareness that she had had a purpose in keeping the weapon beyond the bars and forcing it to follow the swift, darting frenzy of her movements. In the very act of pursuing her, the beam of the flame gun had seared with molten effect across the thick steel bars!

"God!" came the man's thoughts. "Won't it ever die? And where is that damned young one? Another minute now, and I'll have to go. I—"

His thoughts stopped as sixty-five hundred pounds of the hardest organic body in man's part of the galaxy smashed with pile-driver speed at the weakened bars of the cage. The cub strained with his own tautened muscles against the compression of that wall of tendons surrounding him—and lived because even in that moment of titanic attempt, his mother kept those particular muscles relaxed.

Beyond the vastness of her body, he heard and felt the metal bars bend and break where the flame had destroyed their tensile strength.

"Good lord!" the man thought in high dismay. Strangely, then, the preternatural sharpness of his thoughts weakened. The picture of him began to fade, and where the mother ezwal's thoughts had been there was no movement. The young ezwal was aware of her lying above him, a great, flabby dead mass, covering him. The reality of her death struck him swiftly, and it explained why the man's mind and the picture of him had dimmed. It was his own weaker powers that were catching the man's thoughts now.

They were distorted patterns. The man mumbled, "Only got a minute, only a minute . . . then I've got to go . . . and get off the ship before—"

The cub was aware of the man crawling onto his mother's back. He tingled with dismay. It was he who was being searched for now; and if that white flame found him it would deal out equally merciless death. Frantically he pushed deeper into the yielding stomach above him.

And then, all hell broke loose. There was a piercing screaming of air against the freighter's hull. The crash was world-shattering. His six hands were wrenched from their holds. He struck intolerable hardness. And the blackness that came was very real and very personal.

Slowly, the darkness grew alive. Somewhere there was movement, muffled noises, and a confusing sense of many men's thoughts; incredible danger! Alarm leaped along his nerves. In a spasm of movement, he pressed upward into the saving folds of his mother's flesh. And, as he lay there quiveringly still, deep into her, the world beyond and around her enveloping body began to grow clearer. He began to receive thoughts.

"Never saw such an awful mess!" somebody's mind whispered.

"What could have ailed Brenson?" another said. "That fighting instinct got him at last, in spite of his love of life. His body's plain jam . . . what did you say, Mr. McLennan?"

"I'm talking to Kelly," came the curt, savage answer. "Kelly, I said—"

"Just a minute, boss. I was getting an important message

from the patrol's science headquarters. Guess what? Caleb Carson, Professor Jamieson's second in command here on Earth, is coming by air express to take charge. Carson is the grandson of old Blake Carson, who discovered Carson's Planet. He'll arrive at noon . . . that's two hours and—"

"Oh, he is, is he?" McLennan's answering thought, as it penetrated to the ezwal, was truculent. "Well, I don't think he'll be here in time for the kill."

"Kill? What kill?"

"Don't be such a fool, man!" the commander snarled. "We've got a five-hundred-pound ezwal to locate. You don't think a smash-up like this will kill one of those things."

"Lord!"

"It must be alive!" McLennan went on tensely. "And do you know what it means if an ezwal gets loose in this million square miles of wilderness? He'll murder every human being he gets hold of."

"This looks like a hunting party with a vengeance."

"You bet. That's where you come in. Phone down to the reservation superintendent's office, and tell him he's got to round up the biggest, toughest hunting dogs he can get, preferably those who've trailed grizzly bears. Make him realize that this is the most important thing that's ever happened in this forsaken land. Tell him that, on Carson's Planet, where these killers come from, settlers are being massacred in droves, and that men are not even safe in fortified cities. Tell him . . . I don't care what you tell him, but get action! Parker!

"Lower your ship and let down some tackle. I've started the ball rolling for a hunting trip that may be unnecessary. But never mind that. I believe in planning. And now—I think you've got enough power in that bus to hook into this old scoundrel and turn her over. One of the tricks of this tribe is that the young ones can tangle themselves in their mother's skin, and—"

The ezwal let himself sink slowly through the cave of flesh. His lower, combination-feet-and-hands touched something cold and wet, and he stood there for a moment, trembling. His nose caught a draft of air, and savored the scent of cooked flesh from his mother's body. The memory it brought of fire and agonizing death sent a sick thrill along his nerves. He forced the fear aside, and analyzed his chances. Wilderness, their thoughts had said. And in their minds had been pictures of brush and trees. That meant hiding places. Winter? That was harder to picture because there was only a sense of white brightness, and somehow it connected with the unfamiliar cold wetness into which his feet were sinking—a sticky, clinging wetness that would slow him in the swift dash he must make to escape.

Above him there was a sudden *brrr* of power. The weight of his mother seemed to lift from him. Then the weight sagged again.

"Nope!" came a thought.

"Try again!" McLennan replied sharply. "You almost got it. Do a little more horizontal pulling this time, and the rest of you stand back. We may have to shoot fast."

Body taut as a drawn wire, the ezwal poked his square-shaped head out. His three glittering eyes verified the picture he had caught from their minds. The spaceship had broken into three massive sections. And everywhere lay an appalling litter of twisted steel girders, battered metal, and a confusion of smashed cargo. For half a mile in every direction the wreckage sprawled, spotting the snow with splintered wood and miraculously unharmed boxes as well as a vast scatter of dark, chunky things impossible to identify. And each chunk, each piece of metal, each fragment of cargo, offered obstacles to the guns they would use against him.

"*Look!*" Somebody's mind and voice snapped.

It was the most shattering moment in all his world. For a second after the man's yell, the cub was aware that he must expect pain. Not even when the fire was burning away his mother's life had he realized that clearly. But now, abruptly, he knew that the agony was instants away. He shrank. His impulse was to jerk back into the folds of his mother's great, comforting mass of body. Then, even as his eyes blazed at the stiffened men, even as he caught the sudden, tremendous strain in their minds, he remembered what she had said about fighting fear.

The thought caught him in a rhythmic, irresistible sweep. His muscles expanded with effort. He heaved. And was free of the great, crushing body above him. Straight ahead was a run-and-hide paradise. But in that part of his brain, where fear was already vanquished, he dismissed that route as the most dangerous. To his left was a clustered group of unarmed workmen, milling in panic at the appearance of an animal as big as a grown lion. To his right was a little line of men with guns.

It was towards them he plunged. Alert guns twisted towards him, and then were fumbled in dismay as the desperate thought leaped through the minds of the wielders that their fire would burn a path through the workmen to the left.

"You fools!" came McLennan's wail of thought from behind him. "Scatter—for your lives!"

Too late! Hissing in triumph at the completeness of this opportunity to kill these murderous beings, the ezwal crashed into the group. Blood sprayed as he clawed them to the bone in passing. He had a desperate impulse to pause and crunch bodies with his teeth, but there was no time. He was clear of them. The rearing bulk of tattered ship, the harsh cacophony of screaming, fell away behind him. And he was running with all the speed that his six limbs could muster.

A glare of flame from McLennan's gun sizzled into the snow beside him. He dodged, twisted skillfully behind a thick section of shining, bent metal. The beam fought at the metal—and was through, reaching with incandescent violence above him as he dived into a shallow arroyo. A dark-bluish streak, he hurtled through a spread of bush, whipped along for four hundred yards behind a shielding ledge of rock and snow that extended roughly parallel to the ship. He halted on the rock lip of a valley that curved away below him. There were trees there, and brush, and a jagged, rock-strewn land, bright with glaring snow, fading away into the brilliant white haze of distance.

Incredibly, he was safe, untouched, unsinged—and to his brain reached the outer fringe of the storm of thoughts from the men beyond the great hind section of ship that hid them from his view:

"—Parker, yours is the fastest plane. Get these men to the reservation hospital; there's death here if we don't hurry. Kelly, what about those dogs?"

"The superintendent says he can get ten. They'll have to be flown in, and that'll take about an hour."

"Good! We'll all fly to the reservation, and get started the moment this Caleb Carson arrives. With those dogs to do our hunting, a couple of hours' start won't do that thing any good."

The ezwal slid under a spreading bush as the planes soared into the sky. The picture of the dogs was not clear, yet the very blur of it brought doubt. And purpose. Dogs followed trails. That meant they could scent things as easily as he could. That meant the reservation headquarters must be approached upwind if he ever hoped to kill those dogs, if he could ever find the place.

Time went by. He began to doubt that he was heading right. And yet the planes had certainly gone in the direction he was now travelling. Planes! He made a wild leap and safely reached cover as a great, silent plane swooped by over his head. There was the briefest blur of a man's thought—Caleb Carson' thought, the assistant of the mysterious Professor Jamieson. And then the long, shining machine settled behind some trees to his left. The village must be there.

He saw the buildings several minutes later, considerably to the right of the plane. A dark machine—a car—was pushing along from the village toward the plane . . . and he was upwind . . . and if he could attack the dogs now, before that car brought the man, Carson, back to the village, before the men swarmed out to begin their hunt—

With glowing, coal-dark eyes, he stared down at the ten dogs from his vantage point on the hill. Ten . . . ten . . . ten . . . too many, too many. They were chained in a bunch, sleeping now in the snow, but they could all attack him at once. A horrible, alien smell drifted up from them, but it was good that they were on his side of a large out-house; that the men were inside other buildings beyond; and that it would take minutes before they could come out with their irresistible guns.

His thought scattered, and he crouched defiantly as he saw the car push over a hill a quarter of a mile away. It headed almost straight toward him. Caleb Carson would be able to see his whole attack, and even the snow that slowed the car wouldn't hold it more than two minutes—human time.

Two minutes! A time limit was added to all the other things that were against him. But if he could kill the dogs, other animals would have to be flown in. He'd have time to lose himself in these miles of forest and mountain.

The first dog saw him. He caught its startled thought as it lunged to its feet. Heard its sharp warning yelp. And felt the blackness snap into its brain as he dealt it one crushing blow. He whirled. His jaws swung into the path of the dog that was charging at his neck. Teeth that could dent metal clicked in one ferocious, stabbing bite. Blood gushed into his mouth, stingingly, bitterly unpleasant to his taste. He spat it out with a thin snarl as eight shrieking dogs leaped at him. He met the first with a claw-armored forehand upraised. The wolfish jaws slashed at the blue-dark, descending arm, ravenous to tear it to bits. But in his swift way, the ezwal avoided the reaching teeth and caught at the dog's neck. And then, fingers like biting metal clamps gripped deeping into the shoulders. The dog was flung like a shot from a gun to the end of its chain snapped from the force of the blow. The dog slid along in the snow and lay still, its neck broken.

The ezwal reared around for an irresistible plunge at the others—and stopped. The dogs were surging away from him, fear thoughts in their minds. He saw that they had caught his scent for the first time in that one rush, and that they were beaten.

He poised there, making certain. The engine of the motorcar became a soft, close throb, and there were thoughts of men approaching. But still he crouched, exploring the minds of the dogs. And there was no doubt. They were filled with fear of him. Scornfully, swiftly, he turned. With dismay, then, he saw that the car had stopped less than fifty feet distant. There was only one man in it. The other man must have stayed behind to watch the plane.

The human being, Caleb Carson, sat in the open door of the car. He held a long, ugly, shining gun. It pointed at him, un-wavering; and then—incredible fact—a thought came from the cool brain behind the weapon—a thought directed at *him!* "See," it said, "see! I can kill you before you can get to safety. This is an express-flame rifle; and it can blow a crater where you're standing. I can kill you—but I won't. Think that over. And remember this, even though you escape now, in future you live or die as I will it. Without my help you cannot get away; and my price is high. Now, before the others come, run!"

He plunged over the hill, a startled, amazed, wondering, dismayed, six-legged monstrosity. Minutes later, he remembered that those dogs would not dare to pursue him. He sprawled to a stop in the snow. His brain cooled. Jangled emotions straightened. What had happened began to fit into a coherent piece. Time and again on that trip through space his mother had told him: "Man will only accept defeat from one source: blind, natural force. Because we wanted them to leave our land alone we pretended to be senseless, ferocious beats. We knew that if they ever suspected our intelligence, they would declare what they call war on us, and waste all their wealth and millions of lives to destroy us—and now, someone does suspect it. If that knowledge lives, our race dies!"

Someone did suspect! Here in this man Carson was the most dangerous man in all the world for ezwals. The cub shivered involuntarily. It had not been his intention to remain near this dangerous camp an instant after the dogs were neutralized. But now, it was obvious that he must act, no matter what the risk. Caleb Carson must be killed.

"I can't understand those dogs not following that trail!" McLennan's thought came dimly, complainingly, from inside the house. "On Carson's Planet, they use dogs all the time."

"Only dogs that were born there!" was the unemotional reply. And it was the calmness of the mind behind the thought that sent a quiver of hatred through the ezwal, where it crouched under the little berry bush beside the house of the forest reserve superintendent. The confidence of this man brought fear and rage. Carson went on curtly: "That much I gathered for certain from Professor Jamieson's documents. The rest is merely my own deduction, based on my special studies of my grandfather's explorations. When Blake Carson first landed on the planet, the

134

ezwals made no attempt to harm him. It was not until after the colonists began to arrive that the creatures turned so murderous. Mind you, I didn't see the truth on my own. It was only when I heard yesterday that Professor Jamieson was three . . . four now . . . days overdue at the Eristan I base—"

"Eh! Jamieson missing?"

"Sounds serious, too. Some Rull warships are in the vicinity, and of course no spaceship is big enough to carry the Lixon Communicators that make the interstellar telephone possible; so he couldn't send a warning."

Carson paused; then, "Anyway, I thought his documents might show that he had taken a side trip. It was in going through them that I found my first glimpse of the truth. Everything is as vague as possible, but by putting his notes beside my own knowledge, it adds up."

It was all there, the ezwal saw, in Carson's mind. Whether the man called it conjecture, or believed it fully, here was what his mother had feared. Basically, this man knew everything. And if it were true that the master mind, Professor Jamieson, was missing, then in this house was the only remaining person in the world with *the* knowledge.

And he was telling it. Both men therefore, must be killed.

The ezwal's thought scattered as McLennan's mind projected a surprisingly cold, unfriendly thought: "I hope I'm wrong in what I'm beginning to suspect. Let me tell you that I've been to Carson's Planet half a dozen times. The situation there is so bad that no stay-at-home studying documentary evidence could begin to comprehend the reality. Hundreds of thousands of people have been slaughtered."

"I won't go into that," said Carson curtly. "The very number of the dead demands an intelligent and swift solution."

"You have not," said McLennan softly, "visited Carson's Planet yourself."

"No!"

"You, the grandson of Blake Carson—" He broke off scathingly. "It's the old story, I see, of subsequent generations benefiting from the fame of the great man."

135

"There's no point in calling names." The younger man was calm.

McLennan's thought was harsh: "Does this truth you say you deduced include keeping this ezwal cub alive?"

"Certainly. It is my duty and your duty to deliver the young one to Professor Jamieson when and if he returns."

"I suppose you realize that it may be some time before this beast is captured, and that meanwhile it will become a killer."

"Because of the danger of the encroaching Rull enemy of man," replied Carson with abrupt chilliness that matched McLennan's steel hardness, "because of the importance of finding some anwer to the ezwal problem, high government policy requires that all necessary risks be taken."

"Damn government policy!" snarled McLennan. "My opinion of a government that appoints fact-finding commissions at this late date couldn't be properly put into words. A war of systematic extermination must be declared at once—that's the solution—and we'll begin with this scoundrelly little cub."

"That goes double for me!" A harsh thought from a third mind burst out.

"Carling!" McLennan exclaimed. "Man, get back into bed."

"I'm all right!" the young first officer of the smashed warship replied fiercely. "That freak accident that happened to me when we landed ... but never mind that. I was lying on the couch in the next room, and I overheard ... I tell you, sir!" he blazed at Caleb Carson, "Commander McLennan is right. While you were talking, I was thinking of the dozens of men I've met on various trips to Carson's Planet who've simply vanished. We used to talk about it, we younger officers."

"There's no use quibbling," said McLennan sharply. "It's an axiom of the service that the man in the field knows best. Unless he deliberately surrenders his power, or unless he receives a direct order from the commander-in-chief, he can retain his command regardless of the arrival meanwhile of superior officers."

"I shall have the order in an hour," said Carson.

"In an hour," McLennan said, "you won't be able to find me. By the time you do, the ezwal will be dead."

To the ezwal, the words brought a rebirth of murder purpose, the first realization of the immense opportunity that offered here. At this moment, under this one roof, were the three men who were probably the most dangerous of humans to himself and to his kind. There was a door just around the corner. If he could solve its mechanism—to kill them all would be the swift, satisfying solution to his various problems. Boldly, he glided from his hiding place.

In the hallway, the first sense of personal danger came. He crouched at the foot of the stairs, conscious that to go up after the men would leave his way of escape unguarded. And it was vital that he not be trapped up there after killing them. A clatter of dishes from the kitchen distracted him. He suppressed the burning impulse to go in and smash the woman who was there. Slowly, he started up the stairs, his purpose unyielding, but his mind clinging now with fascinated intensity to the thoughts that came from the men.

"—Those things read minds!" McLennan was scoffing. He seemed prepared to go on talking. He was waiting for certain equipment, and every word spoken would delay Carson from radioing for the order he needed. "Professor Jamieson must be crazy."

"I thought," Carling cut in, loyally backing his commander, "that scientists worked by evidence."

"Sometimes," said McLennan, "they get an hypothesis, and regardless of whether half the world is dying as a result of their theory, they go on trying to prove it."

There was an acrid impatience in Carson's thoughts. "I don't say that is Professor Jamieson's opinion. I merely drew that conclusion from a number of notes he made, particularly one which was in the form of a question: 'Can civilization exist without cities, farms, science, and what form of communication would be the indispensable minimum?'

"Besides"— in his mind was the intention to persuade rather than coerce—"while the existence of intelligence in the ezwal would be wonderful, its absence would not constitute a reason for any of us to nullify Professor Jamieson's plans for keeping this young ezwal alive." He broke off. "In any event, there's no

137

necessity for you to go after him. He'll starve to death in three weeks on Earth food. It's practically poison, quite indigestible to him."

Outside the door, the ezwal remembered how bitterly unpleasant the dog's blood had tasted. He cringed, then stiffened. At least, he could kill the men who had brought this fate upon him, and, besides, there was at least one place where food was plentiful. McLennan was saying:

"Men have eaten ezwals."

"Ah, yes, but they have to treat the meat with chemicals to render it digestible."

"I'm sick of this," McLennan said abruptly. "I can see it's no use arguing. So I'm just going to tell you what I've done, and what I'm going to do. A couple of dozen flivver planes will be arriving in about fifteen minutes. We'll scout the country this afternoon. And you can't tell me five hundred pounds of dark-blue ezwal can remain hidden, especially as the thing won't know— What the devil are you pointing that gun at the door for?"

Caleb Carson's directed thoughts came out to the ezwal: "Because just before you came in I saw the ezwal sneaking through the brush. I was sort of expecting him, but I never thought he'd come into the house till I heard claws rattle a few seconds ago. I wouldn't—advise—him—to come—in. Hear that—*you*!"

The ezwal froze. Then, with a rasp of hatred, he launched himself at the stairs. He raced out the door and off through the brush, darting and twisting to evade the flame that poured out the second-floor window from McLennan's pistol. On and on he ran, harder, faster, until he was a great, leaping thing under the trees, over the snow, an incredible, galloping monster. Of all his purposes, the only one that remained after his failure to kill was: He must save his own life. He must have food. And there was food for him only in one place.

The wreck spread before him, a sprawling, skeleton structure, a vast waste of metal. No sounds, no thought-blurs of life reached out to where he lay probing with his mind, listening with his ears. One long, tense, straining moment, and then he was leaping forward, racing into the shelter of the deserted, shattered

138

hulk. Somewhere here was the food that had been brought along for his mother. How long it would keep him even if he could hide it was another matter. He dared not quite think of what must follow if he really hoped to save his life. There was a plane to steal, to operate, a million facts to learn about this alien civilization, and finally a spaceship.

He saw the shadow of the airplane sweep across the snow to his right—and froze to the ground in an instinctive jerk of interlocking muscles. His thoughts disintegrated into a single all-powerful half-thought, half mind-wrecking emotion: He must appear to be another piece of jetsam, one more shattered box, or chunk of metal.

"You needn't try to hide!" came the acrid, directed thought of Caleb Carson. "I knew you'd come up here. Even a full-grown ezwal might have taken the risk. A young one, being simple and honest, needed only the hint. Well, your hour of decision has come."

Snarling, the ezwal watched the plane circle down, down, until it hovered less than a hundred feet above the ground. In angry despair he reared up toward it on his hind legs, as if he would somehow stretch up to it and smash it down beside him. Carson's cold thought came: "That's right! Stand up and be as much of a man physically as you can. You're going to be a man mentally, or die." He broke off. "I'd better inform you that I have just told McLennan where we are, and what I expect will happen. He thinks I'm a fool; and he and Carling will be here in five minutes. Think of that: five minutes! Five minutes to change your whole attitude toward life. I'm not going to try to pretend that this is a fair choice. Men are not angels, but I must know . . . *men* must know about ezwal intelligence. We are fighting a destroyer race called the Rulls; and we must have Carson's Planet in some form as an advance base against those damnable white worms. Remember this, too, it will do you no good to die a martyr. Now that the idea has come of ezwals possibly having intelligence, we'll start a propaganda campaign along those lines. Everywhere on Carson's planet men weary of fighting what they think is a natural force will brace up with that curious military morale that human beings can muster in the face

139

of intelligent enemies. If you yield, I'll teach you everything that man knows. You'll be the first ezwal scientist. If you can read minds, you'll know that I'm sincere in every word."

He was trapped. The knowledge brought fear, and something else! He felt overwhelmed by the tremendousness of the decision he must make.

"The proof of your choice," Carson's thought continued, "will be simplicity itself. In one minute I shall land my plane. It is all-metal construction, divided into two compartments. You cannot possibly smash into my section and kill me. But the door of your section will be open. When you enter, it will close tight and . . . good lord, here comes McLennan"

The big plane almost fell to the ground, so fast did Carson bring it down. It drew up in a clearing a hundred feet away. A door yawned. The scientist's urgent thought came:

"Make up your mind!"

And still the ezwal stood, unyielding. He saw great cities, ships, space liners, with ezwals in command. Then he remembered what his mother had told him and that was like an immeasurable pain.

"Quick!" came Carson's thought.

Flame seared down where he had been; and there was no time to think, no time for anything but to take the initial chance. The flame missed him again, as he twisted in his swift run. This time it reached ahead across the tail of Carson's ship.

The ezwal caught the deliberateness of that act in McLennan's mind; and then he was inside the now unusable machine. The other plane landed. Two men with guns raced toward him. He snarled, as he caught their murder intention, and half turned to take his chances outside. The door clicked shut metallically in his face. Trapped.

Or was he? Another door opened. He roared as he leaped into the compartment where the man sat. His mind shook with this final, unexpected opportunity to kill this man, as his mother had charged him to do. It was the steadiness of the man's mind that made him suppress the impulse to strike one deadly blow. Caleb Carson said huskily:

"I'm taking this terrible chance because everything you've done so far seems to show that you have intelligence, and that you've understood my thoughts. But we can't take off. McLennan's burned the tail struts. That means we've got to have finally clinching proof. I'm going to open this door that leads away from *them*. You can kill me and, with luck, escape—if you hurry. The alternative is to stretch yourself here beside my legs and face them when they come."

With a shuddering movement the ezwal edged forward and stiffly settled down on his long belly. He was only vaguely aware of the cursing wonder of McLennan.

He was suddenly feeling very young and very important and very humble. For he had in his mind the picture of the greatness that was to be his in the world of the ezwals, in that world of titanic construction, the beginning of a dynamic new civilization.

There was silence among us, as the big man finished. Finally, somebody said critically, "This grandson of the discoverer of Carson's Planet seems a pretty cold-blooded sort of chap."

Somebody else said, "Caleb Carson didn't know that the number of dead on Carson's Planet was actually thirty million, the morale situation proportionately more dangerous. He would never have had a real sense of urgency. His solution would have been too late."

"The point is," said the small, thin chap sharply, but with satisfaction, "there's always somebody else who, for various reasons, has special insight into a problem. The accumulated thought on Carson's Planet by its discoverer's grandson is what made it possible for him to read between the rather sketchy lines of Professor Jamieson's notes."

A man said, "Why didn't we hear about this second solution at the time?"

The sharp voice snapped, "That's obvious. It was the very next day that Professor Jamieson's own experiences and fuller solution captured all the headlines. Incidentally, I read last week that a new co-ordinator has been appointed for Carson's Planet. His name is Caleb Carson."

We grew aware of the big man standing up, just as a boy came over to him. The boy said, "Commander McLennan, your ship is calling you. You can take the message in the lounge, sir."

We all stared as the giant headed briskly for the lounge-room door. A minute later, the argument was waxing as hotly as ever.

FILM LIBRARY

THE hundred delegates to the electronic manufacturers' convention, who had attended the showing, were drifting towards the doors. Several wives had been present, and their voices mingled with the deeper tones of the men. The sounds faded swiftly into the distance of the hotel, but Señor Pedro del Corteya, looking up suddenly from what he was doing, saw that he was still not alone.

He continued rewinding the reel, then he put it back into its can, and began to pack away the projector. Out of the corner of his eyes he watched the other with the curious, speculative intentness of the Latin. At last, his job completed, he turned.

"Is it me you wish to speak to, señor?"

The big man hesitated, then he came forward. He was a tall, chunky, fortyish individual with brown eyes and skimpy hair.

"Odd picture you showed us here tonight."

Corteya smiled his personal acceptance of the compliment. "You were amused, señor?"

Again that hesitation; then, "Where did you get it?"

Corteya shrugged. These direct Americans. Did the man expect him to hand over his trade secrets? He said as much.

"Do you think I am a fool, señor? Perhaps you are planning to start up in opposition to my business. You have plenty of money, maybe, and I go broke when you undercut my prices."

The stranger laughed. But he drew out a card and handed it over. Corteya read:

WALTER DORMAN
President
ELECTRONIC COMPANY OF AMERICA

Corteya looked at it, then handed it back. He saw that

Dorman was staring at him hard. The man said finally, with a tiny note of incredulity in his voice, "You still don't believe I'm not after your hide."

Coreya shrugged. "What is it you wish to know, señor?"

"That film?"

Corteya raised his hands in a gesture of deprecation. "A ten-minute novelty."

"Very smoothly done, if you ask me."

"All the world, señor, knows that Hollywood is wonderful."

"Hollywood never made a picture as good as that."

Corteya smiled his if-you-say-so-it-must-be-so smile. For the first time, then, he let his mind go back over the picture he had shown. He couldn't remember it very clearly. It was his custom to watch the audience, not the film. Nevertheless, he recollected that it had been about an automatic electric stove that merely had to be supplied with the appropriate ingredients, and it would mix them, and serve up the finished meal piping hot at any desired time. He had shown the same film two weeks earlier at a local dieticians' meeting, and the audience had laughed heartily at the nonexistent device.

Corteya said, "Señor, I obtain my films from several film libraries. Where they secure them, I do not know. They compete for my business. All I do is look over their catalogues and order films when I need them." He lifted his shoulders. "It is so simple as that."

"Have you had any other novelties like the one tonight?"

"A few. I cannot remember."

"Do they all come from the same film library?"

Dorman's persistence was beginning to wear. "I really cannot remember, señor. To me it is all ordinary business."

"Have you any similar films on hand right now?"

"You mean here? No!"

"I mean at your office."

Corteya looked unhappy. He was a simple, honest man, who could lie as well as the next man, but only if he had started out with a lie, and had to carry on. Having started with the truth, he could not stop.

"At the Aero Club dinner tomorrow," he said gloomily, "I

144

am showing a film about a trip to one of the planets. The catalogue says it is very amusing."

Dorman said, "I know this is a lot to ask, but will you drive over to your office, and show me that picture now?"

"Senor, my wife, she is waiting for me at home."

Dorman said nothing. He took out his pocketbook and peeled off a twenty-dollar bill. As he expected, the other's slim hand reached forth delicately but without diffidence, and accepted the money.

It took only eight minutes to get to Corteya's place of business, and a few minutes after that the young man's projector was set up and purring.

A seascape broke the shadows of a cloudy but brilliantly bright horizon. The sea was flat, a tideless expanse of water. Suddenly, in those murky depths, there was stirring. A creature charged into view. It burst the surface and leaped up, twenty, fifty, a hundred feet. Its enormous, bulbous head and vast, yawning mouth seemed almost to touch the camera. And then it began to fall, still struggling, still furiously determined to grasp the prey at which it had leaped.

It failed. It fell. It hit the water with a splash so gigantic that Dorman was startled. He had been admiring the illusion of stark reality that had been produced with what must be an artificial monster-being mechanically activated in some indoor imitation sea. But those splashes looked *real*. A moment later the narrator said:

"That was a Venusian squid. These creatures, which frequent the depths of the warm seas of Venus, come to the surface only after food. Our camera artist acted as bait, and so enticed the squid to attack him. He was not, however, in danger. Electronic devices protected him at all times."

Dorman smiled twistedly. First an electric stove that prepared meals, now a trip to Venus. Both slick jobs of photography, and, in this case, it was especially clever to suggest there had been no danger. So many of these travelogues about places that actually existed faked suspense and excitement to the point of nausea. He climbed to his feet, his interest close to the vanishing point. He felt very tolerant of himself. Just for a moment, while watching

145

the stove go through its motions, he had had the wild thought that the picture was an advertising stunt for a competitor. The Venusian film put the whole affair into its proper perspective. He saw that Corteya had stopped the machine. The overhead light clicked on.

"Have you learned what you desire?"

"Practically."

The younger man continued to re-wind the reel. While he waited, Dorman glanced around the small room. It had a counter at the front. The projector rested on it near the wall. Behind the counter was a single chair and a small set of shelves. That was all the furniture. The white calcimined walls of the office were decorated with still pictures from one-reel and two-reel films. Printed on each of the pictures was a caption giving the subject and the cost of showing. It was obviously a selling business. No one would come into a place like this without having been previously canvassed or told about it in some way.

"What else, señor?"

Dorman turned. The film was in its can, the projector in its case. "I'd like you to check to see if the two films came from the same film library."

"They did, señor." Corteya had not moved. He was smiling in his deprecating fashion. "I looked in the can," he explained, "when I came in."

Dorman made no move to leave. There was nothing else, really, but he hated to leave unfinished anything he had started. Check on everything, then recheck. That was his method, and he had no intention of changing now. He took out his pocketbook and removed a ten-dollar bill.

"The catalogue of this particular library. I'd like to have a look at it."

Corteya accepted the bill and reached under the counter. He came up with several folders. "They send one of these to me every month. These are for the last four months."

Only the final two contained lists of the novelty films. Dorman ran his gaze down the column, the smile on his lips broadening. There were several travelogues. Venus, a journey through a Martian desert, a spaceship voyage to the moon, an aerial trip

146

over mountainous Europa, one of the moons of Jupiter, a camera examination of the rings of Saturn, a boat trip down a river of liquid oxygen on the far planet, Pluto, and, finally, the size of the Sun as seen from each one of its ten planets.

Dorman glanced swiftly at the remaining score or so films given under the novelty heading. He found the one he wanted instantly. The caption was, "Amusing account of an automatic stove that does EVERYTHING." He closed the folder, and paused to look at the address. Arlay Film Library, Sunset Boulevard, Hollywood, California.

"Thanks," said Dorman.

He went out into the street and climbed into his car. It was getting cooler, so he turned up the window, and sat for a minute lighting a cigaret. He drove unhurriedly back to the hotel. In the lobby, a man hailed him:

"Hey, Wally, come into the bar and have a drink. The boys have been looking for you. Where you been?"

As he settled into a booth a minute later, Dorman said, "I've been wild goose chasing." He explained briefly. One of the other men looked at him.

"Wally," he said, "you're a smart man." He gulped down a drink. "I mean that more than you think. One of the reasons I attended this convention was to find a man who could be the new chairman of the board for our firm. You'd have to buy about a thousand shares, but you'll see what a deal it is when I show you the statements tomorrow. What we're mainly interested in is a good man who doesn't miss any bets. Your action tonight is pure genius, so far as I am concerned, and you're in."

"Waiter," said Dorman, "more drinks."

The ever happy music swelled around them. The voices rose and fell in gyrations of sound. The night dragged on.

Ten weeks before, Mr. Lester Arlay, of the Arlay Film Library, had read the first complaint with a faint frown creasing his already lined forehead. The letter had been shoved inside the can of film, and it began:

"Dear Mr. Arley—"

Mr. Arlay started to scowl right there. He did not approve of his name being misspelled. He read on, grimly:

Dear Mr. Arley:

The sound film, "Food Magic," which you sent me, is entirely different from what I expected. Neither the audience nor I could make head or tail of it. Certainly, it has nothing to do with food. My program for the retailers' convention here was ruined.

The letter was signed by one of his best customers; and Mr. Arlay, who remembered the two-reeler, "Food Magic," perfectly, was dismayed. It was an educational feature turned out by one of the big food distributors. And it was a really dandy job, one of those films which small film libraries could borrow for nothing, and then rent out at a small but profitable rate. It was a film definitely suitable for a grocery retailers' convention.

Frowning, Mr. Arlay shoved the letter back into the can of film and put the can on the "To Be Examined" shelf. He began to open the other ten cans of film that had been returned that morning. Of the ten, four borrowers complained that "This is not the film we asked for." "I cannot understand your sending a film so different from what we ordered." "This is visual gibberish." "Your joke ruined our show."

For several moments, Mr. Arlay stared palely at the letters, and then, with a sudden burst of activity, he examined one of the criticized films. Presently, he slid the reel onto the projector, made the necessary adjustments, switched off the light, and stared with a blank expectancy at the screen.

There was a faraway rustle of music. The music drew closer, but the nearer it came the more uncertainty there was in it. Singing violins played a sweet melody, but swiftly a harsher theme intruded, a trill of doubt. The doubt grew and grew until finally the happy strains were completely dominated. Darkly, almost discordantly, the music played—and retreated into distance.

The screen itself came to life. Color flared over it, an intricate weaving movement of color that never quite formed a recognizable pattern. And the rich, vivid colors grew darker and darker until finally the screen was almost black.

Out of the darkness walked a young woman. She came from the shadows into the light with a casual grace, an agreeable ease, that marked her immediately as one of those marvelous photogenic types. Mr. Arlay had never seen her before, but she quirked her lips into a smile, made a movement with her fingers; and she was a personality.

The trouble was, she had barely appeared when, abruptly, she vanished in a gyrating puff of dark colors. She came on again, and this time she walked along an intense blue hallway into a living room, where a young man sat reading beside a vast window. Mr. Arlay had a flashing glimpse of a city beyond that window; and then the camera angle shifted to the girl.

She was standing behind the man, hesitant. As she stood, the human details of her flesh merged into the dark thematic colors; and it was these colors in human form that moved forward and very obviously kissed the young man on the lips. It was a long kiss, and at the end of it the young man, too, was a color pattern.

The mingled colors began to twist and spin. The screen was a chromatic splendor of gyrating light. It was just beginning to stir with returning music as Mr. Arlay emerged from his puzzlement and held the letter he had received about this particular film in the blazing beam of the projector.

He read: "This is visual gibberish!"

So that was the one! He laid the letter down, and held up the can cover with the title on it: "How to Operate a Chicken Farm."

On the screen, the young woman was walking uncertainly along a street, looking back at the man who was coming along slightly behind her. Mr. Alay clicked it off, re-wound the reel, then took another film out of its can. It was the one about which the complainant had said: "Your joke ruined our show."

He threaded the reel into place, and presently a picture of a machine came onto the screen. It was a very bright, clear picture, without any nonsense about it, but the machine was not one that Mr. Lester Arlay remembered having seen before. The fact did not disturb him immediately. The world was full of machines that he had never seen; and, what was more, that he never wanted to see. He waited; and a quiet baritone said:

"No spaceman should have any difficulty repairing this new space drive."

Mr. Arlay sighed, and lifted the can cover into the light. The title on it was: "How to Operate the American Cogshill Diesel Engine."

What had happened was clear enough, it seemed to Mr. Arlay. Somebody had returned a whole series of wrong films to him; and he had sent them out in their original cans. The fantastically bad-luck angle of the affair was that no less than five wrong films had gone out all at once.

On the screen, the baritone voice was saying, "Now, raise the drive case itself. Since the standard weight of the case is eight tons, care must be taken when near a planetary body to balance the antigravity needles at a similitude of ninety-nine gravitons. Unwringing them becomes a matter of one good shove—"

Mr. Arlay shut the film off, and he was packing it into a can when the thought came: "What did he say? *What* did he say?"

He stood owlishly blinking his realization that something was very wrong.

There was an interruption. The outer door opened, and a young woman came in. She wore a mink coat, and heavily jeweled rings flashed on her fingers. "'Lo, honey," she said in a husky voice.

Mr. Arlay, all extraneous thoughts flying from his mind, came around the counter. His wife skillfully evaded the kiss he attempted to plant on her lips.

"Have you any money?" she asked. "I'm going shopping."

Mr. Arlay said, "Careful, Tania. We're almost at rock bottom."

He said it affectionately. He tried to kiss her again, and this time managed to brush her cheek. His words made her shake her slim body impatiently.

"That's all I ever hear from you," she said darkly. "Why don't you make money like some of the people in this town?"

Mr. Arlay almost pointed out that he did. He refrained. He had no illusions about his hold on this young woman. His business netted him between three and five hundred dollars a week. It was not a terrific amount of money, but it rivaled the salaries of featured movie players. They might make a little more per week, but few of them made it fifty-two weeks a year. It was that income which had enabled him, three years before, to marry a small-part player who was a far more attractive person physically than he could have hoped to marry without money. Mentally—that was another matter. She was a survival type in a sense that would have startled Darwin. Regardless of the variation in his income, she managed to spend it all, month in, month out. Her adaptability sometimes amazed even that defeatist Mr. Arlay.

What he did not realize, and certainly she neither knew nor would she have cared if she had known, was the profound influence she had had on him. All the imaginative qualities that had built his business had been replaced by a complete dependence on experience. He regarded himself as a practical man, and he had no inkling that his habit of thinking of himself as "Mr." was but one compensation for the psychic disaster he had suffered when she entered his life.

Not that he would necessarily have suspected anyway that he had come into possession of films that had been made more than fifty years in the future.

Now that she had come into the office, he strove to keep her there. "Got something here that might interest you," he said eagerly. "Somebody sent me a film of some other library by mistake, and it's quite an odd affair, a sort of a visual freak."

"Now, darling, I'm in a hurry, and—"

Her narrowed eyes saw that this was no moment to refuse him. He needed an occasional crumb, and he was so *completely* unsuspicious. After all, she'd be a nut to let this soft touch walk out on her.

"All right, honey," she crooned. "If you want me to."

He showed her the film with the man and the girl and the swirling colors—and realized the moment the girl appeared on the screen that he had made a mistake. His wife stiffened as that superb actress came into view.

151

"Hm-m-m-m," she said bitingly. "What kind of ham are you serving up now?"

Mr. Arlay let the film run its course without another comment. He had momentarily forgotten that his wife did not admire other actresses, particularly stars. Watching the film, he noticed absently that the reason for the dark tones of music and color seemed to be that the girl was unhappily married, and the twisting colors were designed to show her changing emotions, the doubts that came, and the thoughts that welled up in her mind.

"Interesting," he thought. "I wonder who made it."

As the reel ended, Tania jumped to her feet. "Well, got to be running. I'll cash a check for five hundred dollars. O.K.?"

"Three!" said Mr. Arlay.

"Four," said his wife in a tone of friendly give and take.

Four hundred it was. When she had gone, Mr. Arlay began a check-up to see who had sent him the unusual films. The card index for the film, "How to Operate a Chicken Farm," gave a list of men and schools and institutions that had rented the item. The second last renter would obviously be the one. His gaze flashed down to it.

"Tichenor Collegiate," he read.

Mr. Arlay frowned at the name, and mentally changed the wording in the letter he had intended to write. Tichenor Collegiate was easily one of his best customers. And, what was more, the operator in charge, Peter Caxton, a science teacher, was a thoroughly experienced man. It seemed scarcely possible that Caxton could be guilty.

Quickly, Mr. Arlay examined the card for another of the eccentric films. The second last borrower was Tichenor Collegiate. The same name came up for each of the three other returned films, which didn't belong to his library. Mr. Arlay sat down at his typewriter and, bearing in mind that customers were seldom offended by the facts of the case, wrote:

Dear Mr. Caxton:

A number of films which you have returned to us were not the ones which we originally sent you. Altogether five films—

He paused there Five? How did he know there were only five? Mr. Arlay made a beeline for the Tichenor Collegiate's personal file card. It was a thick one, additions having been glued to it from time to time.

He skipped down to the fifteenth name on the card. That would take it back just a little over two weeks. The title was "Pruning Fruit Trees." The film itself was a fantastic concoction in which a curiously shaped ship seemed to leave the Earth's surface and go to the Moon. The illusions were very realistic, and the photography had a Hollywood slickness.

Mr. Arlay shut it off finally, thinking for the first time that whoever was making those pictures would be well worth representing.

Meanwhile, there was a job to do. One by one, he screened the last nineteen films that had been borrowed by Tichenor. That is, he screened the sixteen that were in. Three had been re-rented, and in due course, no doubt, he would hear from them.

Of the sixteen, seven were travelogues. Travelogues: Unique, incredible creations, filmed by a madman. But mad or not, he was a genius, and he had designed some of the most life-like backgrounds ever conceived for fantasia. Among the first few that Mr. Arlay screened was the one about Venus which, ten weeks later, Pedro del Corteya showed to electronics manufactuer Walter Dorman. Mr. Arlay watched it and the other reels about the solar system with an appraising eye. There was, it seemed to him, much to be said for a skillful motion-picture presentation of what science believed about the various planetary bodies.

Seven travelogues and eight how-to-operate or how-to-repair films—of the eight, one dealt with the operation of a meaningless engine. At least, it seemed meaningless to Mr. Arlay. It had a single extrusion in a strong boxing. There were little chambers in the boxing, and when they were filled with a fine metallic powder, the extrusion could be made to turn with a velocity that did not slow when it was connected to a large machine of intricate construction. Another machine dealt with the repair of what was called an atomic gun. Here, too, the fine metallic powder was tamped into tiny chambers, but there was a transformation tunnel, the purpose of which was not clear. When fired at the end, the gun, a hand weapon, blew a four-hundred-foot-high hill into dust.

Mr. Arlay became impatient as the eight films unreeled onto the screen. This was going a little too far. The travelogues had a certain scientific value, but these operation and repair films, with their pretense to details, strained all credulity. An atomic engine and an atomic gun. How to repair a space drive. Care and operation of the Fly-O, and individual flyer—a combination of straps and a metallic tube that lifted the man in the film off the ground and transported him through the air like Buck Rogers. A radio that was simply a bracelet made of what was called "sensitive metal." The crystalline structure of the sensitivity was shown, and also the radio waves were shown, transformed into sound by ultra-thin bubbles in the metal. There were three rather amusing films about household devices. There was a light that focused wherever desired out of thin air; rugs and furniture that couldn't get dirty; and finally the automatic electric stove that was later to rouse Walter Dorman's competitive instincts. Long before the showing was finished, it had struck Mr. Arlay that there was a type of audience that would be interested in such novelties. It would be important, however, to stress the novelty angle, so that the people would be prepared to laugh.

His best bet, of course, would be to locate their source, and stock a few himself. He phoned Tichenor Collegiate, and asked for Caxton. Caxton said:

"My dear Mr. Arlay, it cannot possibly be we who are at fault. To prevent confusion in bookkeeping, I have long adopted a policy of renting from only one library at a time. For the past two months we have secured our material from you, and returned it promptly. Perhaps you had better re-examine your files."

His tone was faintly patronizing, and there was just enough suggestion in it of an affronted customer to make Mr. Arlay back down permanently.

"Yes, yes, of course. I'll have a look at them myself. My helper must have . . . uh—"

Mr. Arlay hung up, saw that it was nearly one o'clock, and went out to lunch. He drove all the way up to Vine Street for a

154

bowl of tomato soup. The fever in him died slowly, and he realized that it was not actually a difficult situation. He had lost nineteen films, but if he wrote careful letters to the firms that had supplied them to him they would probably send him new ones immediately. And as a sort of compensation for the wear and tear on his nerves, he had sixteen, possibly nineteen, novelty films which might go over rather well.

They did. At least once a week the novelties went out into the mails, and returned again. And by the time they came back there were orders waiting for most of them for the following week. Mr. Arlay did not worry about what the real owner of the films would think when he discovered what was happening. No single library film was worth very much. The owner would probably demand the wholesaler's percentage, and this Mr. Arlay was prepared to pay.

And just in case audience reaction would be required, Mr. Arlay sent printed forms for comments. They came back properly filled out. The size of the audience: 100, 200, 75, 150. The nature of the audience: Retailers' dinner, university astronomy class, the society of physicists, high school students. The reaction of the audience—comments most often made—"Amusing," "Interesting," "Good photography put it over." One common criticism was, "It seems to me the dialogue could be more humorous, befitting the nature of the subject matter."

The situation did not remain static. At the end of the second month, Mr. Arlay had thirty-one more novelty films, and every one of them had been sent him by Peter Caxton of Tichenor Collegiate.

After ten weeks, just about the time that Pedro del Corteya was due to show the stove picture to the electronic manufacturers' convention, two things happened approximately simultaneously. Mr. Arlay raised the rental rate of the novelties fifty percent, and Caxton sent him a letter, which read in part:

"I have noticed in your folders a reference to some novelty films. I would like one dealing with a planet for next Wednesday."

"Now," thought Mr. Arlay, "now, we shall see."

The can came back on Thursday. The film inside was also a novelty type. But it was not the same one he had sent out.

On his way to Tichenor Collegiate for the afternoon classes, Peter Caxton stopped in the corner drugstore and bought a pack of cigarets. There was a full-length mirror just in front of the door. And, as he emerged, he paused briefly to survey himself in it.

The picture he saw pleased him. His tall form was well dressed, his face clean but not too youthful, and his eyes were a smiling gray. The well-groomed effect was accentuated by a neat, gray hat. He walked on, content. Caxton had no illusions about life. Life was what you made it. And so far as he could see, if he worked things right, he ought to be principal of Tichenor in another two years. The time limit was unavoidable. Old Varnish was not due for retirement until then, and Caxton could see no way by which the process could be speeded up.

Tichenor was no super-school, nor did it have the fancy money behind it that some neighboring communities raised every year for education. The smoking-room for the men and women was a joint affair. Caxton settled into one of the chairs and puffed quickly at his cigaret. He was about halfway through when Miss Gregg came in.

She smiled warmly. " 'Lo, Peter," she said. Her gaze flashed significantly to the closed doors of the men's and women's dressing rooms, then back to him.

Caxton said, "Nobody in the men's."

She opened the door to the women's, glanced in, then came over in a gliding motion and planted a kiss on his lips.

"Careful," said Peter Caxton.

"Tonight," she said in a low tone, "at the end of the park."

Caxton could not suppress a faint look of irritation. "I'll try," he said, "but my wife—"

She whispered fondly, "I'll expect you."

The door closed softly behind her. Caxton sat frowning, disturbed. At first it had been pleasant, his conquest of Miss Gregg's heart. But after six months of ever more frequent rendezvous, the affair was beginning to be a little wearing. She had reached the stage where she half anticipated that he would somehow manage to get a divorce, and that somehow it would not hurt his career, and that everything would come out all right. Caxton shared neither her anxiety for such a culmination, nor her vague conviction that there would be no repercussions.

Miss Gregg, he realized too late, was an emotional fool. For a month he had known that he must break off with her, but so far only one method had occurred to him. She must be eased out of the school. How? The answer to that, too, had come easily. A whispering campaign against her and Dorrit. That way he could kill two birds with one stone. Ancil Dorrit was his only serious rival for the principalship, and what was worse, he and Old Varnish got along very well.

It shouldn't be very hard. Everybody except Miss Gregg knew that Dorrit was nuts about her, and Dorrit didn't seem to suspect that his secret was known. The situation amused Caxton. He, a married man, had walked off with Dorrit's dream girl. There was no reason why he shouldn't also snatch the principalship from under Dorrit's nose, so to speak. He'd have to think a little more about the moves, and proceed with the utmost caution.

Caxton rubbed his cigaret into an ash tray with a speculative thoughtfulness, then he headed for the auditorium. His first class was to have a film showing—a nuisance, those things. In the beginning, he had been quite interested, but there were too many poor films. Besides, the dopes never learned anything anyway. He had once questioned some of the brighter students about what they had learned from a film, and it was pitiful. Proponents, however, maintained that the effect was cumulative, the kids preferred it to other methods of teaching, and last week the school board had ordered that Grade Ten, as well as Grade Eleven, was to be shown each film.

That meant that once in the morning, once in the afternoon, he had to handle a swarm of fifteen- to seventeen-year-olds in the darkness of an auditorium. At least, this was the last showing for today. The film had been running for about a minute when Caxton took his first real look at the screen. He stared for a moment blankly, then shut off the projector, turned on the lights, and came down from the projection room.

"Who's responsible for this silly trick?" he asked angrily.

No one answered. The girls looked a little scared, the boys stiffened, except for a few teachers' pets, who turned pale.

"Somebody," Caxton shouted, "has switched films on me over the lunch hour."

He stopped. His own words jarred him. He had charged out of the projection booth without pausing to assess the implications of what had happened. Now, suddenly, he realized. For the first time in his four years at Tichenor he had been the victim of a student's prank, and he was taking it badly. After a moment of further thought, he made an even greater mental adjustment, and the situation was saved.

Caxton swallowed hard. A wan smile lightened his tense face. He looked around coolly. "Well," he said, "if this is what you want, you'll get it."

The second day his smile was grimmer, and it became a matter of discipline. "If this," he said, "happens again, I shall have to report to Old Varn—" He stopped. He had been about to say "Old Varnish." He finished instead, properly—"report to Mr. Varney."

It was a shaken and somewhat mystified Caxton who went into the principal's office the following day. "But where do they obtain the replacement films?" the old man asked helplessly. "After all, they cost money."

The question was not his final word. On Thursday, the film again being different, he trotted dutifully to each of the two classes, and pointed out the unfairness of their action. He also indicated that, since the lost films would have to be paid for, the affair was beginning to take on a decidedly criminal aspect.

The fifth day was Friday, and it was evident that the students had talked things over, for the president of each of the two classes made a brief denial of the suspicions of the faculty. "As you probably know," said one, "the students are usually aware of what is going on among themselves. But this class as a whole is unaware of the identity of the guilty party. Whoever is changing the films is playing a lone hand, and we herewith denounce him, and withdraw any support or sympathy we might normally give to a student who has gotten in wrong."

The words should have quieted Caxton's nerves. But they had the reverse effect. His first conviction, that he was being made game of by the students, had already partly yielded to a wilder thought, and the speeches merely enlivened the newer feeling. That afternoon at recess, without proper forethought, he made the mistake of voicing the suspicion to the principal.

"If the students are not to blame, then one of the teachers must be. And the only one I know who dislikes me intensely is Dorrit," he added grimly, "If I were you, I would also investigate the relationship between Miss Gregg and Dorrit."

Varney showed a surprising amount of initiative. The truth was, the old man was easily tired, and he was already worn out by the affair. He called both Miss Gregg and Dorrit and, to Caxton's dismay, repeated the accusations. Miss Gregg flashed one amazed look at the stunned Caxton, and then sat rigid throughout the rest of the meeting. Dorrit looked angry for a moment, then he laughed.

"This week," he said, "has been an eye opener for most of us here. We have seen Caxton wilt under the conviction that the student body didn't like him. I always thought he was a highly developed neurotic, and now in five days he has shown that he is worse than anything I imagined. Like all true neurotics of the more advanced kind, he failed to make even the most elementary investigations before launching his accusations. For instance, his first charge—I can prove that, for at least two days this week, I could not possibly have been near the projection room."

He proceeded to do so. He had been sick at this boarding house on Tuesday and Wednesday.

"As for the second and more unforgivable accusation, I only wish it were true, though in a different sense than Caxton has implied. I am one of those shy individuals where women are concerned, but under the circumstances I can say that I have long been an admirer of Miss Gregg from a distance."

The young woman showed her first vague interest at that point. From the corner of her eyes, she glanced at Dorrit, as if she were seeing him in a new light. The glance lasted only a moment, then she returned to her tensed contemplation of the wall straight in front of her. Dorrit was continuing:

"It is difficult, of course, to disprove anything so vague as the charge Mr. Caxton has leveled, but—"

Old Varnish cut him off. "It is quite unnecessary to say anything further. I do not for one moment believe a word of it, and I cannot understand what Mr. Caxton's purpose could have been, to introduce such an ill-considered accusation into this wretched affair of the lost films. If the film situation does not rectify, I will report to the school board at their meeting next week, and we shall have an investigation. That is all. Good day, gentlemen. Good day, Miss Gregg."

Caxton spent a confused week end. He was pretty sure that the principal had derived satisfaction from the situation, but there was nothing to do about that except curse himself for having provided the man with an opportunity to get rid of an unwanted heir to his own position. The worst confusion, however, had nothing to do with Varney. Caxton had the sinking feeling that things were happening behind his back. It was a feeling that turned out to be correct.

On Monday morning all the women teachers snubbed him, and most of the men were distinctly unfriendly. One of the men walked over and said in a low tone, "How did you happen to make such a charge against Gregg and Dorrit?"

"I was beside myself with worry," Caxton said miserably. "I was not in my right senses."

"You sure weren't," said the other. "Gregg's told all the women."

Caxton thought grimly, "A woman scorned."

The other man finished, "I'll try to do what I can but—"

It was too late. At lunchtime, the women teachers entered the principal's office in a body, and announced that they would refuse to work in the same school with a male teacher capable of such an untrue story about one of themselves. Caxton, who had already permitted himself flashing thoughts on the possibility of resignation, was now confronted by the necessity of an actual decision. He resigned at intermission, the separation to take effect at the end of the month, the following week end.

His action cleared the air. The male teachers were friendlier, and his own mind slowly and painfully straightened out. By

Tuesday he was thinking savagely but with clarity, "Those films! If it hadn't been for that mix-up, I wouldn't have lost my head. If I could find out who was responsible—"

It seemed to him that the resulting satisfaction would almost compensate him for the loss of his job. He did not go home for lunch. He only pretended to start out. Swiftly, he doubled back to the rear entrance, and, hurrying to the projection room, concealed himself behind a substitute screen that stood against one wall.

He waited during the entire lunch period. Nothing happened. Nobody tampered with the locked doors of the auditorium. No one came near the door of the projection room. And then, after lunch, when he started the projector, the film was different.

In the morning, it had been an ordinary film, concerned with dairy farming. The afternoon film was about the development and use of chemicals to thin or thicken the human blood, and so enable human beings to fit themselves overnight for extreme changes of temperature.

It was the first time that Caxton had closely examined one of the strange novelty films, of which he had ordered several about two weeks before. Examined it, that is, with his mind as well as his eyes. He thought, amazed, "Who is making those pictures? Why, they're wonderful; so full of ideas that—"

He returned to the projection room after school for another look. And received the shock of his life. It was a different film. Different from the one in the morning. Different from the one after lunch. It was a third film, its subject the inside of the sun. With trembling fingers, Caxton rewound the reel—and ran it through again. The perspiration came out on his face as an entirely different, a fourth film, unwound on the screen. The wild impulse came to rush down to the office to phone up Varney. That ended with the realization that the man would refuse. The principal had implied at least twice that the film tangle would probably rectify the moment Caxton left. The burden of weariness that he wore would make him cling to that conviction. "Tomorrow," he would say. "I'll have a look at the projector tomorrow."

It couldn't wait till tomorrow, so it seemed to Caxton. For the

F

first time, he remembered the phone call he had received more than two months before from Mr. Arlay of the Arlay Film Library. The memory cooled him off. His second impulse within minutes—this time to call Arlay—faded before a recollection of what he had said to the owner of the film library. He had been rather snooty. He'd phone Arlay later.

Caxton began swiftly to dismantle the projector. What, exactly, he was looking for he didn't know, and he didn't find it. The machine was in first-class shape, everything as normal as it should be.

He reassembled it slowly, and, shoving it back into position, he once more re-ran the reel. This time there was no switch. It was the same film. He ran it over again, and again there was no change.

Caxton sank heavily into a chair. He had, he realized, made a mistake. Something fantastic had happened—just what, his mind was not quite prepared to consider—but whatever it was, his action in dismantling the projector had nullified the process. Now he couldn't even mention what he had discovered.

He grew angry. Why should he worry about lost films when he was leaving the school shortly? Still angry, he climbed to his feet and strode out of the school, home.

The year was 2011 A.D., and though the automatic projector at Tichenor Collegiate was aware in an electronic sense that something was wrong, it continued functioning. The film distribution machine that operated from Los Angeles was aware that something was wrong, but the disturbance was not great enough to set alarm relays into action. Not at first. Not for about three months. And by then—but here is what happened from the very first moment.

An order came through from Tichenor by the usual electronic channels. The order was of human origin. First, the number of the film was punched, then the assigned number of the school. Usually, when the film was in its place in the library, no other human agency was required. However, if the film and all its duplicates were out on loan, a red light flashed in the projection room at Tichenor, and then it was up to the would-be-renter to order a substitute film.

On this occasion a copy of the film was available. The electronic imprint of the number of the school was stamped onto the container's sensitives, and onto a series of bookkeeping plates. The bookkeeping plates moved through a machine which took information from them, as a result of which money was collected from Tichenor in due time. The film flashed out of its shelf into a tube.

Its speed at the beginning was not great. Instant by instant other film containers clicked into the tube in front of it or behind it, and constant automatic readjustments of speed were necessary, to prevent collisions. The number of *the* film's destination, Tichenor Collegiate, was 9-7-43-6-2-Zone 9, Main Tube 7, Suburban Tube 43, Distribution 6, School 2.

The cut-off at Zone 9 opened in its automatic fashion as the forces from the film container actuated the mechanism. A moment later, the film was in main mail channel number 7. It was the channel of small packages, and they were strung out in an endless train, each in its electronically controlled container. The train never stopped, but it slowed and speeded as new containers were precipitated into the tube, or old ones darted off into cut-offs to their separate destinations.

... 43—6—2. With a click, the film arrived in the receptor. Automatic devices slipped it into position on the projector, and at a set time—in this case about an hour later— the projector's seeing eye attachment opened and surveyed the auditorium. Several students were still in the aisles. It clanged a warning alarm, waited half a minute, then locked the auditorium doors, and once more slid the cover from its "eye." This time a single student remained in one aisle.

The projector clanged its final alarm for the students. The next warning would be a light flash in the principal's office, together with a television picture of the auditorium, which would clearly show the recalcitrant student. This final action proved unnecessary. The youth ceased his capering, and tumbled into a seat. The showing began.

It was not within the capacity of the electronic devices of

163

the projector to realize what happened then. The proper film showed on the screen, but the film that was subsequently put into the container and returned to the film library was an obsolete creation called "Food Magic," loaned to Tichenor by the Arlay Film Library in 1946.

The container likewise was not equipped to discover such errors. By pure chance, neither it nor any other container which subsequently acquired a 1946 film went out on call for nearly three months. When one finally clicked onto a projector in Santa Monica it was already too late. Caxton had dismantled the 1946 projector, and the sequential process of time connection had been broken.

Time is the great unvariant, but the unvariance is no simple relation. Time is here where you are. It is never the same elsewhere. A starbeam penetrates the atmosphere. It brings a picture from seven hundred thousand years in the past. An electron makes a path of light across a photographic plate. It brings a picture from fifty, a hundred years in the future—or a hundred thousand years. The stars, the world of the infinitely large, are always in the past. The world of the infinitely small is always in the future.

This is a rigor of the universe. This is the secret of time. And for one second of eternity two motion-picture projectors in two separate space-time periods lost some of their aspects of separateness, and there was a limited liaison.

It ended, and was never more.

Señor Pedro del Corteya packed away his projector. He was vaguely unhappy. Poor audience response always affected him that way. It was late when he got outside, but he stood for a moment beside his car looking thoughtfully up at the star-filled night. Blue was that sky above, alive with the mystery of the immense universe. Corteya scarcely noticed. He was thinking:

"It is those novelty films that bored them. I have shown too many in this town. No more."

He began to feel better, as if a weight had lifted from his soul. He climbed into his car, and drove home.

ASYLUM

INDECISION was dark in the man's thoughts as he walked across the spaceship control room to the cot where the woman lay so taut and so still. He bent over her. He said in his deep voice:

"We're slowing down, Merla."

No answer, no movement, not a quiver in her delicate, abnormally blanched cheeks. Her fine nostrils dilated ever so slightly with each measured breath. That was all.

The Dreegh lifted her arm, then let it go. It dropped to her lap like a piece of lifeless wood, and her body remained rigid and unnatural. Carefully, he put his fingers to one eye, raised the lid, peered into it. It stared back at him, a clouded, sightless blue. He straightened. As he stood there in the silence of the hurtling ship, he seemed the embodiment of grim, icy calculation. He thought grayly: "If I revived her now, she'd have more time to attack me, and more strength. If I waited, she'd be weaker."

Slowly, he relaxed. Some of the weariness of the years he and this woman had spent together in the dark vastness of space came to shatter his abnormal logic. Bleak sympathy touched him, and he made his decision. He prepared an injection, and fed it into her arm. His gray eyes held a steely brightness as he put his lips near the woman's ear. In a ringing, resonant voice he said, "We're near a star system. There'll be blood, Merla! And life!"

The woman stirred. Momentarily, she seemed like a golden-haired doll come alive. No color touched her perfectly formed cheeks, but her eyes grew alert. She stared up at him with a hardening hostility, half questioning.

"I've been chemical," she said. Abruptly, she was no longer doll-like. Her gaze tightened on him, and some of the prettiness vanished from her face. She said, "It's damned funny, Jeel, that you're still O.K. If I thought—"

165

He was cold, watchful. "Forget it," he said curtly. "You're an energy waster, and you know it. Anyway, we're going to land."

The flamelike tenseness of her faded. She sat up painfully, but there was a thoughtful look on her face as she said, "I'm interested in the risks. This is not a Galactic planet, is it?"

"There are no Galactics out here. But there is an Observer. I've been catching the secret *ultra* signals for the last two hours" —a sardonic note entered his voice—"warning all ships to stay clear because the system isn't ready for any kind of contact with Galactic planets."

Some of the diabolic glee that was in his thoughts must have communicated through his tone. The woman stared at him, and slowly her eyes widened. She half whispered, "You mean—"

He shrugged. "The signals ought to be registering full blast now. We'll see what degree system this is. But you can start hoping hard right now."

At the control board, he cautiously manipulated the room into darkness and set the automatics. A picture took form on a screen on the opposite wall. At first there was only a point of light in the middle of a starry sky, then a planet floating brightly in the dark space, continents and oceans plainly visible. A voice came out of the screen:

"This star system contains one inhabited planet, the third from the Sun, called Earth by its dominant race. It was colonized by Galactics about seven thousand years ago in the usual manner. It is now in the third degree of development, having attained a limited form of space travel little more than a hundred years ago."

With a swift movement, the man cut off the picture and turned on the light, then looked across at the woman triumphantly. "Third degree!" he said softly, and there was an almost incredulous note in his voice. "Only third degree. Merla, do you realize what this means? This is the opportunity of the ages. I'm going to call the Dreegh tribe. If we can't get away with several tankers of blood and a whole battery of 'life,' we don't deserve to be immortal."

He turned toward the communicator; and for that exultant

moment caution was dim in the back of his mind. From the corner of his eye, he saw the woman leap from the edge of the cot. Too late, he twisted aside. The movement saved him only partially. It was their cheeks not their lips that met.

Blue flame flashed from him to her. The burning energy seared his cheek to instant, bleeding rawness. He half fell to the floor. And then, furious with the intense agony, he fought free. "I'll break your bones!" he raged.

Her laughter, unlovely with her own suppressed fury, floated up at him from the floor where he had flung her. She said, "So you did have a secret supply of 'life' for yourself. You damned double-crosser!"

His mortification yielded to the realization that anger was useless. Tense with the weakness that was already a weight on his muscles, he whirled toward the control board, and began feverishly to make the adjustments that would pull the ship back into normal space and time.

The body urge grew in him swiftly, a dark, remorseless need. Twice, he reeled to the cot in a fit of nausea. But each time he fought back to the control board. He sat there finally at the controls, head drooping, conscious of the numbing tautness that crept deeper, deeper. He drove the ship too fast. It turned a blazing white when at last it struck the atmosphere of the third planet. But those hard metals held their shape; and the terrible speeds yielded to the fury of the reversers and to the pressure of air that thickened with every mile.

It was the woman who helped his faltering form into the tiny lifeboat. He lay there, gathering strength, staring eagerly down at the blazing sea of lights that was the first city he had seen on the night side of this strange world. Dully, he watched as the woman eased the small ship into the darkness behind a shed in a little back alley. And, because succor seemed suddenly near, he was able to walk beside her to the dimly lighted residential street near by.

He would have walked on blankly into the street, but the woman's fingers held him back into the shadows of the alley. "Are you mad?" she whispered. "Lie down. We'll stay here until someone comes."

167

The concrete was hard beneath his body, but after a moment of the painful rest it brought, he felt a faint surge of energy, and he was able to voice his bitter thought. "If you hadn't stolen most of my carefully saved 'life,' we wouldn't be in this desperate position. You well know that it's more important that I remain at full power."

In the dark beside him, the woman lay quiet for a while. Then her defiant whisper came. "We both need a change of blood, and a new charge of 'life.' Perhaps I did take a little too much out of you, but that was because I had to steal it. You wouldn't have given it to me of your own free will, and you know it."

For a time, the futility or argument held him silent, but, as the minutes dragged, that dreadful physical urgency once more tainted his thought. He said heavily:

"You realize, of course, that we've revealed our presence. We should have waited for the others to come. There's no doubt at all that our ship was spotted by the Galactic Observer in this system before we reached the outer planets. They'll have tracers on us wherever we go, and no matter where we bury our machine, they'll know its exact location. It's impossible to hide the interstellar drive energies; and since they wouldn't make the mistake of bringing such energies to a third-degree planet, we can't hope to locate them in that fashion. But we must expect an attack of some kind. I only hope one of the great Galactics doesn't take part in it."

"One of *them*!" Her whisper was a gasp. She controlled herself, and snapped irritably, "Don't try to scare me. You've told me time and again that—"

"All right, all right!" He spoke grudgingly, wearily. "A million years have proven that they consider us beneath their personal attention. And"—in spite of his appalling weakness, scorn came—"let any of the kind of agents they have in these lower category planets try to stop us."

"Hush!" Her whisper was tense. "Footsteps! Quick, get to your feet!"

He was aware of the shadowed form of her rising. Then her hands were tugging at him. Dizzily, he stood up.

"I don't think," he began wanly, "that I can—"

"Jeel!" Her whisper beat at him; her hands shook him. "It's a man and a woman. They're 'life,' Jeel, 'life!' "

Life!

He straightened. A spark of the unquenchable will to live that had brought him across the black miles and the blacker years burst into flame inside him. Lightly, swiftly, he fell into step beside Merla, and strode into the open. He saw the shapes of the man and the woman. In the half-night under the trees of that street, the couple came towards them, drawing aside to let them pass. First the woman came, then the man—and it was as simple as if all his strength had been there in his muscles.

He saw Merla launch herself at the man; and then he was grabbing the woman, his head bending instantly for that abnormal kiss.

Afterwards—after they had taken the blood, too—grimness came to the man, a hard fabric of thought and counter-thought, that slowly formed into purpose. He said, "We'll leave the bodies here."

Her startled whisper rose in objection, but he cut her short, harshly. "Let me handle this. These dead bodies will draw to this city news gatherers, news reporters, or whatever their breed are called on this planet. And we need such a person now. Somewhere in the reservoir of facts possessed by a person of this type must be clues, meaningless to him but by which we can discover the secret base of the Galactic Observer in this system. We must find that base, discover its strength, and destroy it if necessary when the tribe comes."

His voice took on a steely note. "And now, we've got to explore this city, find a much frequented building under which we can bury our ship, learn the language, replenish our own vital supplies, and capture that reporter.

"After I'm through with him"—his tone became silken-smooth —"he will undoubtedly provide you with that physical diversion which you apparently crave when you have been particularly chemical."

He laughed gently, as her fingers gripped his arm in the darkness, a convulsive gesture. She said, "Thank you, Jeel. You do understand, don't you?"

II

Behind Leigh, a door opened. Instantly the clatter of voices in the room faded to a murmur. He turned alertly, tossing his cigaret onto the marble floor and stepping on it, all in one motion.

Overhead, the lights brightened to daylight intensity. In that blaze he saw what the other eyes were already staring at: the two bodies, the man's and the woman's, as they were wheeled in. The dead couple lay side by side on the flat, gleaming top of the carrier. Their bodies were rigid, their eyes closed. They looked as dead as they were, and not at all, Leigh thought, as if they were sleeping.

He caught himself making a mental note of that fact, and felt shocked at himself. The first murders on the North American continent in twenty-seven years. And it was only another job. He was tougher than he'd ever believed.

Around him, the voices had stopped. The only sound was the hoarse breathing of the man nearest him, and the scrape of his own shoes as he went forward. His movement acted like a signal on that tense group of men. There was a general pressing forward. Leigh had a moment of anxiety. And then his bigger, harder muscles brought him where he wanted to be, opposite the two heads. He leaned forward, absorbed. His fingers probed gingerly where the incisions showed on the neck of the woman. He did not look up at the attendant as he said softly:

"This is where the blood was drained?"

"Yes."

Before he could speak again, another reporter interjected, "Any special comment from the police scientists? The murders are more than a day old now. There ought to be something."

Leigh scarcely heard. The woman's body, electrically warmed for embalming, felt eerily lifelike to his touch. It was only after a long moment that he noticed her lips were badly, almost brutally, bruised.

His gaze flicked to the man. And there were the same neck cuts, the same torn lips. He looked up. Questions quivered on his tongue. They remained unspoken as the calm-voiced attendant said:

"Normally, when the electric embalmers are applied, there is resistance from the static electricity of the body. Curiously, that resistance was not present in either body."

Somebody said, "Just what does that mean?"

"This static force is actually a form of life force, which usually trickles out of a corpse over a period of a month. We know of no way to hasten the process, but the bruises on the lips show distinct burns, which are suggestive."

There was a craning of necks, a crowding forward. Leigh allowed himself to be pushed aside. He stopped attentively as the attendant said, "Presumably, a pervert could have kissed with such violence."

"I thought," Leigh said distinctly, "there were no more perverts since Professor Ungarn persuaded the government to institute his brand of mechanical psychology in all schools, thus ending murder, theft, war, and all unsocial perversions."

The black frock-coated attendant hesitated, then said, "A very bad one seems to have been missed." He finished, "That's all, gentlemen. No clues, no promise of an early capture, and only this final fact: We've wirelessed Professor Ungarn and, by great good fortune, we caught him on his way to Earth from his meteor retreat near Jupiter. He'll be landing shortly after dark, in a few hours from now."

The lights dimmed. As Leigh stood frowning, watching the bodies being wheeled out, a phrase floated out of the gathering chorus of voices:

"—The kiss of death—"

"I tell you," another voice said, "the captain of this space liner swears it happened—the spaceship came past him at a million miles an hour, and it was slowing down, get that, slowing down—two days ago."

"—The vampire case! That's what I'm going to call it—"

That's what Leigh called it, too, as he talked briefly into his wrist communicator. He finished, "I'm going to supper now, Jim."

"O.K., Bill." The local editor's voice sounded metallic. "And

171

say, I'm supposed to commend you. Nine thousand papers took the Planetarian Service on this story, as compared with about forty-seven hundred who bought from Universal, who had the second largest coverage. And I think you've got the right angle for today, too. Husband and wife, ordinary young couple, taking an evening walk. Some devil hauls up alongside of them, drains their blood into a tank, their life energy onto a wire or something —people will believe that, I guess. Anyway, you suggest it could happen to anybody; so be careful, folks. And you warn that, in these days of interplanetary speeds, he could be anywhere tonight for his next murder. As I said before, good stuff. That'll keep the yarn alive for tonight. Oh, by the way—"

"Shoot!"

"A kid called half an hour ago to see you. Said you expected him."

"A kid?" Leigh frowned to himself.

"Name of Patrick. High school age, about sixteen. No, come to think of it, that was only my first impression. Eighteen, maybe twenty, very bright, confident, proud."

"I remember now," said Leigh. "College student. Interview for a college paper. Called me up this afternoon. One of those damned persuasive talkers. Before I knew it, I was signed up for supper at Constantine's."

"That's right. I was supposed to remind you. O.K.?"

Leigh shrugged. "I promised," he said.

Actually, as he went out into the blaze of the late afternoon sunlit street, there was not an important thought in his head. Nor a premonition.

Around him, the swarm of humankind began to thicken. Vast buildings discharged the first surge of the five o'clock tidal wave. Twice, Leigh felt the tug at his arm before it struck him that someone was not just bumping into him.

He turned and stared down at a pair of dark, eager eyes set in a brown, wizened face. The little man waved a sheaf of papers at him. Leigh caught a glimpse of writing in longhand on the papers. Then the fellow was babbling, "Mr. Leigh, a hundred dollars for these . . . biggest story—"

"Oh," said Leigh. His interest collapsed. He said politely,

"Take it up to the Planetarian office. Jim Brian will pay you what the story is worth."

He walked on, a vague conviction in his mind that the matter was settled. Then, abruptly, there was the tugging at his arm again. "Scoop" the little man said. "Professor Ungarn's log, all about a spaceship that came from the stars. Devils in it who drink blood and kiss people to death!"

"See here!" Leigh began, irritated; then stopped. An ugly chill wind swept through him. He stood, swaying a little from the shock of the thought that was frozen in his brain: *The newspapers with those details of "blood" and "kiss" were not on the street yet, wouldn't be for another five minutes.*

The man said, "Look, it's got Professor Ungarn's name printed in gold on the top of each sheet, and it's all about how he first spotted the ship eighteen light years out, and how it came all that distance in a few hours ... and he knows where it is now and—"

Leigh's reporter's brain, that special, highly developed department, was whirling with a little swarm of thoughts that suddenly straightened into a hard, bright pattern. In that tightly built design, there was no room for any such coincidence as this man coming to him here in this crowded street.

He said, "Let me see those!" and reached as he spoke.

The papers came free from the other's fingers into his hand, but Leigh did not even glance at them. His brain was crystal-clear, his eyes cold. He snapped, "I don't know what your game is. I want to know three things, and make your answers damned fast! One: How did you pick me out, name and job and all, here in this packed street of a city I haven't been in for a year?"

The little man stammered incomprehensible words. Leigh paid no attention. Remorselessly, he pounded on, "Two: Professor Ungarn is arriving from Jupiter in three hours. How do you explain your possession of papers he must have written less than two days ago?"

"Look, boss," the man chattered, "you've got me all wrong—"

"My third question," Leigh said grimly, "is how are you going to explain to the police your pre-knowledge of the details of murder?"

173

"Huh!" The little man's eyes were glassy, and for the first time pity came to Leigh. He said almost softly, "All right, fellah, start talking."

The words came swiftly, and at first they were simply senseless sounds. Only gradually did coherence come. "—And that's the way it was, boss. I'm standing there, and this kid comes up to me and points you out, and gives me five bucks and those papers you've got, and tells me what I'm supposed to say to you and—"

"Kid!" said Leigh; and the first shock was already in him.

"Yeah, kid about sixteen; no, more like eighteen or twenty . . . and he gives me the papers and—"

"This kid," said Leigh, "would you say he was of college age?"

"That's it, boss; you've got it. That's just what he was. You know him, eh? O.K., that leaves me in the clear, and I'll be going—"

"Wait!" Leigh called. But the little man seemed suddenly to realize that he need only run. He vanished around a corner, and was gone forever.

Leigh stood, frowning, and read the thin sheaf of papers. There was nothing beyond what the little man had already conveyed by his incoherent talk. It was a vague series of entries on sheets from a loose-leaf notebook. Written down, the tale about the spaceship and its occupants lacked depth, and seemed more unconvincing each passing second. True, there was the single word "Ungarn" inscribed in gold on the top of each sheet but—

The sense of silly hoax grew so violently that Leigh thought angrily: "If that college kid really pulled a stunt like this, it'll be a short interview." The thought ended. The notion was as senseless as everything else that had happened.

And still there was no real tension in him. He was only going to a restaurant.

He turned into the splendid foyer that was the beginning of the vast and wonderful Constantine's. In the great doorway, he paused to survey the expansive glitter of tables, the hanging garden tearooms. Brilliant Constantine's, famous the world over, but not much changed from his last visit.

Leigh gave his name, and began, "A Mr. Patrick made reservations, I understand."

The girl said, "Oh, yes, Mr. Leigh. Mr. Patrick reserved Private Three. He just now phoned to say he'd be along in a few minutes. Our premier will escort you."

Leigh turned away, puzzled at the way the girl had gushed. Then a thought struck him. He turned back to the girl. "Just a minute," he said, "did you say *Private Three*? Who's paying for this?"

The girl said, "It was paid by phone. Forty-five hundred dollars!"

Leigh stood very still. Even after what had happened on the street, this meeting seemed scarcely more than an irritation to be gotten over with. Now, abruptly, it was become a fantastic, abnormal thing. Forty-five—hundred—dollars! Could it be some fool rich kid determined to make a strong, personal impression?

With cold logic, he rejected that solution. Humanity produced egoists on an elephantine scale, but not one who would order a feast like that to impress a reporter. His eyes narrowed on an idea. "Where's your registered phone?" he asked curtly.

A minute later, he was saying into the mouthpiece: "Is this the Amalgamated Universities Secretariat? I want to find out if there is a Mr. Patrick registered at any of your local colleges, and if there is, whether or not he has been authorized by any college paper to interview William Leigh of the Planetarian News Service. This is Leigh calling."

It took six minutes, and then the answer came, brisk, tremendous, and final: "There are three Mr. Patricks in our seventeen units. All are at present having supper at their various official residences. There are four Miss Patricks, similarly accounted for by our staff of secretaries. None of the seven is in any way connected with a university paper. Do you wish any assistance in dealing with the impostor?"

Leigh hesitated. When he finally spoke, it was with the queer, dark realization that he was committing himself. "No," he said, and hung up.

He came out of the phone booth, shaken by his own thoughts.

There was only one reason why he was in this city at this time. Murder! And he knew scarcely a soul. It seemed incredible that any stranger would want to see him for a reason not connected with his own purpose. He waited until the ugly thrill was out of his system. Then he said to the attendant, "To Private Three, please."

Presently, he was examining the luxurious suite. It turned out to be a splendidly furnished apartment with a palace-like dining salon dominating the five rooms. One entire wall of the salon was lined with decorated mirror facings, behind which glittered hundreds of bottles of liquor. The brands were strange to his inexpensive tastes, the bouquet of several that he opened heady but inviting. In the ladies' dressing room was a long showcase displaying a gleaming array of jewelry. He estimated that there was several hundred thousand dollars' worth, if it were genuine. Leigh was not impressed. For his taste, Constantine's did not supply good value for the money they charged.

"I'm glad you're physically big," said a voice behind him. "So many reporters are thin and small."

The tone was subtly different than it had been over the phone in the early afternoon. Deliberately different. The difference, he noted as he turned, was in the body, too, the difference in the shape of a woman from a boy, skillfully but not perfectly concealed under the well-tailored man's suit. Actually, of course, she was quite boyish in build, young, finely molded. And, actually, he would never have suspected if she had not allowed her voice to be so purposefully womanish. She echoed his thought coolly.

"Yes, I wanted you to know. But now, there's no use wasting words. You know as much as you need to know. Here's a gun. The spaceship is buried below this building."

Leigh made no effort to take the weapon, nor did he glance at it. The first shock was over. He seated himself on the silken chair of the vanity dresser, leaned back against the vanity dresser itself, raised his eyebrows, and said, "Consider me a slow-witted newsman who's got to know what it's all about. Why so much preliminary hocus-pocus?"

He thought deliberately: He had never in his adult life

allowed himself to be rushed into anything. He was not going to
start now.

III

He saw after a moment that the girl was small of build. Which
was odd, he decided carefully. Because his first impression had
been of considerable height. Or perhaps—he considered the
possibility unhurriedly—this second effect was a more considered
result of her male disguise.

He dismissed that particular problem as temporarily insoluble.
Actually, the girl's size was unimportant. She had long, black
lashes and dark eyes that glowed at him from a proud, almost
haughty face. And that was it. That was the essence of her
personality. There was pride in the way she held her head. And
in the poised easiness of every movement, in the natural shift
from grace to grace as she walked slowly toward him. It was not
a conscious pride, but an awareness of superiority that affected
every movement of her muscles, and came vibrantly into her
voice, as she said scathingly:

"I picked you because every newspaper I've read today carried
your account of the murders, and because it seemed to me
that somebody who already was actively working on the case
would be reasonably quick at grasping essentials. As for the
dramatic preparation, I considered that would be more convincing than explanation. I see I was mistaken." She was quite
close to him now. She leaned over, laid her revolver on the
vanity beside his arm, and finished almost indifferently, "Here's
an effective weapon. It doesn't shoot bullets, but it has a trigger
and you aim it like any gun. In the event you develop the beginning of courage, come down the tunnel after me as quickly as
possible, but don't blunder in on me and the people I shall be
talking to. Stay hidden! Act only if I'm threatened."

Tunnel, Leigh thought stolidly, as she walked with a free,
swift stride out of the room. A tunnel here in this apartment,
Private Three. Either he was crazy, or she was.

He realized suddenly that he ought to be offended at the

way she had spoken. He felt annoyed at her trick of leaving the room, leaving him to develop curiosity. He smiled ruefully. If it wasn't for the fact that he was a reporter, he'd show her that such a second-rate psychology didn't work on him. Still irritated, he climbed to his feet, took the gun, and then paused briefly as the odd, muffled sound of a door reluctantly opening came to his ears.

He found her in the bedroom to the left of the dining salon. He felt only the vaguest surprise when he saw that she had the end of a thick green rug rolled back, and that there was a hole in the floor at her feet. The square of floor that was the tunnel-covering lay back neatly, pinned to position by a complicated-looking hinge.

Leigh's gaze reached beyond the opening to the girl. In that moment, just before she became aware of him, there was a hint of uncertainty in her manner. Her right profile, half turned away from him, showed pursed lips and a strained whiteness. The impression he received was of indecision. He had the subtle sense of observing a young woman who, briefly, had lost her superb confidence. Then she saw him, and her attitude changed.

She didn't seem to stiffen in any way. Paying no attention to him at all, she stepped to the first step of the little stairway that led down into the hole, and began to descend without a quiver of hesitation. Yet his first conviction that she had faltered brought him forward with narrowed eyes. And, suddenly, the certainty of her brief fear made this whole madness real. He plunged forward, down the steep stairway, and pulled up only when he saw that he was actually in a smooth, dimly-lighted tunnel, and that the girl had paused, one finger to her lips.

"Sssssh!" she said. "The door of the ship may be open."

That irritated Leigh, a hard trickle of anger. Now that he had committed himself, he felt automatically the leader of this fantastic expedition. The girl's pretensions, her haughty manner merely made him impatient.

"Don't 'Sssssh!' me!" he whispered sharply. "Just give the facts and I'll do the rest."

He stopped. The meaning of the words she had spoken penetrated. His anger collapsed. "Ship!" he said incredulously.

"Are you trying to tell me there's actually a spaceship buried here under Constantine's?"

The girl seemed not to hear. Leigh saw that they were at the end of a short passageway. Metal gleamed dully just ahead. Then the girl was saying, "Here's the door. Now, remember, you act as guard. Stay hidden, ready to shoot. And if I yell 'Shoot,' you shoot!"

She bent forward. There was the tiniest scarlet flash. The door opened, revealing a second door just beyond. Again that minute, intense blaze of red, and then that door also swung open.

It was swiftly done, too swiftly. Before Leigh could more than grasp that the crisis had come, the girl stepped coolly into the brilliantly lighted room beyond the second door.

Leigh poised, undecided, in the shadows, startled by the girl's action. There was deeper shadow against the metal wall toward which he pressed himself in one instinctive move. He froze there. Silently he cursed a stupid young woman who actually walked into a den of enemies of unknown numbers without an organized plan of self-protection. Or did she know how many there were? And who?

The questions disturbed him. Finally, he thought grimly: She wasn't wholly unprotected. At least he was out here with a gun, unnoticed.

He waited tensely. But the door remained open; and there was no apparent movement towards it. Slowly, Leigh let himself relax, and allowed his straining mind to absorb its first considered impressions. The portion of underground room that he could see showed one end of what seemed to be a control board, a metal wall that blinked with tiny lights. He could see the edge of a rather sumptuous cot. The whole was actually so suggestive of a spaceship that Leigh thought, astounded: The girl had not been trying to fool him. Incredibly, here under the ground, actually *under* Constantine's, was a small spaceship.

That thought ended as the silence beyond the open door, the curiously long silence, was broken by a man's cool voice. "I wouldn't even try to raise that gun if I were you. The fact that you have said nothing since entering shows how enormously

179

different we are to what you expected." He laughed gently, an unhurried, deep-throated, derisive laughter that came clearly to Leigh; then he went on, "Merla, what would you say is the psychology behind this young lady's action? You have of course noticed that she is a young lady, and not a boy."

A richly toned woman's voice replied, "She was born here, Jeel. She has none of the normal characteristics of a Klugg, but she is a Galactic, though definitely not the Galactic Observer. Probably, she's not alone. Shall I investigate?"

"No!" The man sounded indifferent. "We don't have to worry about a Klugg's assistant."

Leigh relaxed slowly, but he had a sense of emptiness. For the first time he realized how great a part the calm assurance of the young woman had played in the fabricating of his own confidence. Shattered now! Before the enormous certainties of these two, and in the face of their instant penetration of her male disguise, the effects of the girl's rather wonderful personality seemed a remote pattern, secondary, overwhelmed by a greater power.

He forced the fear from him as the girl spoke. Forced his courage to grow with each word she uttered, feeding on the confidence of her tone. It didn't matter whether she was simulating or not, because they were in this now, he as deep as she. Only the utmost boldness could hope to draw victory from the defeat that threatened them both.

With admiration, he noted the intensity of her voice as she said, "My silence had its origin in the fact that you are the first Dreeghs I have ever seen. Naturally, I studied you with some curiosity. But I can assure you I am not impressed. However, in view of your extraordinary opinions on the matter, I shall come to the point at once: I have been instructed by the Galactic Observer of this system to inform you to be gone by morning. Our sole reason for giving you that much leeway is that we don't wish to bring the truth of all this into the open. But don't count on that. Earth is on the verge of being given fourth-degree rating; and, as you probably know, in emergencies fourths are given Galactic knowledge. That emergency we will consider to have arrived tomorrow at dawn."

"Well, well"—the man was laughing gently, satirically—"a

pretty speech, powerfully spoken, but meaningless for us who can analyze its pretensions, however sincere, back to the Klugg origin."

"What do you intend to do with her, Jeel?"

The man was cold, deadly, utterly sure. "There's no reason why she should escape. She has blood, and more than normal life. It will convey to the Observer with clarity our contempt for his ultimatum."

He finished with a slow, surprisingly rich laughter, "We shall now enact a simple drama. The young lady will attempt to jerk up her gun and shoot me with it. Before she can succeed, I shall have my own weapon out, and be firing. The whole thing, as she will discover, is a matter of nervous co-ordination. And Kluggs are chronically almost as slow-moving as human beings."

His voice stopped. His laughter trickled away. Silence.

In all his alert years, Leigh had never felt more indecisive. His emotions said—*now;* surely, she'd call now. And even if she didn't, he must act on his own. Rush in! Shoot!

But his mind was cold with an awful dread. There was something about the man's voice, a surging power. Abnormal, savage strength was here. Could this really be a spaceship from the stars? His brain wouldn't follow that terrible thought. He crouched, fingering the gun she had given him, dimly conscious that if felt queer, unlike any revolver he had ever had.

The silence from the spaceship control room continued. It was the same curious silence that had followed the girl's entrance short minutes before. Only this time it was the girl who broke it, her voice faintly breathless but withal cool, vibrant, unafraid, "I'm here to warn, not to force issues. And unless you're charged with the life energy of fifteen men, I wouldn't advise you to try anything. After all, I came here knowing what you were."

"What do you think, Merla? Can we be sure she's a Klugg? Could she possibly be of the higher Lennel type?" It was the man, his tone conceding her point, but the derision was still there, the implacable purpose, the high, tremendous confidence.

And yet, in spite of that sense of imminent violence, Leigh felt himself torn from the thought of danger. His reporter's brain twisted irresistibly to the fantastic meaning of what was taking place:

—*Life energy of fifteen men*—

It was all there. In a monstrous way, it all fitted. The two dead bodies he had seen drained of blood and *life energy*, the repeated reference to a Galactic Observer, with whom the girl was connected. He grew aware that the woman was speaking.

"Klugg!" she said positively. "Pay no attention to her protestations, Jeel. You know I'm sensitive when it comes to women. She's lying. She's just a little fool who walked in here expecting us to be frightened of her. Destroy her at your pleasure."

"I'm not given to waiting," said the man. "So—"

There was no delaying now. Leigh leaped for the open doorway. He had a flashing glimpse of a man and woman, dressed in evening clothes, the man standing, the woman seated. He was aware of a gleaming, metallic background. The control board, part of which he had already seen, was now revealed as a massive thing of glowing instruments; and then all that was blotted out as he snapped:

"That will do. Put up your hands."

For a moment he had the impression that his entry was a surprise, and that he dominated the situation. None of the three people in the room was turned toward him. The man, Jeel, and the girl were standing facing each other. The woman, Merla, sat in a deep chair, her fine profile to him, her golden head flung back. It was she who, still without looking at him, spoke the words that ended his brief conviction of triumph. She said to the disguised girl:

"You certainly travel in low company, a stupid human being. Tell him to go away before he's damaged."

The girl said, "Leigh, I'm sorry I brought you into this. Every move you made in entering was heard, observed, and dismissed before you could even adjust your mind to the scene."

"Is his name Leigh?" said the woman sharply. "I thought I recognized him as he entered. He's very like his photograph over his newspaper column." Her voice grew strangely tense: "Jeel, a newspaper reporter!"

"We don't need him now," the man said. "We know who the Galactic Observer is."

"Eh?" said Leigh. His mind fastened hard on those amazing words. "Who? How did you find out? What—"

"The information," said the woman, and it struck him suddenly that the strange quality in her voice was eagerness, "will be of no use to you. Regardless of what happens to the girl, you're staying."

She glanced swiftly at the man, as if seeking his sanction. "Remember, Jeel, you promised."

It seemed so meaningless that Leigh had no sense of personal danger. His mind scarcely more than passed the words. His eyes concentrated tautly on a reality that had, until that moment, escaped his awareness. He said softly, "Just now you used the phrase, 'Regardless of what happens to the girl.' When I came in, you said, 'Tell him to go away before he's damaged.'" Leigh smiled grimly, "I need hardly say this is a far cry from the threat of immediate death that hung over us a few seconds ago. And I have just now noticed the reason.

"A little while ago, I heard our pal, Jeel, dare my little girl friend here to raise her gun. I notice now that *she has it raised*. My entrance did have an effect." He addressed himself to the girl, "Shall we shoot—or withdraw?"

It was the man who answered. 'I would advise withdrawal. I could still win, but I am not the heroic type who takes the risk of what might well be a close call." He added, in an aside to the woman: "Merla, we can always catch this man Leigh now that we know who he is."

The girl said, "You first, Mr. Leigh." And Leigh did not stop to argue.

Metal doors clanged behind him as he charged along the tunnel. After a moment, he was aware of the girl running lightly beside him.

The strangely unreal, the unbelievably murderous little drama was over, finished as fantastically as it had begun.

IV

Outside Constantine's a gray light gathered around them. It was a twilight side street, and people hurried past them with the strange, anxious look of the late for supper. Night was falling. Leigh stared at his companion. In the dimness of the deep dusk, she seemed all boy, slightly, lithely built, striding along boldly. He laughed a little, huskily, then more grimly.

"Just what was all that?" he said. "Did we escape by the skin of our teeth? Or did we win? What made you think you could act like God, and give those tough eggs twelve hours to get out of the solar system?"

The girl was silent after he had spoken. She walked just ahead of him, head bent into the gloom. Abruptly, she turned. She said, "I hope you will have enough sense to refrain from telling what you've just seen and heard."

Leigh said, "This is the biggest story since—"

The girl's voice was pitying. "You're not going to print a word of it because in about ten seconds you'll see that no one in the world would believe any of it."

In the darkness, Leigh smiled tightly. "The mechanical psychologist will verify every syllable."

"I came prepared for that, too!" said the vibrant voice. Her hand swung up toward his face. Too late, he jerked back.

Light flared in his eyes, a dazzling, blinding force that exploded into his sensitive optic nerves with all the agonizing power of intolerable brightness. Leigh cursed aloud, wildly, and snatched at his tormentor. His right hand grazed a shoulder. He lashed out violently with his left, and tantalizingly caught only the edge of a sleeve that instantly jerked away.

"You little devil!" he raged. "You've blinded me."

"You'll be all right," came the cool answer. "But you'll find that the mechanical psychologist will analyze anything you say as pure imagination. In view of your threat to publish, I had to do that. Now, give me my gun."

The first glimmer of sight was returning. Leigh could see her body, a dim shape in the night. In spite of the continuing pain, he smiled grimly. His voice was soft as he said, "I've just now remembered you said this gun didn't shoot bullets. Even the *feel* of it suggests that it'll make an interesting proof of anything I say. So—"

His smile faded abruptly. For the girl stepped forward. The metal that jabbed into his ribs was so hardly thrust it made him grunt.

"*Give me that gun!*"

"Like fun I will," Leigh snapped. "You ungrateful little ruffian, how dare you treat me so shoddily after I saved your life? I ought to knock you one right on the jaw."

He stopped. With staggering suddenness the hard realization struck that she meant it. This was no girl raised in a refined school, who wouldn't dare to shoot, but a cold-blooded young creature who had already proved her determination against a deadlier opponent than he himself.

He had never had any notions about the superiority of man over woman, and he felt none now. Hastily, he handed the weapon over. The girl took it, and said coldly, "You seem to be laboring under the illusion that your entry into the spaceship enabled me to raise my weapon. You're quite mistaken. What you did do was to provide me with the opportunity to let them think that that was the situation, and that they dominated it. But I assure you, that is the extent of your assistance. It was almost valueless."

Leigh laughed out loud, a pitying, ridiculing laugh.

"In my admittedly short life," he said, "I've learned to recognize a quality of personality and magnetism in human beings. You've got it, a lot of it, but not a fraction of what either of those two had, particularly the man. He was terrible. He was the most abnormally magnetic human being I've ever run across. Lady, I can only guess what all this is about, but I'd advise you"—Leigh paused, then finished slashingly—"you and all the other Kluggs to stay away from that couple. Personally, I'm going to get the police in on this, and there's going to be a raid on Private Three. I didn't like that odd threat that they could capture me at any time. Why me?"

He broke off hastily, "Hey, where are you going? I want to

185

know your name. I want to know what made you think you could order those two around. *Who did you think you were?*"

He said no more. His whole attention was concentrated on running. He could see her for a moment, a hazy, boyish figure against a dim corner light. Then she was around the corner. Leigh thought: "She's my only point of contact with all this. If she gets away—"

Sweating, he rounded the corner; and at first the street seemed dark and empty of life. Then he saw the car. A normal-looking, high-hooded coupé, long, low-built, that began to move forward noiselessly and quite naturally. It became unnatural. It lifted. Amazingly, it lifted from the ground. He had a swift glimpse of white rubber wheels folding out of sight. Streamlined, almost cigar-shaped now, the spaceship that had been a car darted at a steep angle into the sky.

Swiftly, it was gone.

Above Leigh the gathering night towered, a strange, bright blue. In spite of the brilliant lights of the city glaring into the sky, one or two stars showed. He stared up at them, empty inside, thinking: "It was like a dream. Those—Dreeghs—coming out of space—bloodsuckers, vampires."

Suddenly hungry, he bought a chocolate bar from a side-walk stand and stood munching it. He began to feel better. He walked over to a near-by wall socket, and plugged in his wrist radio.

"Jim," he said, "I've got some stuff, not for publication, but maybe we can get some police action on it. Then I want you to have a mechanical psychologist sent to my hotel room. There must be some memory that can be salvaged from my brain—"

He went on briskly. His sense of inadequacy waned. Reporter Leigh was himself again.

V

The little glistening balls of the mechanical psychologist whirred faster and faster. They became a single, glowing circle in the darkness. And not till then did the first, delicious whiff of psycho-gas touch his nostrils. He felt himself drifting, slipping. A voice began to speak in the dim distance, so far away that not a word came through. There was only the sound, the faint, curious sound, and the feeling, stronger every instant, that he would soon be able to hear the fascinating things it seemed to be saying.

The longing to hear, to become a part of the swelling, murmuring sound tugged at him, in little rhythmical, wavelike surges. And still the promise of meaning was unfulfilled. Private thoughts ended utterly. Only the mindless chant remained and the pleasing gas holding him so close to sleep, its flow nevertheless so delicately adjusted that his mind hovered minute after minute on the ultimate abyss of consciousness. He lay, finally, still partially awake, but even the voice was merging now into blackness. It clung for a while, a gentle, friendly, melodious sound in the remote background of his brain, becoming more remote with each passing instant. He slept, a deep, hypnotic sleep, as the machine purred on.

When Leigh opened his eyes, the bedroom was dark except for the floor lamp beside a corner chair. It illuminated the darkly dressed woman who sat there, all except her face, which was in shadow above the circle of light. He must have moved, for the shadowed head suddenly looked up from some sheets of typewriter-size paper. The voice of Merla, the Dreegh, said:

"The girl did a very good job of erasing your subconscious memories. There's only one possible clue to her identity and—"

Her words went on, but his brain jangled them to senselessness in that first shock of recognition. It was too much, too much fear in too short a time. For a moment, he was like a child, and strange, cunning, intense thoughts of escape came. If he could slide to the side of the bed, away from where she was sitting, and run for the bathroom door—

"Surely, Mr. Leigh," the woman's voice reached toward him, "you know better than to try anything foolish. And, surely, if I had intended to kill you, I would have done it much more easily while you were asleep."

Leigh lay still, gathering his thoughts and licking dry lips. Her words were not reassuring. "What—do—you—want?" he managed finally.

"Information!" Laconically. "What was that girl?"

"I don't know." He stared into the half-gloom, where her face was. His eyes were more accustomed to the light now, and he could catch the faint, golden glint of her hair. "I thought —you knew." He went on more swiftly, "I thought you knew the Galactic Observer; and that implied the girl could be identified any time."

He had the impression she was smiling. She said, "Our statement to that effect was designed to throw both you and the girl off guard, and constituted the partial victory we snatched from what had become an impossible situation."

The body sickness was still upon Leigh. But the desperate fear that had produced it faded before the implications of her confession of weakness. These Dreeghs were not so superhuman as he had thought. Relief was followed by caution. Careful, he warned himself, it wouldn't be wise to underestimate. But he couldn't help saying:

"I'd like to point out that even your so-called snatching of victory from defeat was not so well done. Your husband's statement that you could pick me up any time could easily have spoiled the picking."

The woman's voice was faintly contemptuous. "If you knew anything of psychology, you would realize that the vague phrasing of the threat actually lulled you. Certainly, you failed to take even minimum precautions. And the girl has made no effort to protect you."

The suggestion of deliberately subtle tactics brought to Leigh a twinge of returning alarm. Deep inside him he thought: What ending did the Dreegh woman plan for this strange meeting?

"You realize, of course," the Dreegh said softly, "that you will either be of value to us alive—or dead. There are no easy alternatives. I would advise alertness and sincerity in your coöperation. You are in this affair without any limitations."

So that was the idea. A thin bead of perspiration trickled down Leigh's cheek. His fingers trembled as he reached for a cigaret on the table beside the bed. He was shakily lighting the cigaret when his gaze fastened on the window. That brought a faint shock. For it was raining, a furious rain that hammered sound-lessly against the noiseproof glass.

He pictured the bleak, empty streets, their brilliance dulled by the black, rain-filled night. Deserted streets—deserted Leigh. For he was deserted here. All the friends he had, scattered over the great reaches of the earth, couldn't add one ounce of strength, or bring one real ray of hope to him in this darkened room. against this woman who sat so calmly under the light, studying him from shadowed eyes.

With an effort, Leigh steadied himself. He said, "I gather that's my psychograph report you have in your hand. What does it say?"

"Very disappointing." Her voice seemed far away. "There's a warning in it about your diet. It seems your meals are irregular."

She was playing with him. The attempt at humor made her seem more inhuman, not less. For, somehow, the words clashed unbearably with the reality of her; the dark immensity of space across which she had come, the unnatural lusts that had brought her and the man to unprotected Earth. Leigh shivered. Then he thought fiercely, "Damn it, I'm scaring myself. So long as she stays in her chair, she can't pull the vampire on me."

Aloud he said, "If there's nothing in the psychograph, then I'm afraid I can't help you. You might as well leave. Your presence isn't adding to my happiness."

In a dim way, he hoped she'd laugh. But she didn't. She sat there, her eyes glinting dully out of the gloom. At last she said, "We'll go through this report together. I think we can safely omit the references to your health as being irrelevant. But there are a number of factors that I want developed. Who is Professor Ungarn?"

"A scientist." Leigh spoke frankly. "He invented this system of mechanical hypnosis, and he was called in when the dead bodies were found because the killings seemed to have been done by perverts."

"Have you any knowledge of his physical appearance?"

"I've never seen him," Leigh said more slowly. "He never gives interviews and his photograph is not available now. I've heard stories, but—" He hesitated. He was giving her general knowledge only, but even that could be dangerous.

"These stories," the woman said, "do they give the impression that he's a man of inordinate magnetic force, but with lines of mental suffering etched in his face, and a sort of resignation?"

"Resignation to what?" Leigh exclaimed sharply. "I haven't the faintest idea what you're talking about. I've only seen photographs, and they show a fine, rather sensitive, tired face."

She said, "There would be no more information in any library?"

"Or in the Planetarian Service morgue," Leigh said, and could have bitten off his tongue for that bit of gratuitous information.

"Morgue?" said the woman.

Leigh explained, but his voice was trembling with self-rage. For seconds now the feeling had been growing on him: Was it possible this devilish woman was on the right track? And getting damaging answers out of him because he dared not stop and organize for lying. He had an incongruous sense of the unfairness of the abnormally swift way she had solved the Observer's identity. Because, damn it, it could be Professor Ungarn.

Ungarn was a mysterious figure, a scientist, great inventor in a dozen highly complicated, widely separated fields. He had a home near one of Jupiter's moons, and he had a daughter named Patricia. Good heavens, Patrick—Patricia!

His shaky stream of thoughts ended as the woman said, "Can you have your office send the information to your recorder here?"

"Y-yes." His reluctance was so obvious that the woman bent into the light. For a moment, her golden hair glittered; her pale blue eyes glowed at him in a strangely humorless, satanic amusement.

"Ah!" she said. "You think so, too?"

She laughed, an odd, musical laugh, odd in that it was at once so curt and so pleasant. The laugh ended abruptly, unnaturally, on a high note. And then—although he had not seen her move —there was a metal thing in her hand, pointing at him. Her voice came at him with a brittle, jarring command, "You will climb out of the bed, operate the recorder, and naturally you will do nothing and say nothing but what is necessary."

Leigh moved slowly to obey the woman's command. As he stood up, the room swayed dizzily. He thought sicklily: If only he could faint. But he recognized that that was beyond the power of his tough body. It was dismay that made him so shivery. Annoyingly, he grew steadier even as he walked to the recorder. For the first time in his life, he hated the resilience of his strength. He set the machine, and said:

"This is William Leigh. Give me all the dope you've got on Professor Garret Ungarn."

There was a pause, then a brisk voice said, "You've got it. Sign the form."

Leigh signed, and watched the signature dissolve into the machine. It was then, as he was straightening, that the woman said, "Shall I read it here, Jeel, or shall we take the machine with us?"

Leigh blinked, and whirled; and then, very carefully, he sat down on the bed. The Dreegh, Jeel, was leaning idly against the jamb of the bathroom door, a dark, malignantly handsome man, with a faint, unpleasant smile on his lips. Behind him—incredibly, behind him, through the open bathroom door, was, not the gleaming bath, but another door; and beyond that door still another door, and beyond that the control room of the Dreegh spaceship!

There it was, exactly as he had seen it in the solid ground under Constantine's. He had the same partial view of the sumptuous cot, the imposing section of instrument board, the tastefully padded floor. *In his bathroom!*

Leigh thought insanely: "I keep my spaceship in my bathroom, of course."

It was the Dreegh's voice that drew his brain from its dizzy contemplation. The Dreegh said, "I think we'd better leave. I'm having difficulty holding the ship on the alternation of space-time planes. Bring the man and the machine and—"

Leigh didn't hear the last word. He jerked his mind all the way out of the bathroom. "You're—taking—me?"

"Why, of course." It was the woman who spoke. "You've been promised to me, and besides, we'll need your help in finding Ungarn's meteor."

Leigh sat quiet, and without plans of his own. He saw after a moment that the rain was still beating against the glass, great sparkling drops that washed murkily down the broad panes. And he saw that the night was dark. Dark night, dark rain, dark destiny—they fitted his dark, grim thoughts. With an effort he forced his body and his mind to relax. When at last he faced his alien captors again, Reporter Leigh was cold with acceptance of his fate, and ready to fight for his life.

"I can't think of a single reason," he said, "why I should go with you. And if you think I'm going to help you destroy the Observer, you're crazy."

The woman said matter-of-factly, "There was a passing reference in your psychograph to a Mrs. Henry Leigh, who lives in a village called Relton, on the Pacific coast. We could be there in half an hour, your mother and her home destroyed within a minute after that. Or, perhaps, we could add her blood to our reserves."

"She would be too old," the man said in a chill tone. "We do not want the blood of old people."

It was the icy objection that brought horror to Leigh. He had a mental picture of a silent, immensely swift ship sweeping out of the eastern night, over the peaceful hamlet. The destroying energy would reach down, and the ship would sweep on over the long, dark waters to the west.

The deadly picture faded. The woman was saying, gently, "Jeel and I have evolved an interesting little system of interviewing human beings of the lower order. For some reason, he frightens people merely by his presence. Similarly, people develop an unnatural fear of me when they see me clearly in a strong light. So we have always tried to arrange our meetings with human beings with me sitting in semidarkness and Jeel in the background. It has proved very effective."

She stood up, a tall, lithely built, shadowed figure in a rather tight-fitting skirt and a dark blouse. She finished, "But now, shall we go? You bring the machine, Mr. Leigh."

"I'll take it," said the Dreegh.

Leigh glanced sharply at the lean, sinewed face of the terrible man, startled at the instant, accurate suspicion of his own desperate intention.

The Dreegh loomed over the small machine, where it stood on a corner desk. "How does it work?" he asked.

Leigh stepped forward. There was still a chance that he could manage this without additional danger to anyone. Not that it would be more than a vexation, unless, as their suggestion about finding the Ungarn meteor indicated, they headed straight out to space. If they did that, then he might actually delay them. He said, "Press the key marked 'Titles,' and the machine will type all the main headings."

"That sounds reasonable." The long, grim-faced head nodded. The Dreegh reached forward, pressed the button. The recorder hummed softly, and a section of it lit up, showing typed lines under a transparent covering. There were several headings.

" '—His Meteor Home,' " read the Dreegh. "That's what I want. What is the next step?"

"Press the key marked 'Subheads.' "

Leigh was suddenly shaky. He groaned inwardly. Was it possible this creature-man was going to obtain the information he wanted? Certainly, such a tremendous intelligence would not easily be led away from logical sequence. He forced himself to grimness. He'd have to take a chance.

"The subhead I desire," said the Dreegh, "is marked 'Location.' And there is a number, one, in front of it. What next?"

"Press Key No. 1," Leigh said, "then press the key lettered 'General Release.' "

The moment he had spoken, he grew taut. If this worked, and there was no reason why it shouldn't, Key No. 1 would impart all the information under that heading. And surely the man would not want more until later. After all, this was only a test. They were in a hurry. And later, when the Dreegh discovered that the "General Release" key had dissolved all the other information, it would be too late.

The thought dimmed. Leigh started. The Dreegh was staring

at him bleakly. The man said, "Your voice has been like an organ; each word uttered full of subtle shadings that mean much to the sensitive ear. Accordingly"—a ferocious smile twisted the lean face—"I shall press Key No. 1. But not 'General Release.' And as soon as I've examined the little story on the recorder, I shall attend to you for that attempted trick. The sentence is—death."

"Jeel!"

"Death!" reiterated the man flatly. And the woman was silent.

There was silence, then, except for the subdued humming of the recorder. Leigh's mind was almost without thought. He felt fleshless, and only gradually did he realize that he was waiting here on the brink of a night darker than the black wastes of space from which these monster humans had come.

He felt a kinship with the black rain that poured with such solid, noiseless power against the glinting panes. His aimless gaze returned to the recorder machine, and to the grim man who stood so thoughtfully staring down at the words it was unfolding. His thought quickened. And, suddenly, there was purpose in him.

If death was inescapable, at least he could try again, somehow, to knock down that "General Release" key. He stared at the key, measuring the distance. Three feet, he thought, perhaps four. If he should fling himself toward it, how could even a Dreegh prevent the dead weight of his body and his extended fingers from accomplishing such a simple mission? After all, his sudden action had once before frustrated the Dreeghs by allowing the Ungarn girl—in spit of her denials—to get her gun into position for firing.

He saw that the Dreegh was turning away from the machine. The man pursed his lips, but it was the woman, Merla, who spoke from where she stood in the gloom:

"Well?"

The man frowned. "The exact location is nowhere on record. Apparently, there has been no development of meteors in this system. I suspected as much. After all, space travel has only existed a hundred years; and the new planets and the moons of

Jupiter have absorbed all the energies of exploring, exploiting man."

"I could have told you that," said Leigh.

If he could move a little to one side of the recorder, so that the Dreegh would have to do more than simply put his arm out—

The man was saying, "There is, however, a reference to some man who transports food and merchandise from the moon Europa to the Ungarns. We will . . . er . . . persuade this man to show us the way."

"One of these days," said Leigh, "you're going to discover that all human beings cannot be persuaded. What pressure are you going to put on this chap? Suppose he hasn't got a mother."

"He has—life!" said the woman softly.

"One look at you," Leigh snapped, "and he'd know that he'd lose that, anyway."

As he spoke, he stepped to the left, one short step. He had an impulse to say something, anything to cover the action. But his voice had betrayed him once. And actually, it might already have done so again. The cold face of the man was almost too enigmatic.

"We could," said the woman, "use William Leigh to persuade him."

The words were softly spoken, but they shocked Leigh. For they offered a distorted hope. And that shattered his will to action. His purpose faded into remoteness. He fought to draw that hard determination back into his consciousness. He concentrated his gaze on the recorder machine, but the woman was speaking again; and his mind wouldn't hold anything except the urgent meaning of her words:

"He is too valuable a slave to destroy. We can always take his blood and energy, but now we must send him to Europa, there to find the freighter pilot of the Ungarns, and actually accompany him to the Ungarn meteor. If he could investigate the interior, our attack might conceivably be simplified, and there is just a possibility that there might be new weapons, of which we should be informed. We must not underestimate the science of the great Galactics. Naturally, before we allowed Leigh his

195

freedom, we would do a little tampering with his mind, and so blot out from his conscious mind all that has happened in this hotel room. The identification of Professor Ungarn as the Galactic Observer we would make plausible for Leigh by a little rewriting of his psychograph report; and tomorrow he will awaken in his bed with a new purpose, based on some simple human impulse such as love of the girl."

The very fact that the Dreegh, Jeel, was allowing her to go on, brought the first, faint color to Leigh's cheeks, a thin flush at the enormous series of betrayals she was expecting of him. Nevertheless, so weak was his resistance to the idea of continued life, that he could only snap: "If you think I'm going to fall in love with a dame who's got twice my I.Q., you're—"

The woman cut him off. "Shut up, you fool! Can't you see I've saved your life?"

The man was cold, ice-cold. "Yes, we shall use him, not because he is essential, but because we have time to search for easier victories. The first members of the Dreegh tribe will not arrive for a month and a half, and it will take Mr. Leigh a month of that to get to the moon, Europa, by one of Earth's primitive passenger liners. Fortunately, the nearest Galactic military base is well over three months distant—by Galactic ship speeds.

"Finally"—with a disconcerting, tigerish swiftness the Dreegh whirled full upon Leigh, eyes that were like pools of black fire measured his own startled stare—"as a reminder to your subconscious of the error of trickery, and as complete punishment for past and—intended—offenses, *this*!"

Despairingly, Leigh twisted away from the metal that glowed at him. His muscles tried horribly to carry out the purpose that had been working to a crisis inside him. He lunged for the recorder—but *something* caught his body. Something not physical.

The pain that struck him seemed mortal. There was no visible flame of energy, only that glow at the metal source. But his nerves writhed; enormous forces contorted his throat muscles; froze the scream that quivered there. His whole being welcomed the blackness that mercifully blotted out the hellish pain.

VI

On the third day Europa began to give up some of the sky to the vast mass of Jupiter behind it. The engines that so imperfectly transformed magnetic attraction to a half-hearted repulsion functioned more and more smoothly as the complication of gravitic pull and counterpull yielded to distance. The old, slow, small freighter scurried on into the immense, enveloping night; and the days dragged into weeks, the weeks crawled their drab course toward the full month. On the thirty-seventh day, the sense of slowing up was so distinct that Leigh crept dully out of his bunk, and croaked, "How much farther?"

The stolid-faced space trucker grinned at him. The man's name was Hanardy, and he said now matter-of-factly, "We're just pulling in. See that spot of light over to the left? It's moving this way."

He ended with a rough sympathy. "Been a tough trip, eh? Tougher'n you figgered when you offered to write up my little route for your big syndicate."

Leigh scarcely heard. He was clawing at the porthole, straining to penetrate the blackness. At first his eyes kept blinking compulsively, and nothing came. Stars were out there, but it was long seconds before his bleary gaze made out moving lights. He counted them with sluggish puzzlement. "One, two, three—seven—" he counted. "And all traveling together."

"What's that?" Hanardy bent beside him. "Seven?"

There was a brief silence between them as the light grew visibly dim with distance and winked out.

"Too bad," Leigh ventured, "that Jupiter's behind us. They mightn't fade out like that in silhouette. Which one was Ungarn's meteorite?"

Hanardy stood up, his heavy face dark with frown. He said slowly, "Those were ships. I never saw ships go so fast before. They were out of sight in less than a minute." The frown faded from his stolid face. He shrugged. "Some of those new police ships, I guess. And we must have seen them from a funny angle for them to disappear so fast."

Leigh half sat, half knelt, frozen into immobility. And after that one swift glance at the pilot's rough face, he averted his own. For a moment, the black fear was in him that his wild thoughts would blaze from his eyes.

Dreeghs! Two and a half months had wound their slow course since the murders. More than a month to get from Earth to Europa, and now this miserable, lonely journey with Hanardy, the man who trucked for the Ungarns. Every day of that time he had known with inner certainty that the danger had not basically altered but had assumed a more hidden form. The one fortunate reality in the whole affair was that he had wakened on the morning after the mechanical psychologist test from a dreamless sleep; and there in the psychograph report was the identification of Ungarn as the Observer, and the statement, borne out by an all too familiar emotional tension, that he was in love with the girl.

Now this! His mind flared. Dreeghs in seven ships. That meant the first had been reinforced by many. And perhaps the seven were only a reconnaissance group, withdrawing at Hanardy's approach. Or perhaps those fantastic murderers had already attacked the Observer's base. Perhaps the girl was dead.

He watched uneasily as the Ungarn meteorite made a dark, glinting path in the blackness to one side. The two objects, the ship and the bleak, rough-shaped mass of metallic stone drew together in the night, the ship slightly behind. A great steel door slid open in the rock. Skillfully, the ship glided into the chasm. There was a noisy clicking. Hanardy came out of the control room, his face dark with puzzlement.

"Those damn ships are out there again," he said. "I've closed the big steel locks, but I'd better tell the professor and—"

Crash! The world jiggled. The floor came up and hit Leigh a violent blow. He lay there, cold in spite of the thoughts that burned at fire heat in his mind. For some reason, the vampires had waited until the freighter was inside. Then instantly, ferociously, attacked. In packs!

"Hanardy!" A vibrant girl's voice blared from one of the loud-speakers.

198

The pilot sat up shakily on the floor, where he had fallen, near Leigh. "Yes, Miss Patricia."

"You dared to bring a stranger with you!"

"It's only a reporter, miss. He's writing up my route for me."

"You conceited fool! That's William Leigh. He's a hypnotized spy of those devils who are attacking us. Bring him immediately to my apartment. He must be killed at once."

"Huh!" Leigh began, and then stiffened. The pilot was staring at him from narrowing eyes, all the friendliness gone from his rough, heavy face. Leigh laughed curtly. "Don't you be a fool too, Hanardy. I made the mistake once of saving that young lady's life, and she's hated me ever since."

The heavy face scowled at him. "So you knew her before, eh. You didn't tell me that. You'd better come along before I sock you one."

Awkwardly, he drew the gun from his side holster and pointed its ugly snout at Leigh.

"Get along!" he said.

Hanardy reached toward an arrangement of tiny lights beside the paneled door of Patricia Ungarn's apartment—and Leigh made a single leap and struck one blow. He caught the short, heavy body as it fell, grabbed at the sagging gun, lowered the dead weight to the floor of the corridor, and then stood like a great animal, straining for sound.

Silence! He studied the blond panels of the doorway to the apartment, as if by sheer, savage intentness he would penetrate their golden, beautifully grained opaqueness. It was the silence that struck him again, presently, the emptiness of the long, tunnel-like corridors. He thought, amazed: Was it possible father and daughter actually lived here without companions or servants or any human association? And that they had some idea that they could withstand the attack of the mighty and terrible Dreeghs?

They had a lot of power here, of course. The earth-like gravity alone would take stupendous energy to maintain. But now, he'd better be on his way before the girl grew impatient and came out with one of her weapons. What he must do was quite simple, unconnected with any nonsense of spying, hypnotic or otherwise.

199

He must find the combination automobile-spaceship in which—
Mr. Patrick—had escaped him that night after they left
Constantine's. And with that tiny ship, he must try to slip out of
Ungarn's meteorite, sneak through the Dreegh line, and so head
back for Earth.

What a fool he'd been, a mediocre human being, mixing with
such people. The world was full of normal girls of his own
general I.Q. level. Why wasn't he safely married to one of them?
Still thinking about that, he began laboriously to drag Hanardy
along the smooth flooring. Halfway to the nearest corner, the
man stirred. Without hesitation, Leigh struck him hard with the
revolver butt. This was no time for squeamishness.

The pilot went limp again, and the rest was simple. He deserted the body as soon as he had pulled it out of sight around the
corner, and raced along the hallway, trying doors. The first four
wouldn't open. The fifth was also locked, but this time Leigh
paused to consider.

It seemed unbelievable that the whole place was locked up.
Two people in an isolated meteorite wouldn't go around perpetually locking and unlocking doors. Carefully, he examined the
door before him. And found its secret. It opened to a slight
pressure on a tiny, half-hidden push button that had seemed
an integral part of the design of the latch. He stepped through
the entrance, then started back with a terrible shock.

The room had no ceiling. Above him was—space. An ice-cold
blast of air swept at him. He had a glimpse of gigantic machines
in the room, machines that dimly resembled the ultra-modern
astronomical observatory on the moon that he had visited on
opening day two years before. That one, swift look was all
Leigh allowed himself. Then he stepped back into the hallway.
The door of the observatory closed automatically in his face.

As he hurried to the next door, it struck him that he had
made a fool of himself. The existence of the cold air showed
that the open effect of the ceiling was only an illusion of invisible
glass. But he decided not to go back.

The sixth door opened into a little cubbyhole. A blank
moment passed before he recognized what it was. An elevator!

He scrambled in. The farther he got away from the residential floor, the less likelihood of quick discovery. He turned to close the door, and saw that it was shutting automatically. It clicked softly, then immediately started up. Leigh frowned. The elevator was apparently geared to go to some definite point. And that could be very bad. His eyes searched for controls; but nothing was visible. Gun poised, he stood alert as the elevator stopped. The door slid open.

Leigh stared. There was no room. The door opened onto blackness. Not the blackness of space with its stars. Or a dark room, half revealed by the light from the elevator. But blackness! Impenetrable. He put a tentative hand forward, half expecting to feel a solid object. But as his hand entered the black area, it vanished. He jerked it back, and stared at it, dismayed. It shone with a light of its own, all the bones plainly visible.

Swiftly, the light faded, the skin became opaque, but his whole arm pulsed with a pattern of pain. He thought: Fool, fool! He laughed bitterly, braced himself. And then it happened.

There was a flash out of the blackness. Something that sparkled vividly, something material that blazed a brilliant path to his forehead—and drew itself inside his head. And then—

He was no longer in the elevator. On either side of him stretched a long corridor. The stocky Hanardy was just reaching for some tiny lights beside the door of Patricia Ungarn's apartment. The man's fingers touched one of the lights. It dimmed. Softly, the door opened. A young woman with proud, insolent eyes and a queen-like bearing stood there.

"Father wants you down on Level 4," she said to Hanardy. "One of the energy screens has gone down; and he needs some machine work before he can put up another."

She turned to Leigh. Her voice took on metallic overtones as she said, *"Mr. Leigh, you can come in!"*

VII

Leigh entered with scarcely a physical tremor. A cool breeze caressed his cheeks; and there was liltingly sweet sound of birds

201

singing in the distance. He stopped as he saw the sunlit garden beyond the French windows. After a moment, he thought:

"What happened to me?"

He put his hands to his head, and felt his forehead, then his whole head. But nothing was wrong, not a contusion, not a pain. He saw that the girl was staring at him, and he realized that his actions must seem unutterably queer.

"What's the matter with you?" she asked.

Leigh looked at her suspiciously. He said harshly, "Don't pull that innocent stuff. I've been up in the blackness room, and all I've got to say is, if you're going to kill me, don't skulk behind artificial night and other trickery."

The girl's eyes, he saw, were narrowed, unpleasantly cold. "I don't know what you're trying to pretend," she said icily. "I assure you it will not postpone the death we have to deal you." She hesitated, then finished sharply, "The *what* room?"

Leigh explained, puzzled by her puzzlement, then annoyed by the contemptuous smile that came into her face. She cut him off curtly, "I've never heard a less balanced story. If your intention was to astound me and delay your death with that improbable tale, it has failed. You must be mad. You didn't knock out Hanardy, because when I opened the door, Hanardy was there, and I sent him down to Father."

"See here!" Leigh began. Then he stopped. Because Hanardy *had* been there as she opened the door! And yet earlier—
When?

Doggedly, Leigh pushed the thought on: Earlier, he had attacked Hanardy. And then he—Leigh—had gone up in an elevator; and then, somehow, back. He began to feel unbalanced. With trembling fingers, he felt his head again. And it was absolutely normal. Only, he thought, there was something inside it that sparkled and tingled.

With a start, he saw that the girl was drawing a gun from a pocket of her simple white dress. He stared at the weapon, and he thought, "I've got to delay her some more."

He said urgently, "I'm going to assume you're puzzled by my words. Let's begin at the beginning. There is such a room, is there not?"

202

"Please," said the girl wearily, "let us not have any of your logic. My I.Q. is 243, yours is 112. So I assure you I am quite capable of reasoning from any beginning you can think of." She went on, her low voice curt, "There is no 'blackness' room, as you call it, no sparkling thing that crawls inside a human head. There is but one fact: The Dreeghs in their visit to your hotel room hypnotized you; and this curious mind illusion can only be a result of that hypnotism—don't argue with me—"

With a savage gesture of her gun, she cut off his attempt to speak. "There's no time. For some reason, the Dreeghs did something to you. Why? What did you see in those rooms?"

As he explained and described, Leigh realized that he would have to attack her, and take all the attendant risk. The purpose was a taut thing in his mind as he obeyed her motion and went ahead of her into the corridor. It was there, an icy determination, as he counted the doors from the corner where he had left the unconscious Hanardy.

"One, two, three, four, *five*. This door!" he said.

"Open it!" the girl said.

He did so; and his lower jaw sagged. He was staring into a fine, cozy room filled with shelf on shelf of beautifully bound books. There were comfortable chairs, a magnificent handwoven rag rug, and a desk.

It was the girl who closed the door firmly and once more motioned him ahead of her. They came to the sixth room.

"And this is your elevator?"

Leigh nodded mutely; and because his whole body was shaking, he was only dimly surprised that there was no elevator, but only a long, empty, silent corridor. The girl was standing with her back partly to him; and if he hit her, it would knock her hard against the doorjamb.

The sheer brutality of the thought was what stopped him, held him for an instant. And then it was too late. The girl whirled and looked straight into his eyes.

Her gun came up and pointed steadily. "Not that way," she said quietly. "For a moment I was wishing you would have the nerve to try it. But that would be the weak way for me." Her eyes glowed with pride. "After all, I've killed before through necessity, and hated it. You can see that, because of what the Dreeghs have done to you, it is necessary."

Her voice was curt again. "So back to my rooms. I have a space lock there to get rid of your body. Move!"

It was the emptiness, the silence except for the faint click of their shoes that caught at Leigh's nerves. He felt hopeless as he walked back to the apartment. He was trapped in this meteorite, hurtling darkly through the remote wastes of the Solar System. Here in this prison, pursued and attacked by deadly ships from the fixed stars, he was under sentence of death, the executioner to be a girl. That was the devastating part. He couldn't argue with this young woman. Every word would sound like pleading, and that he would not do.

The singing of the birds, as he entered the apartment, brought him out of his mental depression. He walked to the stately French windows, and stared at the glorious summery garden. At least two acres of grass and flowers and trees spread before him. There was a wide, deep pool of green, green water. Everywhere gorgeously colored birds fluttered and trilled, and over all blazed the glory of brilliant sunshine.

It was the sunshine that held Leigh longest. Finally, it seemed to him that he had the solution. He said in a hushed voice, without turning, "The roof—is an arrangement—of magnifying glass. It makes the Sun as big as on Earth. Is that the—"

"You'd better turn around," came the hostile, vibrant voice from behind him. "I don't shoot people in the back. And I want to get this over with."

It was the moralistic smugness of her words that enraged Leigh. He whirled. "You damned little Klugg. You can't shoot me in the back, eh? Oh, no! And you couldn't possibly shoot me while I was attacking you because that would be the weak way. It's all got to be made right with your conscience."

He stopped so short that, if he had been running, instead of talking, he would have stumbled. Figuratively, almost literally, he saw Patricia Ungarn for the first time since his arrival. His mind had been so concentrated, so absorbed by deadly danger—

—For the first time as a woman.

Leigh drew a long breath. Dressed as a man, she had been

204

youthfully handsome. Now, she wore a simple, snow-white sports dress. It was scarcely more than a tunic, and came well above her knees. Her hair shone with a brilliant brownness, and cascaded down to her shoulders. Her bare arms and legs gleamed a deep, healthy tan. Pure white sandals graced her feet. Her face gave the impression of extraordinary beauty. And then, amazed, he saw that her perfect cheeks were flushing vividly.

The girl said, "Don't you dare use that word to me."

She must have been utterly beside herself with rage. Her fury was such an enormous fact that Leigh gasped. Abruptly, he realized his tremendous opportunity.

"Klugg!" he said. "Klugg, Klugg, Klugg! So you realize now that the Dreeghs had you down pat, that all your mighty pretension was simply your Klugg mind demanding pretentious compensation for a dreary, lonely life. You had to think you were somebody, and yet all the time you must have known they'd only ship the tenth-raters to these remote posts. Klugg, not even Lennel; the Dreegh woman wouldn't even grant you Lennel status, whatever that is. And she'd know. Because if you're I.Q. 243, the Dreeghs were 400. You've realized that, too, haven't you?"

"Shut up! Or I'll kill you by inches!" said Patricia Ungarn. And Leigh was amazed to see that she had blanched under her tan. Stronger than before, he realized that he had struck, not only the emotional Achilles' heel of this strange and terrible young woman, but the very vital roots of her mental existence.

"So," he said deliberately, "the high morality is growing dim. Now you can torture me to death without a qualm. And to think that I came here to ask you to marry me because I thought a Klugg and a human being might get along."

"You what?" said the girl. Then she sneered. "So that was the form of their hypnotism. They would use some simple impulse for a simple human mind." She broke off, visibly fighting for calmness. "I think we've had just about enough. I know just the type of thoughts that come to a male human in love. Even knowing you're not responsible makes the idea none the less bearable. I feel sickened, insulted. Know, please, that my future husband is arriving with the reinforcements three weeks from now. He will be trained to take over Father's work—"

"Another Klugg!" said Leigh, and the girl turned shades whiter.

Leigh stood thunderstruck. In all his life, he had never seen anyone so violently affected as was this young girl. The intellectual mask was off, and underneath was a seething mass of emotions bitter beyond the power of words to express. Here was evidence of a life so lonely that it strained his imagination. Her every word showed an incredible pent-up masochism as well as sadism, for she *was* torturing herself as well as him. But he couldn't stop now to feel sorry for her. His life was at stake, and only more words could postpone death—or bring the swift and bearable surcease of a bullet fired in passion. He went on grimly:

"I'd like to ask one question. How did you find out my I.Q. is 112? What special interest made you inquire about that? Is it possible that, all by yourself here, you, too, had a special type of thought, and that, though your intellect rejected such lowly love, its existence is the mainspring behind your determination to kill, rather than cure me? I—"

"That will do," interrupted Patricia Ungarn.

It required a moment for Leigh to realize that in those few short seconds she had pulled herself completely together. He watched her tensely as her gun motioned toward a door he had not noticed before. She said curtly, "I suppose there is a solution other than death. That is, immediate death. And I have decided to accept the resultant loss of my spaceship."

She nodded at the door. "It's there in the air lock. It works very simply. The steering wheel pulls up or down or sideways, and that's the way the ship will go. Just step on the accelerator, and the machine will go forward. The decelerator is the left pedal. The automobile wheels fold in automatically as soon as they lift from the ground. Now, get going. I need hardly tell you that the Dreeghs will probably catch you. But you can't stay here. That's obvious."

"Thanks." That was all Leigh allowed himself to say. He had exploded an emotional powder keg, and he dared not tamper with it further. There was a tremendous psychological mystery here, but it was not for him to solve. Suddenly shaky from the realization of what was still ahead of him, he walked gingerly toward the air lock. And then—

It happened!

He had a sense of awful nausea. There was a wild swaying through blackness.

And then he was standing at the paneled doorway leading from the corridor to Patricia Ungarn's apartment. Hanardy stood beside him. The door opened. The young woman who stood on the other side of the threshold said strangely familiar words to Hanardy about going down to the fourth level to fix an energy screen. Then she turned to Leigh, and in a voice hard and metallic said:

"Mr. Leigh, you can come in."

VIII

The crazy part of it was that he walked in with scarcely a physical tremor. A cool breeze caressed his cheeks. And there was the liltingly sweet sound of birds singing in the distance. Leigh paused uncertainly. By sheer will power he shook the daze out of his mind, and bent mentally into the cyclone path of complete memory. Everything was there suddenly, the way the Dreeghs had come to his hotel apartment and ruthlessly forced him to their will, the way the "blackness" room had affected him, and how the girl had spared his life.

For some reason, the whole scene with the girl had been unsatisfactory to—Jeel; and it was now, fantastically, to be repeated.

That thought ended. The entire, tremendous reality of what had happened yielded to a vastly greater fact: There was—something—inside his head, a physical something. In a queer, horrible, inexperienced way, his mind instinctively fought against it. The result was ghastly confusion. Whatever it was, rested inside his head, unaffected by his brain's feverish contortions, cold, aloof, watching.

Watching.

Madly, then, he realized what it was. Another mind. Leigh shrank from the fact as from destroying fire. He tensed his brain. For a moment, his frenzy was so great that his face twisted with the anguish of his efforts. And everything blurred.

Exhausted finally, he simply stood there. And the thing-mind was still inside his head. Untouched.

What had happened to him?

Shakily, Leigh put his hands up to his forehead. Then he felt his whole head. There was a vague idea in him that if he pressed hard, it would be affected. He jerked his hands down with an unspoken curse. Damnation on damnation, he was even repeating the actions of this scene. He grew aware of the girl staring at him. He heard her say:

"What's the matter with you?"

It was the sound of the words, exactly the same words, that did it. He smiled wryly. His mind drew back from the abyss where it had teetered. He was sane again.

Gloomily, he recognized that he was still far from normal. Sane yes, but dispirited. Clearly, the girl had no memory of the previous scene, or she wouldn't be parroting. That thought ceased, too. A strange thing was happening. The mind inside him stirred, and looked through his eyes. Looked intently.

Intently.

The room and the girl in it changed, not physically, but subjectively, in what he saw, in the details. The details burned at him. Furniture and design that a moment before had seemed a flowing, artistic whole, abruptly showed flaws, errors in taste and arrangement and structure. His gaze flashed to the garden, and in instants tore it to mental shreds. Never in all his existence had he seen or felt criticism on such a high, devastating scale.

Only it wasn't criticsm. Actually. The mind was indifferent. It saw things. Automatically, it saw some of the possibilities. By comparison the reality suffered. It was not a matter of anything being hopelessly bad. The wrongness was frequently a subtle thing. Birds not suited, for a dozen reasons, to their environment. Shrubs that added infinitesimal discord, not harmony, to the superb garden.

The mind flashed back from the garden; and this time, for

the first time, studied the girl. On all Earth, no woman had ever been so piercingly examined. The structure of her body and her face, to Leigh so finely, proudly shaped, so gloriously patrician —he found low grade now.

An excellent example of low-grade development in isolation.

That was the thought, not contemptuous, nor derogatory, simply an impression by an appallingly direct mind that saw overtones, realities behind realities, a thousand facts where one showed.

There followed crystal-clear awareness of the girl's psychology, objective admiration for the system of isolated upbringing that made Klugg girls such fine breeders; and then—

Purpose!

Instantly carried out. Leigh took three swift steps toward the girl. He was aware of her snatching at the gun in her pocket. There was startled amazement on her face. Then he had her. Her muscles writhed like steel springs. But they were useless against his superstrength, his superspeed. He tied her with some wire he had noticed in a half-opened clothes closet.

Then he stepped back, and to Leigh came the shocked personal thought of the incredible thing that had happened, comprehension that all this, which seemed so normal, was actually so devastatingly superhuman, so swift that—seconds only had passed since he came into the room.

His private thought ended. He grew aware of the mind, contemplating what it had done, and what it must do before the meteorite would be completely under control.

Vampire victory was near.

There was a phase of walking along empty corridors, down several flights of stairs. Leigh thought dully, his own personal thought, that the Dreegh seemed to know thoroughly the interior of the meteorite. Somehow, during the periods of transition, of time manipulation, the creature-mind must have used his captive body to explore the place completely. And now, with simple, deadly purpose, he was heading for the machine shops on the fourth level, where Professor Ungarn and Hanardy labored to put up another energy defense screen.

He found Hanardy alone, working at a lathe that throbbed, and the sound made it easy to sneak up—

The professor was in a vast room, where great engines hummed a strange, deep tune of titanic power. He was a tall man, and his back was turned to the door as Leigh entered. But his reactions were much quicker than Hanardy's, quicker even than the girl's. He sensed danger. He whirled with a catlike agility. And succumbed instantly to muscles that could have torn him limb from limb. It was during the binding of the man's hands that Leigh had time for an impression.

In the photographs that Leigh had seen, as he had told the Dreegh, Merla, in the hotel, the professor's face had been sensitive, tired-looking, withal noble. He was more than that. The man radiated power, as no photograph could show it, *good power* in contrast to the savage, malignant, greater power of the Dreegh.

The sense of a powerful personality faded before the aura of cosmic weariness. It was a lined, an amazingly lined face. In a flash, Leigh remembered what the Dreegh woman had said. It was all there: deep-graven lines of tragedy and untold mental suffering, interlaced with a curious peacefulness. Like resignation. On that night months ago, he had asked the Dreegh woman: Resignation to what? And now, here in this tortured, kindly face was the answer: *Resignation to hell*.

Queerly, an unexpected second answer trickled into his consciousness: Morons; they're Galactic morons. Kluggs. The thought seemed to have no source; but it gathered strength. Professor Ungarn and his daughter were Kluggs, *morons* in the incredible Galactic sense. No wonder the girl had reacted like a crazy person. Obviously born here, she must have guessed the truth only in the last two months.

The I.Q. of human morons wavered between seventy-five and ninety, of Kluggs possibly between two hundred and twenty-five and, say, two hundred and forty-three. What could be the nature of Galactic civilization if Dreeghs were four hundred, and Kluggs of the lowest I.Q. range were on the highest genius level by Earth standards? Somebody, of course, had to do the dreary, routine work of civilization. Kluggs and Lennels and their kind were obviously elected. No wonder they looked tired with that weight of inferiority to influence their very nerve and muscle structure. No wonder whole planets were kept in ignorance.

Leigh left the professor tied hand and foot, and began to turn off power switches. Some of the great motors were slowing noticeably as he went out of that mighty engine room. The potent hum of power dimmed.

Back in the girl's room, he entered the air lock, climbed into the smal automobile spaceship, and launched into the night. Swiftly, the gleaming mass of meteorite receded into the darkness behind him. Suddenly, magnetic force rays caught his tiny craft, and drew it remorselessly toward the hundred-and-fifty-foot, cigar-shaped machine that flashed out of the darkness. He felt the spy rays; and he must have been recognized. For another ship flashed up to claim him. Air locks opened noiselessly, and shut again. Sickly, Leigh stared at the two Dreeghs, the tall man and the tall woman. He explained what he had done. Dimly, hopelessly, he wondered why he should have to explain. Then he heard Jeel say:

"Merla, this is the most astoundingly successful case of hypnotism in our existence. He's done everything. Even the tiniest thoughts we put into his mind have been carried out to the letter. And the proof is, the screens are going down. With the control of this station, we can hold out even after the Galactic warships arrive, and fill our tankers and our energy reservoirs for ten thousand years. Do you hear, *ten thousand years*!"

His excitement died. He smiled with sudden dry understanding as he looked at the woman. Then he said laconically, "My dear, the reward is all yours. We could have broken down those screens in another twelve hours, but it would have meant the destruction of the meteorite. This victory is so much greater. Take your reporter. Satisfy your craving—while the rest of us prepare for the occupation. Meanwhile, I'll tie him up for you."

Leigh thought, a cold, remote thought: The kiss of death. And shivered in appalled realization of what he had done.

IX

He lay on the couch, where Jeel had tied him. He was surprised, after a moment, to notice that, though *the* mind had withdrawn into the background of his brain, it was still there, cold, steely, abnormally conscious.

He wondered: what possible satisfaction could Jeel obtain from experiencing the mortal thrill of death with him? These people must be ultimately sadistic. The wonder died like dry grass under a heat ray as the woman came into the room and glided toward him. She smiled. She sat down on the edge of the couch.

"So here you are," she said.

She was, Leigh thought, like a tigress. There was purpose in every tense muscle of her long body. In surprise he saw that she had changed her dress. She wore a sleek, flimsy, tight-fitting gown that set off in startling fashion her golden hair and starkly white face. He watched her with fascination. He said, "Yes, I'm here."

Silly words. But he didn't feel silly. He stiffened even as he spoke. It was her eyes that did it. For the first time since he had first seen her, her eyes struck him like a blow. Blue eyes, and steady. So steady. Not the steady frankness of honesty. But steady like dead eyes. A chill grew on Leigh, a special, extra chill, adding to the ice that was already there inside him. He had the unholy thought that this was a dead woman, artificially kept alive by the blood and *life* of dead men and women. She smiled, but the bleakness remained in those cold, fish eyes. No smile, no warmth could ever bring light to that chill, beautiful countenance. But she smiled the form of a smile, and she said:

"We Dreeghs live a hard, lonely life. So lonely that sometimes I cannot help thinking our struggle to remain alive is a blind, mad thing. We're what we are through no fault of our own. It happened during an interstellar flight that took place a million years ago—" She stopped, almost hopelessly. "It seems longer. It must be longer. I've really lost track."

She went on, suddenly grim, as if the memory, the very

telling, brought a return of horror, "We were among several thousand holidayers who were caught in the gravitational pull of a sun, afterward called the Dreegh Sun. Its rays, immensely dangerous to human life, infected us all. It was discovered that only continuous blood transfusions, and the life force of other human beings could save us. For a while we received donations; then the government decided to have us destroyed as hopeless incurables. We were all young, and in love with life, of course. Some hundreds of us had been expecting the sentence, and we still had friends in the beginning. We escaped. We've been fighting ever since to stay alive."

And still he could feel no sympathy. It was odd, for all the thoughts she undoubtedly wanted him to have, came. Picture of a bleak, endless existence in spaceships, staring out into the perpetual night. Life processes circumscribed by the tireless, abnormal needs of bodies gone mad from ravenous disease. It was all there, the emotional pictures. But no emotions came. She was too cold. The years and that devil's hunt had stamped her soul and her eyes and her face.

And besides, her body seemed tenser now, leaning toward him, bending forward closer, closer, till he could hear her slow, measured breathing. Even her eyes suddenly held the vaguest inner light. Her whole being quivered with the chill tensity of her purpose. When she spoke, she almost breathed the words, "I want you to kiss me, and don't be afraid. I shall keep you alive for days, but I must have response, not passivity. You're a bachelor, at least thirty. You won't have any more morals about the matter than I. But you must let your whole body yield."

He didn't believe it. Her face hovered six inches above him. And there was such a ferocity of suppressed eagerness in her that it could mean only death. Her lips were pursed, as if to suck, and they quivered with a strange, tense, trembling desire, unnatural, almost obscene. Her nostrils dilated at every breath. Surely no normal who had kissed as often as she must have in all her years could feel like that, if that was all she expected to get.

"Quick!" she said breathlessly. "Yield, yield!"

Leigh scarcely heard. For that other mind that had been lingering in his brain surged forward in its incredible way. He heard himself say. "I'll trust your promise because I can't resist such an appeal. You can kiss your head off. I guess I can stand it—"

There was a blue flash, an agonizing burning sensation that spread in a wave to every nerve of his body.

The anguish became a series of tiny pains, like small needles piercing a thousands bits of his flesh. Tingling, writhing a little, amazed that he was still alive, Leigh opened his eyes.

He felt a wave of purely personal surprise. The woman lay slumped, lips half twisted off of his, body collapsed hard across his chest. And the mind, that blazing mind was there, watching, as the tall figure of the Dreegh man sauntered into the room, stiffened, and then darted forward.

He jerked her limp form into his arms. There was the same kind of blue flash as their lips met, from the man to the woman. She stirred finally, moaning. He shook her brutally. "You wretched fool!" he raged. "How did you let a thing like that happen? You would have been dead in another minute, if I hadn't come along."

"I—don't—know." Her voice was thin and old. She sank down to the floor at his feet, and slumped there like a tired old woman. Her blonde hair straggled and looked curiously faded. "I don't know, Jeel. I tried to get his life force, and he got mine instead. He—"

She stopped. Her blue eyes widened. She staggered to her feet. "Jeel, he must be a spy. No human being could do a thing like that to me. Jeel"—there was sudden terror in her voice—"Jeel, get out of this room. Don't you realize? He's got my energy in him. He's lying there now, and whatever has control of him has my energy to work with—"

"All right, all right." He patted her fingers. "I assure you he's only a human being. And he's got your energy. You made a mistake, and the flow went the wrong way. But it would take much more than that for *anyone* to use a human body successfully against us. So—"

"You don't understand!"

Her voice shook. "Jeel, I've been cheating. I don't know what got into me, but I couldn't get enough life force. Every time I

214

was able, during the four times we stayed on Earth, I sneaked out. I caught men on the street. I don't know exactly how many because I dissolved their bodies after I was through with them. But there were dozens. And he's got all the energy I collected, enough for scores of years, enough for—don't you see?—enough for *them*."

"My dear!" The Dreegh shook her violently, as a doctor would an hysterical woman. "For a million years, the great ones of Galactic have ignored us and—"

He paused. A black frown twisted his long face. He whirled like the tiger man he was, snatching at his gun as Leigh stood up.

The man Leigh was no longer surprised at anything. At the way the hard cords fell rotted from his wrists and legs. At the way the Dreegh froze rigid after one look into his eyes. For the first shock of the tremendous, the almost cataclysmic truth was already in him.

"There is only one difference," said Leigh in a voice so vibrant that the top of his head shivered from the unaccustomed violence of the sound. "This time there are two hundred and twenty-seven Dreegh ships gathered in one concentrated area. The rest —and our records show only a dozen others—we can safely leave to our police patrols."

The Great Galactic, who had been William Leigh, smiled darkly and walked toward his captives. "It has been a most interesting experiment in deliberate splitting of personality. Three years ago, our time manipulators showed this opportunity of destroying the Dreeghs, who hitherto had escaped by reason of the vastness of our galaxy. And so I came to Earth, and here built up the character of William Leigh, reporter, complete with family and past history. It was necessary to withdraw into a special compartment of the brain some nine-tenths of my mind, and to drain completely an equal percentage of life energy.

"That was the difficulty: How to replace that energy in sufficient degree at the proper time, without playing the role of vampire. I constructed a number of energy caches, but naturally at no time had we been able to see all the future. We could not

215

see the details of what was to transpire aboard this ship, or in my hotel room that night you came, or under Constantine' restaurant. Besides, if I had possessed full energy as approached this ship, your spy ray would have registered it And you would instantly have destroyed my small automobile spaceship. My first necessity, accordingly, was to come to the meteorite, and obtain an initial control over my own body through the medium of what my Earth personality called the 'blackness room.

"That Earth personality offered unexpected difficulties. In three years it had gathered momentum as a personality, and that impetus made it necessary to repeat a scene with Patricia Ungarn, and to appear directly as another conscious mind in order to convince Leigh that he must yield. The rest, of course was a matter of gaining additional life energy after boarding your ship, which"—he bowed slightly at the muscularly congealed body of the woman—"which she supplied me.

"I have explained all this because of the fact that a mind will accept complete control only if full understanding of defeat is present. I must finally inform you, therefore, that you are to remain alive for the next few days, during which time you will assist me in making personal contact with your friends."

He made a gesture of dismissal. "Return to your normal existence. I have still to coördinate my two personalities and that does not require your presence."

The Dreeghs went out blank-eyed, almost briskly; and the two minds in one body were alone!

For Leigh, the Leigh of Earth, the first desperate shock was past. The room was curiously dim, as if he were staring out through eyes that were no longer—his! He thought, with a horrible effort at self-control: "I've got to fight. Some *thing* is trying to possess my body. All the rest is lie."

A soothing, mind-pulsation stole into the shadowed chamber where his—self—was cornered: "No lie, but wondrous truth. You have not seen what the Dreeghs saw and felt, for you are inside this body, and know not that it has come marvellously *alive*, unlike anything that your petty dreams on Earth could begin to conceive. You must accept your high destiny, else the sight of your own body will be a terrible thing to you. Be calm, be braver than you've ever been, and pain will turn to joy."

Calm came not. His mind quivered in its dark corner, abnormally conscious of strange and unnatural pressures that pushed in at it like winds out of unearthly night. For a moment of terrible fear, it funked that pressing night, then forced back to sanity, and had another thought of its own, a grimly cunning thought: The devilish interloper was arguing. Could that mean —his mind rocked with hope—that coördination was impossible without *his* yielding to clever persuasion?

Never would he yield.

"Think," whispered the alien mind, "think of being one valuable facet of a mind with an I.Q. twelve hundred, think of yourself as having played a rôle. And now you are returning to normalcy, a normalcy of unlimited power. You have been an actor completely absorbed in your rôle, but the play is over. You are alone in your dressing room removing the grease paint. Your mood of the play is fading, fading, fading—"

"Go to hell!" said William Leigh loudly. "I'm William Leigh, I.Q. one hundred and twelve, satisfied to be just what I am. I don't give a damn whether you built me up from the component elements of your brain, or whether I was born normally. I can see what you're trying to do with that hypnotic suggestion stuff, but it isn't working. I'm here. I'm myself. And I stay myself. Go find yourself another body, if you're so smart."

Silence settled where his voice had been. And the emptiness, the utter lack of sound brought a sharp twinge of fear greater than that which he had had before he spoke.

He was so intent on that inner struggle that he was not aware of outer movement until, with a start, he realized he was staring out of a port window. Night spread there, the living night of space.

A trick, he thought, in an agony of fear; a trick somehow designed to add to the corroding power of hypnotism. A trick! He tried to jerk back. And, terrifyingly, couldn't. His body wouldn't move. Instantly, then, he tried to speak, to crash through that enveloping blanket of unholy silence. But no sound came.

Not a muscle, not a finger stirred; not a single nerve so much as trembled.

He was alone.

Cut off in his little corner of brain.

Lost.

Yes, lost, came a strangely pitying sibilation of thought, lost to a cheap, sordid existence, lost to a life whose end is visible from the hour of birth, lost to a civilization that has already had to be saved from itself a thousand times. Even you, I think, can see that all this is lost to you forever.

Leigh thought starkly: The *thing* was trying by a repetition of ideas, by showing evidence of defeat, to lay the foundations of further defeat. It was the oldest trick of simple hypnotism for simple people. He couldn't let it work.

You have, urged the mind inexorably, accepted the fact that you were playing a rôle; and now you have recognized our oneness, and are giving up the rôle. The proof of this recognition on your part is that you have yielded control of—our—body.

—Our body, *our* body, OUR body—

The words re-echoed like some Gargantuan sound through his brain, them merged swiftly into that calm, other-mind pulsation:

—concentration. All intellect derives from the capacity to concentrate; and, progressively, the body itself shows *life*, reflects and focuses that gathering, vaulting power.

—One more step remains: You must see—

Amazingly, then, he was staring into a mirror. Where it had come from, he had no memory. It was there in front of him where, an instant before, had been a black porthole—and there was an image in the mirror, shapeless at first to his blurred vision.

Deliberately—he felt the enormous deliberateness—the vision was cleared for him. He saw. And then he didn't.

His brain wouldn't look. It twisted in a mad desperation, like a body buried alive, and briefly, horrendously conscious of its fate. Insanely, it fought away from the blazing thing in the mirror. So awful was the effort, so titanic the fear, that it began to gibber mentally, its consciousness to whirl dizzily, like a wheel spinning faster, faster.

The wheel shattered into ten thousand aching fragments. Darkness came, blacker than Galactic night. And there was—

Oneness!

Other Panthers For Your Enjoyment

Asimov in Panther

☐ **THE STARS LIKE DUST**   30p
A great Utopian story of a chase through the length and breadth
of the galaxy in search of a secret document which may be the key
to the overthrow of tyranny.

☐ **THE END OF ETERNITY**   30p
Mankind is spreading through the galaxy – and meets an alien
intelligence which is moving in from the shadowy 'outside'. How to
stop them? Simple – you modify the past: except that nothing ever
is as simple as that in Isaac Asimov's stupendous cosmology.

☐ **THE CAVES OF STEEL**   30p
Many writers have tried to merge science fiction with the
detective story, but only Asimov has supremely succeeded.
THE CAVES OF STEEL has a detective – an unusual one –
operating in the deep-down warrens of an over-populated metropolis
– and if you think you know what over-population means . . . read
Asimov.

☐ **THE NAKED SUN**   30p
Another science fiction/detective story masterpiece. A tec from
over-crowded Earth has to take off to a sparsely populated
way-out planet. After the teeming dens of Earth – a sort of womb
existence – the wide open spaces make him literally sick.
Nevertheless, there's a killer on the loose – to be run down.

☐ **ASIMOV'S MYSTERIES**   30p
Short, sharp stories about murders, mayhems, crooks and
detectives fouling up Asimov's cleanly organised science fiction
worlds. This deep, dark space collection rounds off the author's
excursion into the s.f./thriller field.

☐ **THE MARTIAN WAY**   30p
Four novellas by Asimov. The author races along – taking Mars
in his stride (the title is a misnomer) as he slams his penetrating
imagination into the deeps of space and time.

Asimov in Panther

☐ **FOUNDATION**   30p
The first volume of an astounding sweep through 30,000 years
of galactic history. A shadowy figure – called Hari Seldon –
establishes a mysterious foundation. Its objective – to save
galactic civilisation from coming disaster.

☐ **FOUNDATION AND EMPIRE**   30p
The galaxy is rent by space adventurers staking out their claims to
ephemeral kingdoms. Then a mutant known as The Mule makes
his appearance and imposes his brutal overlordship across the
whole galaxy.

☐ **SECOND FOUNDATION**   30p
To the entire galaxy comes the grim final reckoning. The Seldon
Foundation reveals itself and its cosmic aims, and order is at last
imposed on chaos. As the magazine *Vector* wrote, 'The *Foundation*
trilogy is the prime example of straight SF published to date. No
other work can compare with the magnificent scope that this
series offers'.

☐ **I, ROBOT**   30p
Almost single-handed Isaac Asimov invented 'robotics', and
practically every famous author in the SF field has acknowledged
his indebtedness to this splendidly imaginative novel and its
famous sequel –

☐ **THE REST OF THE ROBOTS**   30p
Although these stories can be read in their own right they also
complete Asimov's fantastic imaginings of a robot universe.

☐ **EARTH IS ROOM ENOUGH**   30p
Fifteen stories, each one built on an impeccable set of facts (which
is the only way to write really convincing SF). And Dr Asimov, a
practising scientist himself, is a master of bizarre facts.